WINGS OF
THE NORTH

wings of the north

HANCOCK HOUSE PUBLISHERS
Saanichton — Seattle

ISBN 0-919654-61-4 Hardcover
ISBN 0-88839-060-2 Soft Cover

Canadian Cataloguing in Publication Data

Turner, Dick, 1911-
        Wings of the north

        ISBN 0-919654-61-4
        ISBN 0-88839-060-2

1. Turner, Dick, 1911-   2. Air pilots-
Correspondence, reminiscences, etc. 3.
South Nahanni Valley, N.W.T. I. Title.
TL540.T87A3   629.13 ′092 ′4
               C76-016059-7

Third Printing
First Soft Cover 1980
Second Soft Cover 1982

Published by:

HANCOCK HOUSE PUBLISHERS LTD.
19313 Zero Avenue, Surrey, B.C., Canada V3S 5J9

HANCOCK HOUSE PUBLISHERS
1431 Harrison Avenue, Blaine, WA, U.S.A. 98230

Table of Contents

Chapters

1	Into the Air and Down	9
2	Back in the Air Again	25
3	Turbulence and Toothache	39
4	New Airstrips	53
5	Vera's Diary	59
6	Headless Valley	71
7	Floats and Fishing	81
8	Prospecting	87
9	Do It Yourself	93
10	The Group of Eight	99
11	The Search Goes On	109
12	River Running	115
13	Victims and Near Victims	173
14	Barge Out—Charter In.	189
15	Aerial Antics	201
16	The Polaris	209
17	Trapping	223
18	Northern Development	235
19	Courting Hunters—Courting Hunted	245
20	The Quest I	257
21	The Quest II	273
22	At Last	283
	Glossary	288

DEDICATION

To the memory of George Bayer who exemplified the best spirit of man and pilot.

PRELUDE

From beside a fleecy cloud where the icy mountain top hides a rising sun that will in moments bathe the little emerald lake with warmth and splendor, I dedicate this book to the 'esprit de corps' that exists among the bush pilots of the north.

Knowing that I am not competent to do justice to all aspects of bush flying, I ask forgiveness from all the bush pilots who are my friends for the errors and omissions in this chronicle.

I do not pretend that this is a complete treatise on the history of northern aviation. That must be left to others who are more capable than I. If this poor effort of mine brings back nostalgic memories of the north to those of you who have experienced the thrills, the terrors, the delight and exhilaration of being with the eagle of the sky; if there are any words in this book that will enable the young men and women now entering the world of aviation to become better and safer pilots; if it brings interest and excitement to others, then I will be well satisfied and content that I have not failed in my objective.

Dick Turner

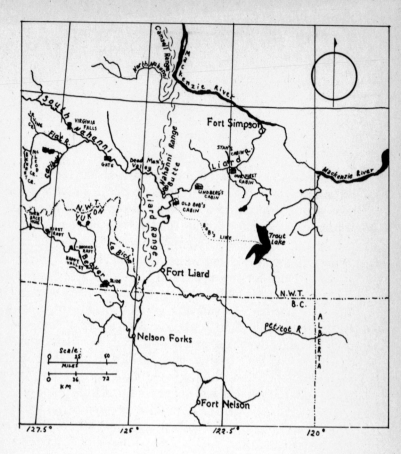

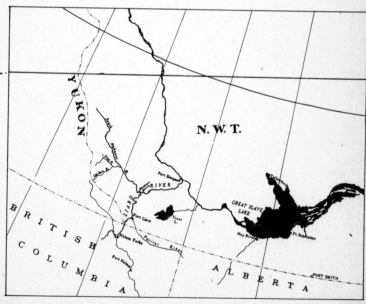

1

Into the Air and Down

The little aircraft banked and turned away from the mountain, heading south over the rolling timbered bushland toward the British Columbia border and Fort Nelson. The Nahanni Valley was left behind and we were headed for southern civilization and the city of Vancouver where, rumor had it, grass was green all year round and people mowed their lawns in February. I thought, "At least it will be a change from the north where the Liard ice is still three feet thick, the days short and the temperature is forty below."

It was February 2nd, 1958, with my forty-seventh birthday coming up. After almost thirty years of trapping, fur trading and river boating, was I going to be able to adjust to 'outside' life for a month or more? Was I going to be able to learn to fly? Could I pass the Department of Transport examinations at the termination of ground school? Could I find a suitable aircraft to purchase with the limited funds I had available? If those hurdles were surmounted, could I fly the aircraft home from the coast to Calgary, Edmonton, Fort St. John, Fort Nelson and the last one hundred and sixty-five miles north to Nahanni Butte: over a thousand miles through mostly mountain and wilderness?

Doubts began to assail me of the wisdom of this venture. While I felt this trip outside was necessary and beneficial for my wife Vera and the two smaller children (Martha nine, and Rolf twelve), it also meant taking the kids away from their correspondence lessons for a month or more. But if the venture was successful we would have an aircraft at Nahanni and would not be as isolated as before. With the aircraft equipped with skis from November to April I would be able to fly to Fort Nelson to get our mail and supplies on a regular basis. We would be able to have fresh fruit in the winter time and other supplies needed for the trading post; and most important of all, we could ship the fur from the trading post to the outside market for the monthly auction sales, thus up-grading the operation of our business.

Looking down at the timbered hills and ice-bound lakes I vowed to go ahead with my plans to become a bush pilot with whatever determination I could muster and take whatever obstacles there might be one by one.

Jack Norcross turned from the controls of his Stinson and said to me, "Would you like to take the controls for a while, Dick?"

"No, thanks," I replied. "I think I'll wait 'til I get to the flying school. Handling the controls in the air is not much use. What I need is instruction in landing and takeoff and I sure don't want to bend your little bird."

"OK," Jack laughed, "but don't worry, you'll make out all right."

All small light planes are noisy, making conversation difficult, and we did not continue talking.

At Fort Nelson, Rolf and I transferred to a four engine D C 6B of Canadian Pacific Airlines.

We broke through the clouds over Vancouver and I saw the waters of the Pacific for the first time: the green islands of the gulf set in the blue, blue waters with the snow-capped mountains rising right out of the sea. No wonder it is called Beautiful British Columbia.

With our parkas, moccasins and heavy clothing we felt conspicuous as we stepped from the Terminal building into the balmy air. There I noticed a green carpet at the edge of the walk.

"Ah-Ha," I thought. "That looks like grass all right, but I'm no fool, I'll bet it is artificial turf. They can't fool me, even if I am from the north," and in what I hoped was not a furtive manner I bent down and pulled at some of it. "Bless my soul," I said out loud. "It is grass, good green natural grass."

My son Rolf who despite his twelve years thought he was pretty worldly wise, was often embarrassed by the naivete of his father.

"Don't be stupid Dad, of course it's grass," he said.

To tease the members of my family I often spread it on a bit thick and this maneuver serves as an escape hatch in case I really do make a 'boo-boo.' I can then smile as if to say, "it was just a joke, I'm really not so dumb."

We were to meet Vera and Martha, who had arrived in Vancouver some days before, at the Fraser Arms Hotel. While waiting in the lobby someone came up behind me, hit me a wallop and said, "Dick Turner, what the hell are you doing here?" Picking myself up I saw a familiar face.

"Bill Cormack you old buzzard, when did they let you out? Are you tending bar here? You can't possibly still be flying for C.P. Air."

"You'd better believe I am. I'm flying a Six on the Tokyo run. And who is this big boy here? Obviously your son eh? Come in and have a drink. I'm off for three days now. We've got lots to talk about."

When friends from the north meet in the outside world it must seem to onlookers that the northerners are a bit out of their minds. They are so happy to see someone from home that they slap one another around something scandalous. Once while I was standing on the sidewalk in Hay River, a man came up behind me and taking me for a long lost pal, hit me a wallop that sent me staggering. On seeing his error he was terribly embarrassed and full of apologies.

"It's OK," I said, "I have done the same thing myself."

In fact I almost did something that might have had frightening consequences. I saw a girl I knew, a very good friend of long standing, walking ahead of me in a town. I came up behind her to plant a kiss on her neck, and just in the nick of time saw that she was a complete stranger. I almost died of heart failure, but I was able to collect myself sufficiently to walk on in what I hoped was a casual and nonchalant manner. I had visions of being hauled away by the gendarmes and being charged with goodness knows what. But, boy, oh, boy, since then I have never even said "Hello" to a girl without examining her in great detail fore, aft and sideways.

When the glasses were filled and toasts were drunk, Bill Cormack said, "OK, unburden yourself, what the hell's a trapper doing out here so far from home?"

"I'm going to take flying lessons," I replied. "I hope to buy a T-Craft or something similar and fly it home. I'm having a hell of a time getting my fur out to the auction sales before the bottom drops out every spring, and I'm determined to get an airplane of my own."

"Are you going to a flying school here in Vancouver?"

"No, I think I'll go out to Skyway Flying Services at Langley."

"Yes," Bill said, "I think that is a pretty fair flying school: you'll do all right but for God's sake don't fly your little plane back to Calgary through the mountains. We call the region east of Hope, 'The Graveyard of the World'. You will only have a few hours flying time and you should get an instructor to fly the plane over the mountains and you can take it from there."

Bill continued in this vein for half an hour or more. He had me convinced and I promised to take his advice. I told him his words were not falling on deaf ears, and I was not likely to over estimate my flying capabilities.

Bill and his brother George had trapped in the Fort Simpson area for a year or so, then Bill had taken flying lessons and had flown a Norseman bush plane based in Norman Wells. He had upgraded himself with a multi-engine and instrument rating and was now flying Sixes on the Tokyo run.

In the course of conversation I said, "I hear your brother George is a big shot with Shell Oil now."

Bill replied, "How did you spell that?"

Which goes to show you never get much sympathy from a brother.

Up in our rooms at the Fraser Arms I found that sitting on the bed was somewhat different from sitting on the bunks in my line cabins on the trapline. Instead of feeling something solid under you, you seemed to sink in and float around as on a cloud on a windy day. Sleeping on the damned thing was out of the question. I put the mattress on the floor and even then slept fitfully. When Rolf told Bill Cormack about this later he thought it was a great joke.

The following day we rented a U-Drive and the four of us drove out to Langley and established ourselves in a motel a mile or so from the flying school.

My medical examination turned out well and the card came back from the Department of Transport marked with a 1-1-1-1 profile, and I have fortunately maintained that to this day. (1-physical; 1-vision; 1-color perception; 1-hearing.)

Next I drove out to the flying school where I put down my money and Ed Batchelor took me in hand and began the up-hill job of teaching me to fly. The three trainer planes the school had at that time were 90 HP Super Cubs, high wing monoplanes.

Ed took me out and we examined the airplane in detail, he pointing out and naming the various parts of the empenage, the controls and the instruments and their functions.

"You must inspect the airplane carefully, before each and every flight," he explained. "You must never, but NEVER take anything for granted. When you are a pilot in command of an aircraft and prepare to leave the ground, you are considered by the Department of Transport to have acknowledged the aircraft to be airworthy. In flying an aircraft for the first time you must inspect the log books and also make a thorough inspection of the airplane. Now then, in this case I am the pilot in command; I have satisfied myself that the airplane is airworthy. Let's go flying."

We had spent half an hour in examining the airplane and I thought, "Hmmmm, there is a lot more to flying than just driving the machine."

The Cub is a two place tandem seated airplane. Ed said, "You sit in front, I will get in the back and drive. We'll do a short flight and then you can do some circuits and bumps."

"Now why did he say, 'circuits and bumps' " I thought. "Airplanes come down and land and that's it." I was soon to discover what bumps were.

Ed taxied into position, opened the tap and the Cub, picking up speed was soon in the air.

"Nothing to it," I thought. "That is easy enough."

"At 500 feet," Ed said, "You start a climbing turn to the left. At the present all circuits are left hand here. At 1000 feet you reduce throttle and level off. Now we are clear of the circuit. These are the functions of the controls: the stick controls the ailerons and the elevator like this: feet on the rudder pedals control the rudder, like so; both aileron and rudder must be used at the same time to do a proper turn. Avoid crossing your controls. You will find there is nothing to it. After a time it will come easy."

"There is the hospital," Ed continued. "You're to keep away from that. They don't like noise. And there is the town of Langley, you are to stay away from there, they also do not like noise. In all cases you must fly at least a thousand feet above ground except when landing or taking off. Now we'll go back to the field and you can take over. You follow me through a landing or a 'bump' and then you can take it."

"So I can take it eh?" I thought. "With all this weaving about and gypsy-doodling I'm feeling sick already and my head is swimming with all these instructions. I wish to hell I was back home with my feet on the ground, driving my team of dogs." How far away that was. "I wish I could back out of this." I mumbled under my breath.

Ed was talking, "At a thousand feet you enter the circuit, watching carefully for other aircraft, keeping a safe distance from those ahead of you and when you land get off the runway as soon as you slow down so that you do not impede any aircraft coming in behind you. Soon all our machines will be equipped with two-way radio and will be able to keep in touch with the tower and other airplanes."

We glided to a smooth landing, turned around and were ready to go. "You have control," Ed said.

'You have control' was the most false and misleading statement that has ever been made. What Ed meant was, "I HOPE you have control." I truly think that Winnie the Pooh could have done a better job than I did my first circuit. In fact it was not a circuit. A circuit according to Webster is 'part of a circle'. What I did was in no way part of a circle. I'm sure nothing in the world like it has ever been done before. You may have heard of the man who mounted his horse and galloped off in all directions. Well, it was not a horse, it was an airplane, and the man was me. Poor Ed was an unwilling passenger. If he wasn't out of his mind he had to be unwilling. A roller coaster ride would have been mild compared with what poor Ed went through.

I opened the tap (advanced the throttle) as Ed had done on our first flight. But from there on the similarity ended. The plane leaped forward and off to the right. I corrected the rudder; the plane swung violently to the left, I pushed right rudder, too much; off the runway to the right again; back to the left again. Now we were in the air and the nose was pointed straight up.

"Down with the nose," Ed shouted. I dumped the stick ahead. Down we went almost to the ground. The runway was gone. We were over the fence, dangerously close. Up again. Too much. Down again. Miraculously the airplane had not stalled; we were still in the air. Now I had swerved away to the right. There was the hospital down there. Ed said to keep away from it. A mad swerve to avoid flying over the hospital. A wild thought entered my head.

"Maybe I should head directly at the hospital, as I'm sure as hell going to end up there anyway; if I don't kill myself today it will certainly be tomorrow."

Ed was speaking, he was amazingly calm. And did I detect a note of humour in his voice? My God, he was laughing! He was probably hysterical with fear.

"Climb to a thousand feet, throttle back and level off. Now make a gradual turn to the left. Now turn down-wind keeping a sharp lookout for other aircraft. There is someone on final now, you are number two, you have lots of room. Now do your cross-wind. Easy now, easy. Keep your altitude and do not chase your airspeed. YOU ARE CHASING YOUR AIRSPEED. You do not make a turn with only your rudder; use your aileron. Just a light pressure now, all right. Carb. heat on and throttle back. Don't forget Carb. heat. Control your speed with your elevator and your rate of descent with throttle. OK now, keep her at about seventy miles an hour. You are too fast and too high, I'll help you a little. We were over the fence, now the field, touched down and came to a halt at the end of the runway. I was trembling and soaked with sweat.

"I guess that's enough for today," Ed said. "We'll give it another go tomorrow."

We taxied to the parking area, got out and walked over to the office.

"What a terrible mess I made of it," I thought. "The other students and instructors will be laughing in derision. They will know I'm a 'frozen brains' from the north."

We entered the building. No one so much as noticed us. Students were busy with instructors; some planning a flight; some discussing tomorrow's instruction, and one student who had already soloed was entering up his log books.

"We'll start a log book for you now Dick, and see what there is down for tomorrow. We'll enter up our flight in the aircraft's log books. This is the Journey Log Book and this is the Engine Log. And this is your own private log book. I make the entries as your instructor and after you solo you will enter your own time when you are the pilot in command."

Ed went to the desk where the flights for the next day were booked, glanced down the page and said, "There's an aircraft free tomorrow at ten. We'll put you down for an hour in the morning and an hour in the afternoon, OK?"

"Sure, OK," I said, swallowing and trying to sound enthusiastic.

"And by-the-way, Dick, ground school is Monday and Wednesday nights from seven to nine in room four in the building past the hangar. You can prepare yourself by studying 'from the ground up' in the evenings."

Back at the motel, Vera asked, "How did it go?"

"Not too bad," I replied, "I've got a good instructor. Ed Batchelor, he's cool."

That evening I kept thinking, "I've sure got to get a grip on myself and quit being so nervous. Some of those young guys say they have soloed in three hours. It's going to take me thirty at least unless I smarten up. And after thirty-five hours I'm supposed to be a pilot and will be writing the D.O.T. exams. I can see it's going to be a full time job if I am to do it in a month."

The next day Ed and I logged two hours of circuits and bumps and I made one or two landings without Ed having to help me. I was inclined to come in too hot and would bounce before coming to a stop.

At ground school Ed started out by telling us about Great Circles, and leading on to map reading and navigation. Then he went to flight controls, explaining the forces acting upon an aircraft in flight—thrust, drag, lift and gravity. Then an explanation of the terms—pitch, yaw, turn, bank, slip, etc. and the proper use of the controls. I saw that ground school was mainly a matter of memorizing the right answers in Navigation, Air Regulations, Weather and Aircraft Maintenance. I had plenty of time to study in the evenings and made sure I would not fail the written exams.

After Ed had given me about six hours of dual instruction he said to me one morning, "Let's go up and practice some spins and steep turns. Take her up to four thousand feet, go over to the area where we were yesterday and we'll go through a spin or two."

If he had said, "Now we'll go and do some loops under the Patullo bridge," he couldn't have unnerved me more. "Well, this is it then, I only have to die once, so let's go."

When we were over the area of farmlands he had indicated, Ed said, "All right, I have control." He sounded so nonchalant I thought he had abandoned the idea of doing spins. But he continued, "We do a right turn, all clear; now we do a left turn, again all clear, no aircraft in sight. This is how we induce a spin. Pull back on the controls until she is headed almost straight up, then when we are on the point of a stall we throttle back, kick right rudder and at the same time give a little opposite aileron and over we go."

And over we went. Not now, but right now. Spinning to the earth clockwise like a leaf falling to the ground. I found my hands clinging to the engine supports in the cockpit. Ed laughed, and said, "We make one then two and three complete turns, and as she comes up on the third turn we dump the stick ahead, neutralize the controls and before the airspeed builds up pull back on the stick until we are flying straight and level. You see, there is no problem and no danger, and the airplane comes out of it so easily. Now you have control Dick, take her back up to 4000 and you do one."

Surprisingly enough after the first initial fright a coolness and confidence set in and I tightened my seat belt for the third time, and wonder of wonders, went up to altitude, looked carefully to right and left, found all clear, lined up with a road on the ground, put the nose in the air and did a passable anti-clockwise spin, making two complete revolutions and coming out on the third.

Ed then showed me how to do steep turns. You put one wing high in the air and with the nose on the horizon you come around in a tight turn with not too much pressure on the stick trying to hit your slip-stream each time 'round. Since that time I have heard experts disagree on how much throttle should be used when doing steep turns and have heard some maintain that steep turns can be accomplished 'hands off' by utilizing only trim and rudders. It can be done with some aircraft, perhaps not with all.

After this I would practice spins and steep turns at every opportunity as I found that doing so did wonders for my self-confidence.

The next day we did stalls and precautionary landings.

Ed said, "Take her over to where we were yesterday and up to about three thousand feet." I did so, then he reached ahead and said, "I am chopping the throttle and pulling Carb. heat now. Pick out a farm field and make a dead engine approach with the intention of landing in the field."

I did as he instructed me to do beforehand. Picking out a large enough cow pasture nearby I zigged and zagged back and forth losing altitude at 500 feet per minute, always keeping the field in sight and up-wind. The wind direction was indicated by smoke rising from the ground. On final approach over the field and just about to touch down, Ed said, "OK, that's good, pour on the coal, go 'round and do it again."

The next day after an hour of circuits and bumps Ed announced, "Taxi to the end of the strip and turn around." I did so. He opened the door and got out. "All right," he smiled, "You're on your own, I'm going in to have coffee, make a couple of circuits and come on in."

My heart started to pound and my hands became clammy.

"This is it, Dick Turner," I thought. "This is what you wanted now let's see if you can get this bird in the air and down again without killing yourself."

I taxied onto the runway, put on the brakes, did the mandatory checks, mixture rich, all clear, let out the brakes, opened the tap, dumped the stick ahead to raise the tail and then eased back gently as speed was gained, and became airborne.

"Ed's not here to help me now," I thought. "I've just got to do things right." Before I knew it I was at 500 feet. Now a climbing turn; WHOOPS, at 1000 feet already, throttle back, level out. There's where I turn for cross-wind, so far so good; there's the clump of trees where I turn for down wind. A bit further a slight panic hit me, where the hell is the building below where I turn on base leg? There it is. Good. Reduce power, now turn on final and line up for approach. Carb. heat's on, OK. Rate of descent about right. Maybe a little too low, some throttle. Chop it again. Over the fence, not bad, a mite too high, let her settle gently, stick back, more, MORE, all the way. She's on. A three pointer. One little bounce and I roll to a halt. WOW! I did it. I can fly.

Ed came out grinning and shook my hand. I did two more circuits, not as good as the first but passable. I got out of the airplane walking on air. I could hardly wait to tell Vera and the kids.

"I soloed, all by myself and Ed says I did all right, I'm going to be a pilot at last."

Vera seemed amused, "Isn't that the point of the whole thing? If you are going to fly an aircraft you'll be a pilot won't you?"

"But this is the biggest day of my life," I replied. "I was doubtful for a while if I was going to be able to solo. Some kids do it in six hours and I took eleven and twenty minutes. But Ed says that your time to solo doesn't always indicate the true measure of a man's flying ability. There are many things that determine the making of a good pilot. Only time will tell but I am certainly going to work hard at it."

On the days which were not suitable for flying I drove into Vancouver to find a light aircraft to purchase. The ones suitable for bush flying and within the price range of my pocket book were limited. At last I settled on a two place Taylorcraft. It was a fabric airplane with wooden spars, painted yellow and her registration was CF-HAL.

The next two weeks were spent in trying to get my landings a little smoother and in cross country flying. At last one of the other instructors gave me a check ride and I was ready to go to Vancouver to write the D.O.T. examinations.

The exams were a series of multiple choice questions and you had to check off the answer you thought was the right one. They seemed to be straightforward questions and there was nothing surprising about them. Sometime later I was told that I had passed and received my Private Pilot Licence number VRP-5186, dated March 5, 1958.

I found the T-Craft was different to fly than the Super Cub I had trained on. It had less power and was slow to accelerate. It did have a tremendous wingspan and would float and float. Its stall was the most gentle I have ever seen in an aircraft. With the engine shut down and with a fairly good load, you could hold the stick full back and at forty miles an hour the nose would drop, she would pick up speed, the nose would come back up and she would stall again with never any tendency for one wing or the other to fall off. The T-Craft had what we call gentle characteristics. But her top speed was about ninety-three miles per hour. She had a lot of drag for that little 85 HP engine. I purchased a pair of skis to go with her and shipped them to Fort Nelson by truck to be there when Rolf and I arrived later.

It was on March 9 that Ron Elmore, an instructor at the flying school and I set off for Calgary. Vera and Martha had left to fly home to Nahanni and Rolf went with them as far as Calgary and would go on with me from there.

Going into McCall Field (now the Calgary International Airport) was a bit of a headache as the radio in HAL had only the LF (low frequency) band and a Mickey Mouse one at that. A decent two-way radio at that time would have cost over a thousand dollars and was a luxury I could not afford. Ron, who was flying the plane had difficulty in making out the tower transmissions, but they seemed to be able to hear him all right.

Compared to the little airstrip at Langley the vast hard-surfaced runway at Calgary seemed endless. We needed only one tenth of it for our requirements.

The next morning Rolf and I taxied out for the flight to Edmonton and points north. I'm blessed if I could make out the instructions from the tower but when they gave me a green light I was on my way.

The weather was clear, we had maps with a scale of eight miles to the inch with our route marked out and with the highway underneath navigation was simple. A few miles from Penhold two Harvard trainers came buzzing at us like a pair of hornets and missed us by a distance that was far too close for comfort. The roar of their engines surged above ours as we met. I was flying straight and level and minding my own business. They gave me such a fright I would have shot them down if I had anything to shoot with. They were probably smart alec kids training for the Air Force.

At Edmonton the weather delayed us for a day. We had a good set of maps and I resolved to follow the railroad to Whitecourt, then the highway for fifty miles more at which point we would cut across to Grande Prairie. From there the road would take us right to Fort Nelson. From Edmonton to Whitecourt the ceiling was very low and we flew at treetop level. Rolf held the maps and checked off each town as we went by. Past Whitecourt we were able to climb to five thousand feet and were able to pick up Grande Prairie long before we arrived. We fueled at Grande Prairie and Fort St. John. We bumped down on runway 025 at Fort Nelson late in the afternoon and we were both glad to be getting near home.

After some waiting around we got the wheels removed from HAL and the skis put on. I could now see that the skis I had bought in Vancouver were not quite the right ones for northern conditions. They were called A1500A and were the most useless damned things you ever did see. A duck's webbed foot could support more weight in the snow than those skis could. They were possibly four and a half feet long and not more than eight inches in width. They came to a very sharp point and had a slight turn-up.

I made a couple of circuits with the skis on the ski-strip near the hangar. There was no difference in the flying characteristics of the aircraft except that of course there was no braking action, which mattered not at all except in a rare case when a landing was made on glare ice.

We got away about noon one day and as we headed for Nahanni 165 miles north, I wondered about the depth of snow on the river ice of the snye where we would be landing in front of our house. I had asked Gus Kraus to have the natives tramp out a landing strip on this side channel of the Nahanni which was two hundred feet wide and was protected from the winds more than the main river channel.

It was a little hazy with a light wind and as I circled over Nahanni I could make out everything on the ground except the airstrip on the ice. "It is probably drifted over with snow," I thought. However it would not matter much as the surface seemed smooth and the depth of snow I felt sure was not over two feet.

The wind seemed to be drifting the smoke from the cabin chimney right across the river so I circled once and lined up with the snye and came in from the east for a landing. Knowing the surface was smooth I was surprised to feel a bump when we touched down. We settled into the twenty inches of snow and the aircraft started to pull off sharply to the right. I applied left rudder but to no effect. We went about two hundred feet and were almost stopped when the tail came up and right over and poor HAL was on its back in the snow. Rolf and I crawled out and examined the situation. The starboard ski had hit the frozen hard packed trail and had bent the landing gear off forty-five degrees to the right and that was why the plane had wanted to pull over.

Neither of us had the least scratch but I could see the airplane would need extensive repairs before it flew again. My flying days were over for this winter at least.

Martha had been standing on the river bank and had seen the aircraft go over on its back. She was in tears, and I couldn't blame her for crying as it is a sad thing to see a bird from the sky crumple its wing.

We proceeded to dig out our baggage and odds and ends and carry them up to the house. I cannot remember the exact words I used at the time but I can assure you that the air was a deep purple for miles around. I cursed Gus for not having marked out a landing strip as I had asked. I cursed my own foolishness for not dragging the intended landing area more carefully and for forgetting about the tobaggan trail that I knew would be as hard as a steel rail. And I complained about he perversity of Fate in general, and particularly the stupid bastards who had designed those A1500A skis with such colossal ineptitude. The points were like needles and were obviously designed to penetrate an obstacle instead of riding over it.

Up at the house Vera tried to console me. "Take it in your stride, you'll get it flying again. Be glad no one was hurt."

"Big help Irvin." I snarled. "It would have been a damned sight better if I had run slam into the Butte. Not hurt. Not hurt? Christ Almighty, the AIRPLANE is hurt, that's what's hurt. And how am I going to fix it here, that's what I'd like to know? It will be next winter and two thousand dollars later before I get it flying again. And I stamped around almost out of my mind with grief and fury. It had taken every dollar I could scrape up for the trip outside, flying lessons and the airplane. Now it seemed it was all for nothing. My hopes of getting the fur to market were shattered. Again we would sit and wait until June to get the fur to the auction sales and wait until September for the money to buy our trade goods and supplies that had come in by water transport in August. Wherever I turned I could see money going down the drain.

Coping with adversity had taken ninety per cent of my effort in the north so far, and the other ten per cent went to put bread on the table. I thought, "A setback like this is after all a normal turn of events, but if I can hang on and keep pressure applied perhaps when the tide turns something will start coming my way."

I notified the Department of Transport regarding the accident as that had to be done within forty-eight hours. I also informed the insurance company that I would have the aircraft in Fort Nelson to be shipped out for repairs about May 20th following.

Somehow we got back to normal and I was soon busy getting the tug and barge ready for open water and the trip to Fort Nelson as soon as the ice moved out of the rivers.

2

Back in the Air Again

Although HAL was covered with insurance to the full value I soon found out the hard way that I had a lot to learn about insurance and insurance companies. I had $250 deductable on hull coverage and ended up having to pay another $200 on top of that to the firm that repaired the machine and which the insurance company refused to pay. On consulting a law firm in Vancouver I was advised to pay the two hundred extra or face a lengthy and expensive court procedure when I had no guarantee the ruling would be in my favour. I wonder how many other aircraft owners have been ripped off this way?

On October 1st HAL was back in Fort Nelson on wheels ready to go again. Here a strange thing happened which I had not forseen. When I got into the airplane for a test flight I was so nervous that I was afraid I would bend it if I tried to take it up alone and concluded it would be a safety measure to get another pilot to check me out. Steve Villers and Jim Burroughs offered to give me a few circuits. It took longer than I had thought to feel comfortable in the aircraft again. Steve gave me several hours of his time and made a trip with me to a sandbar airstrip on the Liard River a hundred miles northwest.

The next day I loaded up and headed for Nahanni, hoping for better results than the last time HAL set off for the Butte. It was lovely fall weather. The leaves with no snow on the ground as yet. There was no man made landing strip at Nahanni in those years and I planned on using sandbars on the rivers as landing strips.

The bar across from the house was long enough but a bit soft as yet but there was one on the Liard about four miles upstream that appeared hard and serviceable. That was the one I would use until the weather turned cold, at which time I would utilize the one nearer home.

On arriving at Nahanni I buzzed Jack Norcross to come and get me with his boat, then flew back to the sand bar for a landing. This time I flew back and forth until I was sure there were no obstructions in the touch-down area. The surface of sand and small stones was smooth and the landing was good. I taxied over to a sheltered place near the trees and tied the aircraft down to stakes driven into the ground, and locked the controls so that the wind would not flip the ailerons and elevators around.

Now I felt much better, as the aircraft was handy to home and in another month it could be brought down to the bar on the Nahanni where it would be visible from the yard.

By November 1st the wet sand of the exposed bars was frozen solid making the landing strip as firm as tarmack. When the snow became deep enough I removed the wheels and installed the skis, which had been widened and shaped properly. Ted Taylor and Hilton Burry had supervised the job for me at Fort Nelson.

That fall the Nahanni River froze over early in November a mile below the house and a mile above leaving two miles of open water in between which had to be crossed to reach the airplane on the sandbar. The shore ice extended out for a hundred feet or so and on a cold day there was much to get back and forth across the open water to the aircraft. To get away by nine in the morning when a faint light was appearing in the east, I had to be up at six. After breakfast I would bundle up in warm clothes and carry down to the water's edge all the necessary equipment and baggage for a flight to Fort Nelson. There would be a keg of gas, strainer and funnel, the aircraft battery that had been warming in the house, a blow-pot to preheat the engine, a packsack with spare clothing, outgoing mail, bedroll to keep freezables in for the trip home, and emergency equipment including food, axe and rifle. These items were loaded into the canoe on the edge of the ice, and the canoe lifted gently and slipped into the water. Then I would step carefully in and paddle across a hundred yards to the other shore. On a morning when it was twenty or more below there would be a fog rising from the water and it was an eerie feeling paddling in the dark through the stream and moving cakes of ice to the opposite shore that could barely be seen.

Across the river I would unload the canoe, pull it across the ice and up onto the beach where a sudden rise of water could not reach it. (When rivers are freezing over they can often drop or rise two or three feet overnight.) Then the supplies were piled on a small hand toboggan and pulled down stream to where the aircraft was parked. I always fueled up after a flight as the danger from condensation inside the tanks would thus be eliminated. First I would light the blow-pot and set it inside the engine tent directly under the oil pan. For an hour while the engine was warming I would sit inside the engine tent where it was comfortable and to see that nothing caught on fire. Unless it was colder than forty below, after an hour's heating the engine was warm enough to start. A cold engine will often fire up but unless the oil is warm a cold start is not advisable. Aircraft mechanics have warned repeatedly against starting an engine when the oil is too cold to circulate. It is well to heed their advice, for a pilot's life depends on the trouble free operation of his engine.

Next the warm battery was placed inside and hooked up, wing covers removed and folded in the airplane, engine tent, packsack, mail bag, axe and gun placed in the baggage compartment. Then an inspection of the aircraft was made, gas caps locked, air vents open, all ice and snow removed from the elevators, oil filler cap tight, cowlings properly fastened and the skis kicked loose from the poles or brush underneath them. All pilots did not bother with wing covers as they are heavy to cart around and a nuisance to put on and off. But it does assure the wings and most importantly, the leading edges are free of ice and snow when you take off.

When it was warm the engine would always fire up immediately and after a warm up period when the oil temp. needle came off the peg, checks were done and with the dawn appearing in the eastern sky the tap was opened and HAL was away.

Before the winter was far advanced I noticed a big difference in the performance compared to the warm weather of the summer. On a hot day the engine develops less power and coupled with less lift from the expanded air it often seems to take forever and a day to become airborne. On a cold day the engine develops full power and at forty below the air seems as thick as water and with this terrific lift you are in the air right now.

Fort Liard was less than halfway to Fort Nelson and during these years I had a trading post there and the man managing it that winter for me was Ernie Carriere, an old trapper. I usually stopped there to pick up the mail and to check for any small items needed for the store. Most winters the ice on the Liard was too rough to permit landing with an aircraft, and we used the ice at the mouth of the Black River for an airstrip.

With the hours of daylight so short during December and January I was seldom able to get my errands done and mail and supplies picked up in time to get home before dark, and I would have to overnight at Fort Nelson.

During these years the burden of my company fell upon Ted Taylor and his wife Melvina. Ted was the base engineer for Canadian Pacific Airlines and also had the airport gas agency for Imperial Oil. The whole deal turned out to be pretty rough on poor Ted. In order to sell me gasoline for the airplance (it burned four gallons an hour) he found he was doing the maintenance on HAL and putting me up for the night when I stayed over.

When Ted and Melvina eventually moved to a more southern clime, Ross Clark and Hilton Burry found themselves with a star boarder on occasion. As all four of us, with some others, were flying types it later transpired that we had some interesting times, but more of that later.

Martha, now ten years old, was going to school at Fort Nelson that winter and now that we had an airplane we could get her home for Christmas. The trip home was uneventful except that it was very cold inside the aircraft. There is almost no heat at all in those old bush airplanes and even if you bundle up as much as possible, at thirty below, after sitting for two hours you get so cold that if someone kicks you, you shatter.

It must have been at least thirty below when we landed at Nahanni. By now the river had tightened up and there was a trail across to the house. I told Mart that she had better run along to the house right away and I would throw the wing covers on, put some poles under the skis and be along later. In order to get warmed up I dashed around gathering up poles to put under the skis. One likely looking pole was bent over in a hoop with each end frozen in the sand under the snow. It wouldn't come loose and instead of getting the axe from the airplane I was determined to break it loose with my hands. I put all my strength into the job and gave it a mighty tug. It came all right, but just the big end and it caught me squarely across the bridge of the nose. It just about set me on my butt. I hung tough for a while, saying to myself, "I won't go down, I WILL NOT go down," and slowly I sank to my knees in spite of my efforts not to give in.

It was the strangest feeling; my knees seemed to turn to jelly and crumple under me like well-cooked spaghetti. On my knees I began to recover. One hand from my mit went to my face and came away covered with blood. I stood up; one eye was dim but I was getting my strength back. Now I grabbed that stick and with wild fury I smashed it to bits, which did make me feel much better.

I looked up and Gus was coming along the trail to help me with the airplane and carry the load over to the house.

"Whatever you been doing?" he enquired. "Trying to kill yourself?"

"That damned log," I answered. "I'm lucky it hit me on the head, somewhere else might have hurt."

We soon had the engine tent and the wing covers on and were over at the cabin warming up. Vera looked at me and asked, "What in the world have you been doing to yourself?"

Before I could answer Gus replied, "Oh, he went to give me some 'lip' and I let him have it."

Which goes to show that in the north we laugh at anything short of death and destruction.

Over a late lunch I told Vera and Gus that my poor nose was having a rough history. When I was ten years old I had been hit in the face with a hockey puck twice in the same day, and it has been somewhat awry ever since. Now today it had received another blow, nearer to the bridge this time so perhaps it would have two bumps now. On looking in the mirror it seemed I was wearing a green and purple mask.

This brought to mind the case of Jack Mulholland, who was Bill Epler's partner when Bill and Jack's brother Joe went into the Nahanni and never returned. Both had trapped in the lower Liard area in the 1930s. Jack was what I would term a colorful character and had been raised in the tough school of the hobo jungles of the 1920s. He was known for his quick wit and both he and Bill Epler were said to be very tough opponents in a poker game.

Jack was repairing his boat engine one June in Fort Simpson. It was a 25 HP Universal inboard and did not have an electric start. As the engine sat low in the boat the hand cranking was difficult and a bit touchy. The crank had become worn and was inclined to slip out of the locking mechanism when pressure was applied. Bill and I were watching Jack start the engine one evening when the engine was in a non-starting mood. Jack was bent over the engine and was obviously becoming frustrated when he gave the crank a vicious upward heave. The heavy knobby end of the crank slipped from the engaging pin and coming around caught him squarely on the nose at about the middle point. Poor Jack didn't even have strength enough to swear; he knelt there with his hands to his face groaning.

With the help of Bill and me he was soon able to get to his feet and we walked him up to Dr. Truesdell's house close by. Art Truesdell sat him in a chair and as a sculptor would with a bit of clay he pressed the nose back into shape, standing back once in a while to assess his work. Jack's face was not as white as a sheet but it did remind me of uncooked bread dough. On seeing this the Doctor said, "Run in the house Dick and get him a drink."

And I immediately thought, "A glass of rum now is just what the Doctor ordered, there will never be a better time for it."

Art spoke again, "The water barrel is in the corner."

A dipperful of water did restore Jack somewhat and in a short time he was able to walk on back to the cabin, and he was soon joking about his poor wounded nose.

"You would think," he said, "that in time I would learn to keep my snoot out of the way of flying objects. Last winter I was wrapping a cracked hammer handle with tape and I was pulling like hell on the hammer handle. The tape broke and the hammer head landed smack on my nose, right in this very same place." And with a poor attempt at a chuckle he put his hand gingerly to the swollen blob that at other times was his nose.

Gus volunteered, "I guess a man's nose is there to protect his eyes. If a man's eyes stuck out like his nose most of us would soon be blind."

"Better the nos than the ayes," I said and nobody laughed.

Rolf and Mart had never attended a regular school and during the summer Vera and I had decided to send Mart to Fort Nelson to take grade seven and Rolf to Yellowknife for grade nine. Yellowknife was the largest settlement in the Northwest Territories and was reported to have a good high school with an excellent staff. Jack Norcross had flown Rolf to Yellowknife in late August and I planned on flying over there to bring the boy home for the Christmas holidays. It was a 335 mile trip one way; 100 to Simpson and 235 from there. On December 23rd I set off and at Simpson was forced to turn back for weather and did not attempt the trip again until a day or two after Christmas. This time I made it through to Yellowknife; it was twenty below with a low ceiling and no wind.

There was a big ski-plane base in a bay of the big lake close to town and that is where I landed. There were many planes sitting on the ice; among them another T-Craft, Cessna 180s, Norsemen, Beavers and Otters. There were about five operators running charter businesses out of Yellowknife as there was some mining exploration work to the north and many Artctic communities were served from the base.

Rolf was thirteen years old at this time and quite a tall lad. I was very surprised to find him thin and worn looking. He seemed to be getting enough food where he was boarding and after considering the situation overnight I put him in the hospital for a day or two for a thorough check-up, as I thought he might have contracted T.B. or some other debilitating disease. The doctors could find nothing wrong so we went back to the hotel and planned on leaving for home when the storm abated. The wind had risen to a gale and a real blizzard had developed. We stayed for a time with Vera's brother Art and his wife Jossie, who had three daughters.

The girls who were all school age told me that Rolf was a very good student and was in fact doing too well for his own good. The miners' kids, with a number of toughs among them said he was making them appear dumb and were trying to slow him down by beating him up regularly. Rolf had said nothing of this to me but now things were starting to fall into place. I went over to the school and had a talk with his teacher who said that Rolf was a very good student and even corrected the teacher in class on occasion. He said he was unaware of the treatment by the tough miners' kids. I listened, offered no comment and left.

"That is it," I concluded, "the kid is going home and will take correspondence." If we had lived at Yellowknife I would have found some other solution to the problem. I love a battle as well as anyone providing I have a just cause, but there was no way I was going to leave him here to submit to such treatment.

For many years after this I avoided Yellowknife as I would have a skunk.

I mention this incident to illustrate the price paid to bring children up in the bush. In going out to school to a large center the experience for most kids is almost traumatic. A friend of ours who taught primary school at Fort Liard for a number of years sent his boys to Edmonton for high school. When he visited them six months later one of the boys was on the verge of a mental breakdown as a result of the treatment by some of his classmates.

For three days the wind blew and it became colder each day. On the morning of January 2nd the wind had died and it was fifty-five below at the skiplane base, a scene of frustrated activity. Pilots and crews were out with blowpots heating their engines; some had their motors going and were trying to get moving; some had shut down temporarily and were pushing and pulling on their skis to break them loose from the drifted snow which was now as hard as cement. One pilot had returned from a flight north because the oil temperature had dropped to a dangerous level. A bulldozer was out on the bay pushing down the drifts and smoothing the surface to allow the planes to take off.

I thought it was a mite too cold to fly, so I shut it down and went back to the hotel.

The following morning it had warmed up to forty-two below with a heavy haze hanging low over the lake. I borrowed a large blowpot and in two hours we had HAL warmed up and ready to go. Rolf and I took turns in watching the blowpot so that one of us could stay inside to keep warm. We put on all the clothes we had for we knew it would be colder than a banker's smile inside that T-Craft. We were in for a bitter two and a half hour's flight to Fort Simpson.

Taxiing over the drifts to the cleared strip I was afraid the little plane would tip over. The drifts were so high that one wing would almost touch the surface as we bumped along. Miraculously the oil temperature needle came off the peg and stayed in the green. I opened the tap, we picked up speed and were in the air. The ceiling was low with the visibility not over four miles and to see ahead at all we had to stay right over the trees. The only navigating instrument the T-Craft had was a compass which pointed east all the time, so there was nothing for it but to follow the lakeshore around until we hit the MacKenzie River which would take us into Fort Simpson. This would take us many miles out of our way but seemed the safest thing to do.

My God, but it was cold in that airplane; the wind came in around the doors and through the cracks. The small engine heater had no effect at all. Rolf almost froze his hands when he had to take off his mitts to get out a map for me. And what the hell was wrong with the controls? The trim was set as far ahead as it would go but the plane was still tail heavy. I had to keep a constant pressure on the control column to keep the nose down. Something was very wrong, but I was damned if I was going to turn and go back to that dump of a Yellowknife.

I had never followed the lakeshore before, and it was all strange country to me. Watching the map carefully, after an hour and a half we checked our position at Wrigley Harbour with Beaver Lake coming up. The thermometer registered just forty below and I could see that Rolf was pretty cold although he did not complain. I was dressed warmer than he was yet my hands and arms were becoming so cold and stiff that I could not maintain sufficient pressure on the control and had to bring up my knee to keep it in the forward position.

"If we can last out to Providence," I said, "we'll land and get warmed up. I think there is a strip there, it can't be more than fifty miles now." Rolf nodded in approval. I think he was too cold to speak.

There was an airstrip at Providence about three miles from town that looked like it had never been used and the drifts seemed two feet high.

"They'll be hard as rocks too," I thought. "But we have to land; we must warm up and we'll need more gas to get to Simpson."

I flew low over the strip in a maneuver that pilots call 'dragging the strip' to look for obstructions, bumps, holes and anything that might impede a landing.

"It sure as hell is rough," I said to Rolf, "but we have to go down, that's for sure." I lined up with the strip, made a low approach under power and as we touched, chopped the power and held back on the stick. We bumped along to a stop with no harm done. I taxied to one side and we got out, stiff with cold.

"Now what?" I asked Rolf. "It is three miles to town, there are no buildings in sight and we had better start walking before we freeze to death."

"Look, Dad," Rolf exclaimed, "there's someone coming."

A vehicle drove up, a man got out and said, "You'd better come in and get warm, I live right close."

Only once in my life before and never since have I been so cold, and never have I been so glad to see the inside of a warm house. There is a myth which says that when you are cold you wish to lie down and fall asleep. Don't ever believe it. When you are really cold you are in pain, almost like having a toothache in every bone in your body.

I cannot for the life of me recall that man's name, but wherever he is I hope that he is blessed with all the good things that life can hold. He took us in and fed us after we had thawed out. We stayed all night and in the morning he provided a propane torch to heat the engine of the T-Craft and gasoline for refueling.

As I write this the room is warm and comfortable, but I have just gone over and turned the heat up from 72 to 82. I still shiver when I think of that day.

After we fueled up I examined the plane and in checking over the tail section I found well over twenty pounds of packed snow had been sucked into the fuselage directly above the elevators, during the blizzard. This additional weight was the cause of the airplane flying tail heavy. More weight here would have put the center of gravity far enough back so that the plane would have stalled after take-off with possibly very unpleasant consequences.

The next day was noticeably warmer and we arrived safely at Nahanni where the four of us had a delayed New Year's feast and celebration.

The holidays were over and it was time to get Mart back to school. At our house when any of the kids were leaving for school to be away for five months or so it was always an unhappy and tearful time. This was no exception.

When we left for Fort Nelson it was ten below with a solid cloud cover. The T-Craft hummed along merrily and never missed a beat as long as I remembered to pull Carb. heat when necessary. The strip at the Black River was in good condition: it was hardly ever drifted in for it was protected by the deep river bed and tall trees on each side and did not get the blast from the wind that howled up or down the Liard River. After taking off from Liard I saw the clouds were right down on the surrounding hills and I chose to follow the river valley south although it was forty miles farther than cutting straight across.

Fifty miles south of Fort Liard we hit snow showers and patches of fog. In one patch of what looked like a snow shower we picked up drops of rain that froze to the windshield. I looked at the thermometer, which showed eight degrees below. No doubt about it, there was forty-two degrees of frost and yet it was raining. It was the first time I had encountered 'super cooled' moisture that froze to the aircraft on impact. The moisture in the air should have been frozen into visible snowflakes and pellets but seeing is believing and I began to skirt around those innocent looking showers. At Pretty Hill we passed through a harmless looking one and instantly the windshield was covered with ice and in a short time had obstructed the forward view and seemed to be about an eighth of an inch thick. The side windows were clear and I could see that the wings and the spars were starting to build up a perceptible amount of ice.

"Nothing to worry about there," I thought. "She'll fly with a lot more ice than that but it would be more to my liking to see where I'm going so I had better turn and get out of this."

Looking out the side I made the turn and headed back to Liard. I looked to see how Mart was taking all this and saw that she had covered herself with a blanket and had her head buried.

"You're OK," I told her. "You can look out the side window."

"It scares me," she replied. "I feel better like this."

"All right then, I'll wake you up at Liard."

But I wasn't feeling too relaxed myself. There were more light showers to go through before we got back and as I prepared to land the forward view was completely obscured. There was no wind however and I was able to make a nice long final approach over the Liard River into the mouth of the Black in a sort of side-slipping maneuver which enabled me to see ahead until I straightened out to touch down.

When we came to a stop Mart came out of hiding and said, "I wasn't really scared Daddy, but I felt better where I was warm and not bothering you. I knew you'd make it all right." And she gave me a kiss.

Experienced pilots told me later that if a stubborn pilot persists in boring his way through those kind of icing conditions he could possibly end up killing himself and his passengers, for ice forming on the leading edges of the wings could destroy the lift characteristics and the airplane would cease to fly.

3

Turbulence and Toothache

I was averaging about thirty hours of flying time each month now and had one hundred and fifty hours of time logged. As my hours built up I was realizing more and more that being a competent pilot was a continuous learning process. With one or two noticeable lapses I did not become bold and over-confident. If I erred it was mostly on the over cautious side. Old pilots have said that an occasional fright, if you learn from it, will make a better pilot of you. Of the many bush pilots I knew who have killed themselves, most should have known from experience not to allow themselves to get into such situations.

Fort Nelson, Fort Liard and Nahanni Butte are all on the eastern edge of the mountain front. The prevailing winds are from the west and throughout the year we get many days of hot west winds that come boiling over the mountains from six and eight thousand feet down to six hundred feet above sea level at Nahanni Butte. The air is heated by pressure and by the time it gets this far it is often from forty to sixty degrees above. These are called Chinook winds and are as common in the winter months as at other times of the year. They can last from two hours to ten days. The velocity is often fifty mph and can go to seventy mph. It has been my experience that velocities higher than these come from the north and east and are extremely rare.

A strong wind coming from the west moves over very rough terrain and the air becomes turbulent just as water does when passing swiftly over boulders. Experts in this field have informed me that at sufficient velocity, the air on leaving a mountain range will start to roll downward and around in a series of onrushing loops. This movement will continue onto the plains for many miles depending on the velocity. The insidious feature of this condition is that in contrast to the violent and very dangerous up-drafts of the anvil-shaped thunder heads (cumulo-nimbus) which are obvious to the eye, the cloud warnings of the Chinook condition are not always noticeable. Often the air is clear with little white innocent looking clouds at from six to ten thousand feet.

My first and almost fatal encounter with a violent Chinook wind was on March 5, 1959 when I had less than 200 hours flying time. The days were getting long and the weather was warm and balmy when I loaded the T-Craft (which handled 300 pounds of cargo easily) at the Fort Nelson Airport, took off on the ski strip and headed home. My load consisted of a case of cigarettes and tobacco for the store, cases of groceries and canned goods, a parcel of fresh fruit and vegetables stuffed inside the bedroll, a sack of mail for ourselves and our neighbours and a 100 pound sack of feed oats for Mart's horse. This last item was in the cockpit beside me, resting against the passenger's seat. I climbed to 5000 feet and leveled off. The outside temperature was forty above, the roar of the engine was reassuring and I felt fat and happy. (Since that episode whenever I realize that I am fat and happy I tighten my seatbelt and check thoroughly for signs of danger.)

After passing the Sixty Mile Ridge I could see the long mountain to the west of Liard and directly ahead in the distance the 5000 foot mountain we call Nahanni Butte. At this time the turbulence was becoming pronounced but not severe and a crab to the left was necessary in order not to drift off track. There were no black Chinook clouds over the mountains to the west but the little white puffs above me seemed to be rolling along like balls of yarn on a floor.

Becoming a bit apprehensive I tightened my seat belt for the third time. The turbulence increased and I recalled Ed Batchelor's advice, "If you encounter severe turbulence reduce power and maintain your attitude." Meaning keep the aircraft straight and level. I did so, or rather I tried to do so.

The airspeed needle was swinging from eighty to one hundred mph and the sound of the engine would roar and then disappear then roar again. The tail would rise in the air and be slammed to the right; one wing would drop off suddenly, then rise again much higher than it should. To correct this behaviour I tried to compensate by using aileron control. The effect was almost nil: I was being tossed around like a leaf in the wind. My hands were wet with sweat and my grip on the control column would have done credit to a trapeze artist.

When the turbulence was at its worst it was useless to direct my eyes to the instrument panel. The shuddering of the aircraft coupled with the violent movement of the wings prevented me from searching out any instrument and pinning it down for long enough to get a reading. I did know the airspeed needle was swinging violently. The gas gauge was a dip needle on a floating cork and it was leaping madly up and down. The ball and needle of the turn and bank indicator were both wobbling in an uncertain manner, with the rudders being used for directional control. The RPM needle was constant when I looked at it on first reducing power. The altimeter was working full time as it tried to keep pace with the updrafts and subsequent downdrafts. There was no rate-of-climb dial on the T-Craft which is just as well for I am certain the mechanism would have been horribly twisted and useless after that hammering.

Except for trying to get a reading on the airspeed indicator occasionally, I had no interest in the instruments anyway. My eyes were directed on the horizon in a grim attempt to keep the plane in some semblance of a normal flying attitude.

I did consider turning back to Fort Nelson but I was not sure I could turn without the aircraft going over on its back. And besides I was ashamed to tell Ted and the boys that I was afraid of a little turbulence. By this time I was past Liard and not over fifty miles from home and for a time I was truly doubtful if those long wings with their wooden spars could hold on much longer.

The sack of oats would leave the floor and come down again filling the cockpit with dust. The fuselage creaked and groaned and twice I heard a 'snap' from the direction of the main spar. I knew that wings had been known to come off in the air and was not sure how much of a snap it would take to do it. After considering that this was probably my last day of life I resigned myself to my fate, merely using some rudder to stay right side up, and at the same time keeping one hand on the sack of oats so that it would not slam into the instrument panel.

One thought was now becoming firmly fixed in my mind and it was this: if by any chance I survived this ride, I would renounce flying, sell the aircraft, throw away my log book and try to forget I ever wanted to be an aviator. I was just NOT cut out to be a pilot.

As I approached the Butte the violence decreased and the plane was responding a bit more to the controls and I was able to leave the sack of oats to take care of itself. I could see that the aircraft was going to hang together and I would have to give all my attention to the landing. I was using the snye in front of the house for a strip and it was protected by trees. The wind appeared to be straight down the snye and though the gusts were violent I might get it down right side up. Hope began to revive and as I approached the Butte I resolved to fly the plane onto the strip and not let it fly me. One characteristic of Chinook winds is the fluctuation from sixty mph. to a dead calm with five to ten second intervals, and I was prepared to use full power when necessary to keep from hitting the ground.

I started the final approach well back from the snye and found the wind was directly in line, but the gusts were furious. Trimmed out to come down at 200 feet per minute the T-Craft would suddenly drop away as if in a vacuum, then go straight up for a hundred feet, then down again. Low over the river it was more stable and with power applied at just the right instant I held it off until I was over the strip then chopped the power and holding the tail high, it stayed down. Rolf came down from the house to help me and with him holding a wing we got it turned around and tied down in the parking area.

"We were worried, Dad, on account of the wind. How was it?"

"Son, it was rough as hell and I'm soaked with sweat, but I'll tell you about it later."

There was water under the snow on the ice, the steps up the bank were sloppy with mud and the roofs of the buildings were pouring with water. When I had left home the day before it was ten below.

We carried the groceries up to the house and I sat down to eat.

"There is no need to tell Vera right now that I have quit flying," I thought. "I'll tell her tomorrow." Tomorrow came and I waited another day. I never did tell her, and three days later I was flying again. As long time northern bush pilot George Dalziel once said to me, "None of us will live forever anyway, and we might as well die in an airplane as anywhere else."

High winds and turbulence to a flyer are similar to death and taxes, you have to live with them. They cannot be avoided. You submit to the buffeting and shaking up when you must. In time you learn your limitations and those of your aircraft, and you do not go beyond them. If a situation starts to develop that you cannot handle, you get the hell out of there; you land or go home. Don't be proud; pride and heroes are buried together in the same grave. As Ernest Gann says, 'Fate is the Hunter' and I think those of us who survive many hours of bush flying are the lucky ones.

Perhaps the best known of all air currents and the most dangerous to small aircraft are those associated with anvil shaped thunder heads. Severe ones have been known to cause light planes to disintegrate in the air. One such case was documented by the D.O.T. some years ago. In this case the vertical air movements were so sudden and violent that a Cessna 180 was seen by witnesses to come apart in the air. Strange to say the first structural failure to occur was the leading edge of the wings which parted in a downward direction. Much more was torn free before the airplane fell to the ground. All students are warned repeatedly of these dangers to light aircraft and still a few insist on tempting fate.

In my opinion the next most dangerous wind condition is the dreaded down-draft. There is always a down-draft on the lee (sheltered) side of a hill or mountain, the severity of which is dependent upon the strength of the wind. If the air is clear the downdraft obviously cannot be seen but a pilot at all times must be aware of where the updrafts and downdrafts are. Another D.O.T. Accident Report of recent years relates how five men met their death in a Beaver aircraft. A contributing factor to the cause of the accident was presumed to be a downdraft, perhaps coupled with the pilot's mishandling of the controls. The aircraft was float equipped and was coming in to land on a fast-flowing northern river. The wind was crossways to the river and the pilot on his downwind leg was low and in the lee of a hill and would have been subject to a downdraft. On the turn to come around for the final approach the aircraft ceased to fly and contacted the ground under full power. The conclusion must be that a downdraft added to a low flying speed and a steep bank in the turn caused the airplane to stall.

Doug Rae an experienced bush pilot who flew a Beaver for many years in our area told me that during what he thought was only a mild Chinook wind he came in from the east on floats to land at our place at the Butte. He came in on his downwind leg under the cliffs of the mountain to make a rather sharp banking turn to land on the snye. A gust of wind caught him before he could act, one wing was vertical and he was going over onto his back. With quick presence of mind he applied aileron and rudder to keep the airplane in a roll until it came around right side up. Luckily he was not heavily loaded and had plenty of altitude for this maneuver. Doug said that never again did he come under those cliffs to make his turn.

I have heard a lot about air currents and their effect upon aircraft from helicopter pilots who must understand air movement thoroughly to survive. In fact they make use of updrafts in their daily flying operations. They often work in hilly or mountainous terrain where there are usually currents of air that do move in almost any direction. In taking his load to the top of the mountain he will approach it on the windward side, get close to the rock wall and allow the upward flow of air to carry him to the top. In the afternoon when the wind has died and the sun is beating on the southern slope, he will maneuver the chopper into the upward movement of warm air to help him to the top. Chopper pilots will tell you that they have to know at all times what the wind is doing and precisely what effect it will have on an airplane. A helicopter is as much an airplane as a fixed wing, the only difference is that the chopper has rotary wings.

George Dalziel told me of a similar experience over Dead Mans Valley. It was in July, during a very strong Chinook. A violent gust caught him and flipped the aircraft onto its back. He also like Doug, forced it to keep rolling until it was right side up again. In both these cases the airplane did a complete roll.

Updrafts sometimes occur in clear air on hot days and almost every pilot has at some time or other gone up a thousand feet before he could catch his breath, but more frightening are the downdrafts, when the bottom drops out and you find yourself heading for the ground at a thousand feet per minute, with the nose up and full power on. In my experience the airplane has always regained normal flight before tree top level.

One very competent pilot, we'll call him Alphonse, told me that he once got into a down-draft in the mountains and did not come out of it until he was almost touching the ground. Alphonse was and is a very good pilot and I envied him his poise and confidence, but he met his match one day in the Nahanni canyons. He did not broadcast this episode but word does get around.

Alphonse had in his employ another pilot by the name of Dolfuss, probably a better pilot than Alphonse, who one very windy day twice returned a distance of two hundred miles from trying to deliver a load of groceries with a float equipped 180. He said the turbulence was too great to risk landing.

There is what seems to me a false pride in most pilots which will not permit them to admit they can not deliver a load because of rough air. Dolfuss knew he was good and had no qualms about admitting he had faced an impossible situation.

His boss Alphonse said nothing but next morning he announced he would take the trip himself, letting it be known by implication that Dolfuss couldn't handle a 180 in a wind. On returning to Fort Simpson with an empty plane Alphonse admitted he had not delivered the load, but had dropped it off at Nahanni Butte instead on the way back. The intended destination was a survey camp on the Nahanni River midway in the first canyon. Although the canyon walls are broken and irregular they rise to well over three thousand feet above the river level. There is as much chance of landing an aircraft in this canyon, right side up, in a Chinook wind of high velocity, as you would have of delivering a basket of eggs to center ice in the Montreal Forum when the Canadiens are warming up.

There is a mountain valley twelve miles west of Nahanni Butte where an oil company drilled a hole some years ago. They constructed a very nice dirt airstrip about 5000 feet in length and much of their supplies was brought in by air. The valley is perhaps six miles in diameter and is surrounded by sharp mountains rising to three thousand feet above the valley floor. One day a DC-4 (a four engined aircraft) was hired to bring in a load of heavy equipment. Unfortunately a healthy Chinook wind was blowing that day with the general direction at right angles to the airstrip. In a situation of this kind the surface winds are actually as inconsistent as a basketball in a hard fought game. I have many times seen wind-socks at opposite ends of an airstrip standing straight out and pointing in opposite directions.

The pilot of the DC-4 was new to the area and he must have had guts. He made three passes at the strip before he was able to land. He was silent and grim while the airplane was being unloaded. The 'Tool-Push' then said, "How soon can you be back with the next load?"

"I'm not coming back," was the terse reply. And I am quite sure he never did.

There is one aspect of flying that was never mentioned to me when I was a student and that was if you were to become an aircraft pilot you must get used to being shook up, and for periods of several hours at a time. In many cases small planes cannot climb above the turbulence as the jets can and you must submit to the buffeting. It is a common experience to have your head hit the roof of the cockpit even when your seat belt is so tight it is making welts on your thighs. Anything loose in the cockpit will rattle around like a dried pea in a cigar box. My friend and fellow pilot Bob Ward once on a flight from Fort Simpson turned back ten miles from Nahanni Butte because he said the aircraft instruments were coming loose from the panel. It is possible he merely felt they were coming loose.

For some years now I was getting more and more interested in the Nahanni and Flat River mountains as a prospecting area. Some of the Indians whom I had known for almost thirty years told me of certain places to the north and west where mineral showings had been found. Paul Tesou who was now in his seventies volunteered to show me from the aircraft where minerals outcropped near Moose Horn Lakes. His knowledge of geology was very limited but for all that he had an intelligent grasp of the basic tenets of mineralization. He knew what a quartz vein was and that some minerals were often associated with these veins. In Slavey a quartz vein is called 'rock fat'. And he knew that valuable minerals were often heavy compared with the country rock. Another man, Emil Lenoir who had spent many of his younger years trapping in the Nahanni mountains told me that over twenty years ago he had stumbled across a fresh rock slide that had revealed a heavy metal in small black, heavy square cubes half an inch across. Others in the band had seen the cubes he had brought back to camp but did not know the location. Emil died and took the secret with him. Another man told me of picking up what he considered was silver ore on the side of a mountain in the Yukon.

All of these men knew as I did that Big Charlie had picked up a gold nugget the size of a walnut, but could not remember where. He had reportedly given it to a Bishop who had a watch fob made of it. As near as I could find out, this happened near the turn of the century.

All these locations were over a hundred miles from any road and most were not near a navigable river. To check the reported finds with a float plane would cost money and would be time consuming. Many miles of walking and back-packing would be entailed. But first a floatplane must be acquired.

The T-Craft was a little too light and lacking in horse power to be able to get in and out of mountain lakes on floats. The

150 HP Super Cub was reported to be ideal for this purpose: its only drawback was limited space for cargo. Anything bigger meant going into a lot of money and I decided on a Super Cub.

In January of 1960, CF-LCZ was flown to Fort Nelson for me and I saw HAL fly away south. Pilots get sentimentally attached to their airplanes and I felt a tug at my heart when HAL left, but when I test flew LCZ I fell in love with it. I had thought the 90 HP Super Cub I had trained in was a hot machine but the 150 HP was a lot better. It had sixty more horses in basically the same airframe and when you opened the tap you got action.

LCZ was similar to HAL in one respect only: on a hot day in July they were both warm and comfortable but on a cold day a Polar Bear would freeze inside them.

The skis I had widened for HAL I now installed on LCZ and with the power of a Super Cub I could get in and out of lakes where the snow was often two feet deep. I started taking my trading post customers out to their trapline base camps and picking them up. I wanted to build up my flying hours and took every opportunity to do so when I could in some way be compensated for the cost of the trip. One month toward spring I got in one hundred hours flying.

One problem developed that I never did solve completely. In the village of Nahanni Butte there were up to eighty people including nine or ten native families. It was inevitable that children and others would develop cuts and bruises and various illnesses that needed medical attention. For some years there was no radio transmitter at the village and it would rest upon Jack Norcross with his Stinson or me to take the patient to Fort Simpson where the hospital and doctor were located.

Private pilots are not supposed to fly for hire or reward, but an aircraft is costly to maintain. In my case it was imperative that the trading post and barge business show a profit every year and the aircraft was a necessity in our isolated region. This meant that the airplane had to carry its own weight and could not be a burden on other aspects of the business.

The village peoples' supply of money was never over-abundant and you could hardly ask for payment when someone had to go to the hospital. So for a time, what happened was that whenever I brought a patient into town the doctor in Simpson would (in his capacity as an official of the Federal Health Services) sign a purchase order allowing me to get a barrel of gas from the Imperial Oil Agent. This was satisfactory to me as I believe it was to Jack Norcross. Jack was a missionary pilot and while we used our planes for different purposes we both felt that we could not ignore a case where medical attention was required. And the Medical Health Services were always willing to contribute to a mercy flight.

The problem that arose was: how could we tell when hospitalization was necessary. When a native trapper for instance would say, "I'm sick and have to see the doctor, will you take me to Simpson?" How were we to know if he really was sick or if he merely wanted a free trip to Simpson to buy a bottle of whisky? Other pilots have reported that a patient would moan and groan something scandalous until he or she got out of the aircraft at Simpson or Fort Nelson and immediately disappear in the direction of the pub.

All northern pilots, as far as I know, took the view that if there was an indication at all that the person needed to see the doctor he would be taken to town and if the patient's self-diagnosis proved to be erroneous, it was put down to profit and loss. Better to err nine times in that direction than to refuse one trip to someone who did need medical attention. One hospital was a hundred miles away and the other a hundred and sixty-five.

The Fort Simpson hospital was staffed by a series of young doctors who did about a two year stint there. Most of these young men were well qualified, intelligent and dedicated to their work. All took their Hippocratic Oath seriously and would go anywhere to help anybody. They were a credit to their profession and I thought highly of them. They often told me, "The least we can do is to contribute to the fuel for the aircraft when you bring a patient in."

One fine March day a young native man of nineteen or so, whom I liked and respected, came over to the store with a swollen jaw and a haggard look and asked me if I could take him to Simpson to have his tooth pulled by the doctor. He had not slept for two nights and was obviously in pain.

I said, "You get right over here with your hat and coat and I'll have you in Simpson within the hour." I have suffered so much with tooth-ache that just looking at him made mine start to hurt.

We were an hour in getting to town and at the airstrip someone said, "You're in luck, there's a dentist at the hospital now." I dropped Raymond off at the hospital and went over to the clinic to get my gasoline. In the office a young lady approached me and said, "I am Dr. so and so, what can I do for you?"

"And I'm Dick Turner," I replied, "that infamous flyer from Nahanni Butte, and I have just brought a young native in from Nahanni with a tooth-ache, he's at the hospital now." I am always at my best when talking with a pretty lady, and so my voice was quite pleasant.

She looked at me in a puzzled manner and said, "well, what about it?"

"The other doctors usually give me a purchase order for a barrel of gasoline," I replied, "when I bring a patient in."

"I couldn't possibly sign a purchase order for fuel for a flight for merely a tooth-ache. That would be like waving a red flag at a bull. The Medical Services would never go for that at all. Oh, no."

Foolishly I asked, "Did you ever have a tooth-ache? I have and they are damned painful."

"It doesn't matter," she replied, "a charter trip for a tooth-ache is not warranted, but I just might pay you fifteen dollars for your trouble."

I almost laughed in her face. Possibly I smiled, for her color mounted.

"Now just don't bother yourself about it," I said. "Let's forget the whole thing. I can easily afford the gasoline and I'll bring in anyone at any time who has a tooth-ache." And I turned and left. Strange to say that lady doctor and I never did become friends; and after that I never asked for gasoline from the Health authorities. The Medical Services also went down in my regard.

With further mercy flights my policy was if the patient could pay something toward the gasoline for the trip, he did;

if not we forgot about it. The people at the village did favors for me too and in the long run we came out about even.

4

New Airstrips

I think it was in February of 1960 that a caterpillar tractor train came through from Fort Simpson, making a road through the bush to haul supplies to a seismic camp. For a few days the trailer camp was right behind our house and we visited back and forth. As soon as I saw those beautiful Caterpillar D-7s with their blades that could push down a tree as easily as I could a wheat stalk, I got ideas. So I asked the foreman, "I wonder what it would cost me to have you clear an airstrip behind my house? I think we could get fifteen hundred feet there and that would be enough for the Super Cub."

"Sure, I believe we can manage that," the foreman replied. "Perhaps we'll have time tomorrow or the next day."

I was chortling. I filled his cup with coffee until it ran over, gave him a cigar and lit it for him, and opened the door and bowed when he left the house.

Things were looking up; using sandbars and rivers for landing strips had its disadvantages. A landing strip behind the house where the Cub could be tied down in the back yard was something I had hardly dared dream of.

An ice bridge was being constructed across the Liard River

and the foreman needed a tent and some diesel fuel and other items which I gladly supplied. He suggested the clearing of the airstrip was about equal to the value of the supplies. I agreed and that was that; I got the best of the deal. But later on I was able to square things up by doing some flying for him with my Super Cub.

By March the depth of snow in the bush had built up to thirty inches or more and on the big lakes the wind had drifted the snow into large drifts which made landing with a skiplane hazardous. On some rivers and lakes where the snow lay undisturbed, water had been forced from underneath out onto the surface of the ice and with the protection of the blanket of snow, lay unfrozen to the depth of a foot. In all the bush camps where the trappers had to be delivered or picked up landings had to be made on lakes and rivers where I had never been before. A pilot if he wanted to avoid damage to his aircraft had to be extremely cautious in picking a landing spot. If he landed on a lake well out from shore where the snowdrifts were large he could damage the undercarriage or the tailski. If he picked a shoreline where the snow lay deep and undisturbed, he could find himself in a foot of water that would freeze instantly to the skis, which if nothing worse would cause delay and inconvenience.

If the sun were shining the shadow would bring out the drifts quite clearly, and the smooth grey patches would indicate water under the snow. But with a hazy, grey or snowing condition the surface was indistinct and a pilot had to be tensed right up, using all his knowledge and perception of northern snow conditions and at the same time hoping his mind would be receptive to a sixth sense warning system or premonition that would alert him to any danger that could be lurking unseen.

All bush pilots have had many close calls and narrow escapes in landing on unmarked snow surfaces. The lucky ones have escaped bending their aircraft and have been able to take off again with nothing worse than a fright and a warning. The unlucky ones have met with misfortunes ranging from a broken ski to a sunken aircraft and sometimes death. Some aircraft have gone through the ice when only a hundred feet away the ice was two feet thick. Most of the sunken aircraft were recovered later at great labor and expense. On some rare occasions they went right down with the loss of all on board.

A common occurrence in winter conditions was to get caught in water under the snow, the insidious condition we term 'overflow'. A typical case is that related to me by Chris Van Toole, a one-time bush pilot who now flies multi-engine aircraft. In this case Chris was on a charter flight in to a mountain lake with a load of groceries for an elderly trapper. He had a Cessna 180 on skis loaded with seven hundred pounds of groceries.

It was early in January with few hours of daylight and the weather was bitterly cold. It was a routine trip except that Chris had never been into this lake before in winter. He found the cabin near the lakeshore, circled once or twice looking for obstructions and came around for a final approach. The touchdown was smooth as the snow was very deep; the plane settled and came to a stop very quickly. Chris got out and stepped into two feet of snow over a foot of water. Any water or slush now exposed to the bitterly cold air froze immediately.

After the load was removed he found the engine could not budge the airplane; it was held solidly by the deep snow and slush. There was nothing for it but to tramp down the snow so that the plane would be able to gather enough speed for take-off, but first he had to cut poles to put under the skis. He had no snowshoes in the airplane but he did have a change of footgear. It took several hours of slogging back and forth to prepare a take-off path. He had completed very little when the sun went down and the temperature became colder. The sky was clear and the moon came up with one of those brilliant star-lit nights that are almost as bright as day. It was not far off midnight when Chris, tired, hungry and almost exhausted, climbed aboard and fired up. When the engine was warm he made his check, opened the tap, kicked the rudders to break her loose, started to move and gaining speed was soon in the air. Forty minutes later he landed in Simpson and I believe to this day he has never been back to Carlson Lake.

For my part, having been in overflow many times with my

dogteam when trapping, I was well aware of the dangers. Many times on final approach to land on a snow covered ice surface a sixth sense warned me of WATER. I would 'pour on the coal'; go around again, and find another place to land. So once more I began to feel 'fat and happy' and soon got my come-uppance. Early in April on a nice bright sunshiny day I took a trapper sixty miles to his base camp. Over the cabin I could see I had a choice of landing on the Fort Nelson River or on a sandbar to one side. I felt the snow would be much deeper on the bar than on the ice, and that late in the year most overflow would be frozen solid, as crystallized snow makes poor insulation. The river ice was long and straight and very white, indicating no water underneath. I touched down very gently, went a hundred feet and crashed through a three inch frozen crust into eighteen inches of snow and water. The throttle was closed for landing; mercifully my reflexes flew into action and I opened the tap and held down the tail and the poor little Cub came to a shuddering halt. The air was warm and balmy and the slush did not freeze to the skis. We were able to walk ahead of the airplane and break down the crust with our feet, then taxi up onto the sandbar with the propeller picking up the slush and blasting it back onto the airplane. I still don't know what kept us from going over on our back when we broke through the crust. From then on I had a deep and abiding affection for my little red and white bird which almost amounted to reverence.

My love for the Cub was so great that Vera said to me, "Why don't you take it to bed with you?"

I disdained to answer. What a silly question to ask. The bed was much too small for the three of us.

In early September when the barge work was wound up for the season I brought LCZ down from Fort Nelson and landed in the cleared space behind the house. During the summer we had chopped out roots and cleared the ground for a strip twenty feet wide and nine hundred feet long. With good approaches at either end, it was enough. And every day now when there was any time to spare I filled in holes, raked up branches and chunks of wood, until we had a passable little airstrip.

Around this time the Regional Administration of the

Northwest Territories for our area wanted to have dirt airstrips made at the villages surrounding Fort Simpson. This was a necessary and a sensible move as it would enable the outlying communities to be served by air pretty well the year round. As the Department of Northern Affairs would not come up with the money for such a program, the local officials then asked for funds to build fire guards to protect these same communities from forest fires. The money was forthcoming. The fire guards were made with a bulldozer, smoothed and crowned with a grader and the villages had their airstrips. The cost of the grader I am sure was hidden and added to the bulldozer time. Which seems to show that honesty doesn't ALWAYS pay.

While all the airstrips at the villages were pretty well flat, there were some strips in the surrounding area which were much higher at one end than at the other, and one of the lessons a bush pilot must learn is the danger of landing on a down-hill slope. If the incline is very pronounced you must always land uphill unless the velocity of the wind is extreme, otherwise you will not get stopped in time and will go humping and bumping along off the end of the strip and into the trees and the rubble.

I had about two hundred hours time when the foreman of a bush camp asked me to fly him where his Caterpillar train was waiting, a location where he was to build a long airstrip to service an oil rig. His men had radioed that they had a small strip freshly made that was long enough for the Super Cub. This was in August and the road into camp was impassable so I said, "Hop aboard my flying machine and in fifteen minutes we will be there." In fifteen minutes we were over the camp all right but it took me longer than that to complete the landing. After 'dragging the strip' my first approach was too high and too fast. I poured on the coal and went around again. I could see that I was going to have to round out over the rubble and roots and stumps if I were going to touch down and get stopped in time. The strip looked very short indeed. The next time round was a bit better but the airspeed was still too high as I was about to land so round we went once again. The third time I made a long, low final approach, let the airspeed fall right off and came in over the rubble with power on and the nose high. Now, chop it man, and stand on the brakes! This I did and we came to a stop with fifty feet to spare. I got out and looked around.

"My God, what have I done?" I thought. "Like a blooming idiot I landed down hill." I could now see that there was a very noticeable slope to the ground. There were hills and mountains around, and in the air I was thinking only of the wind direction and the surface of the newly plowed airstrip and had not observed that the strip was on an incline. That must be lesson No. 136, and another one I must never forget. I said nothing to those around me and they did not know that I had pulled a 'boo-boo'.

5

Vera's Diary

The only recorded document we have of our family activities is Vera's diary of the 1960s. For Christmas of 1959 one of the children bought her a five year pocket diary with four lines for a daily entry. When this was filled, another one was procured; consequently from 1960 to '69, with a few gaps here and there, there is a variety of oddments of information on weather conditions, goings and comings of members of the family and neighbours, the making of bread, doing a washing, planting the garden etc. Because my memory as to specific dates and names is often hazy I find Vera's diary helpful in placing events in their proper chronological order, and in jogging my memory for interesting items to be recorded.

Some entries I would like to record verbatim to help with the picture of our life at Nahanni. This brings up a subject which I had hoped to keep hidden, and another that needs further explanation.

As to the first—boys in their infancy are sometimes dubbed with pet names or nicknames such as Bud, Tubby, Sonny, Chubby, Chuggie or Boomer. As they grow older it is usual for their rightful and more formal name to gain precedence. In my case the members of my family and close friends have continued to use the name I somehow acquired in childhood. It is Dixie. Vera continues to refer to me as Dixie as she does in the diary. When speaking of me, if she prefaces her remarks with "Dick", I brace myself for a reprimand, and if on rare occasions it is "Dick Turner", then I get the dog and head for the door, for I know where we both will be for awhile.

Some of her references are to 'hauling hay' or 'feed for the horse', thus giving one to understand that we had an animal of that description at Nahanni. Alas! Such was indeed the case. It came about this way. Our first two children, Nancy and Donald we thought to bring up 'properly'. The third one Rolf we gave up on, and the fourth one Martha, we never tried to bring her up and indulged her every whim; of course, she will not agree with this. It is well known that small girls have an affinity for horses. And it is also no secret that fathers are easy 'pushovers' when daughters have some objective in view. So when Mart got the idea she wanted a horse, even though— "Well, you'll have to ask your mother," then, "You'll have to see your father about it," it was a foregone conclusion she would get her horse. I was beaten down by both girls at home. (Nancy was away at school.) Martha said, "If you can have airplanes Daddy, why can't I have a horse?"

And Mother said, "If Dad can spend money on airplanes, he can buy you a horse."

We got the horse. A four year old mare, a chunky bay that had never been ridden. I bought her at Rolla in the Peace River country. I paid ninety dollars for her with saddle and bridle thrown in. She was trucked three hundred miles to Fort Nelson, put on the stern deck of our barge, and brought another three hundred miles to Nahanni Butte. The poor beast had never been in a truck or on a barge before and fought tooth and nail getting on and off. At last we got her on solid ground at home and I wondered if Mart was ever going to be able to ride her. I needn't have worried; before long the animal had submitted to saddle and bridle. Mart named her 'Honey' and to my consternation I would see them careening through the bush leaping over barrels and piles of rubble.

"What in hell are you doing with that horse?" I would say in exasperation.

"Making a jumper out of her of course."

"Oh, a jumper, yes, of course, a jumper. My God child, do you want to break every bone in your body and kill the horse as well?"

"Don't be silly, Daddy, Honey always waits for me when I fall off and besides I don't ask her to go over anything much over four feet yet." And she smiled sweetly at me and patted Honey's neck.

"Do you realize what that child of yours is doing?" I said to Vera. "She's bloody well making that horse jump over great piles of barrels and logs and things."

"Yes, I know," she replied. "I have seen them take some tumbles, but soon they are racing around again. A ten year old girl's bones are soft."

"Yes, and so is her head," I mumbled as I turned away.

To keep that blessed horse from wandering away (she did swim both the Nahanni and the Liard Rivers that first summer in an attempt to return to her home pastures) we fed her all sorts of goodies, tasty morsels such as candy, cake and cinnamon buns. She became so greedy that she would gobble up anything that was offered to her. I think HP sauce and cigars were the only things she refused. R.M. Patterson (author of *DANGEROUS RIVER*) tried her with oysters and down they went. The boys from the various geological crews who were camped in our yard from time to time would tempt her with a great variety of food from the kitchen; beef steaks, sausages, cheese and many kinds of fruit and vegetables were gladly accepted. The men would roll oranges along the ground and had the horse trotting after them.

It got to the point that whenever Honey heard the crinkling of paper she would come running, much to the consternation of local natives who left the trading post with their purchases in a paper bag. The horse would come trotting toward them and they would take off on the run toward their boats at the river bank, the horse right behind them with her head at times over their shoulders. Once poor Jimmy Betsaka leaped to safety over the garden fence where the horse held him at bay until Vera dashed out and escorted Jimmy to the river where he made his escape into his boat and across to the Village.

With Mart tutoring her to be a 'jumper' Honey soon learned

to leap the fence and come to the kitchen door when she felt in need of a bit of a snack. She would stamp on the doorstep until her demands were met. If there was a delay she would twirl the doorknob with her lips and would sometimes open it and put her head and front feet inside the house and would whinny softly thinking perhaps she had not been noticed up to this point. Cinnamon buns were her favorite. Vera's cinnamon buns were large, brown and crunchy with much brown sugar syrup cooked into them. Honey would accept a whole bun at a time, lift her head high in the air and with a look of ecstacy, close her eyes and munch on the bun for the longest time, smacking her lips as the last bit went down.

The taste for odd and exotic foods eventually got Honey into trouble, or at least got her into the bad books of some people. One morning on examining LCZ before going flying I found that the blessed animal had eaten a section from the elevators. The fabric is treated with a preservative 'dope' which she must have found attractive.

I came into the house stomping and lamenting loudly, "The perfidious mutations that resulted in the warped characteristics that allowed an animal shaped like a horse to have the appetite of a goat."

When I had cooled somewhat Vera said, "There's no real harm done, fix it up and take it in your stride." She was right of course and I was later ashamed of my outburst.

Some weeks later just before Christmas, I arose early in the morning (8:00 am) to prepare breakfast for the rest of the family, which on rare occasions I did. I stoked up the living room fire, lit the propane stove for the kitchen table and went to step outside.

Many Christmas goodies recently flown in from Fort Nelson filled the refrigerator which stood in the kitchen porch just outside the door: there were such items as turkey, sausages, T-bone steaks, cheeses, fresh frozen peas, frozen strawberries, ice cream and other oddments. The storm door which opened outward seemed to be blocked by something piled against the door. I squeezed outside, closed the door and took in the scene of destruction. At first glance it looked as if someone had dumped a load of garbage on the doorstep. But on closer examination it proved to be the contents of the refrigerator that was strewn about. Fresh hoofprints near the door indicated that the blessed horse had jumped the fence again, opened the door of the frig with her teeth, pulled out each and every item and removed the paper wrappings in search of a tasty morsel. There seemed to be some sausages missing but otherwise, if you don't count teeth marks, nothing was missing or damaged. I wrapped up the things as best I could, piled them back in the frig, and closed the door.

"Poor Mother," I thought, "she'll be furious, but I must tell her immediately."

In the bedroom, Vera was snuggled down having a last delicious snooze before I called her for breakfast. I touched her shoulder and said quietly, "Vera, Honey jumped the fence, got into the frig, pulled everything out and scattered it around. I don't know how much is missing."

I do believe that if someone had dropped a bomb on the house there would have been less violent reverberations. I was sorry now that I had not consulted the children on a plan of breaking the news to Mom in a less sudden and a more gentle manner.

From a sound sleep she was instantly awake and had grasped the situation precisely and immediately. She sat up in bed, and with her hands pushing on the bed, bounced up and down exclaiming vehemently, "That God damned horse, you'll have to shoot that horse. That God damned horse, you'll have to shoot that horse."

"Now, now," I replied soothingly, "there is no real harm done, just take it in your stride." I bent over and kissed her saying, "I think she only ate the sausages, the other things seem OK."

An hour later we were all eating breakfast and laughing over the antics of 'that beast'.

1960 - RANDOM NOTES FROM VERA'S DIARY

January 31
Sky overcast. Dixie left with LCZ for Nelson. Norcross flew in from Nelson 5:00 pm.

February 2
Cloudy and cold. Dick and Gus [Kraus] went to Simpson. Turned back for weather.

Feb. 3
Very cloudy. Butte fogged right in. All Netla Indians were here to the store. Dixie hauled hay.

Feb. 7
Very cloudy. Snowing. Dixie took Fr. Lizzie to Liard from Simpson with LCZ. Back at 3:45 pm.

Feb. 9
Dixie and I flew out to Grange Lake [trapline] where we tramped out runway for LCZ.

Feb. 14
Clear quite warm. An Otter landed at Gus's. Dixie hauled hay. Norcrosses were over for supper.

Feb. 15
Dixie left with LCZ for Fort Nelson.

Feb. 19
Clear. Lovely morning. LCZ came in 3:00 pm. I took mail across river.

April 22
Clear and warm. Froze a little overnight. Helped Dick paint boats and barge. The Liard ice moved a little.

May 1
Ice jammed in the Nahanni.

May 6
Ice running thick this pm.

May 8
Weather unsettled. Dick loaded barge for trip to Fort Nelson. I washed, baked etc.

May 9
Dick and Rolf left for Fort Nelson with barge.

May 10
Slightly cloudy, rained a little. R.C.M.P. called in going up Nahanni. Butte starting to look green. Dug flower garden.

May 18
Beautiful morning. Search and rescue airplane flew over again today.

May 19
Leaves are bursting. Planted garden.

May 27
Bullock Wings flew in with their camp. [our yard] Steve Villers flew in with Monty Alford. [Water Res.]

May 28
Dixie, Don and Rolf got in with barge from Fort Nelson [probably about midnight]

May 29
No entry for this day.

But we were all busily engaged unloading the barge, carrying the supplies up the river bank and wheeling it all to the store with a wheelbarrow, a distance of a hundred yards. Our customers usually came in a drove from the village when they saw the barge come in, to purchase fresh items, to watch the unloading and to sometimes help with the work.

It would take one or two days to get the barge unloaded and the freight sorted and piled in the warehouse. Then quite often Don and Rolf would be off somewhere with the barge on a charter trip.

The last of the hunters were coming in now with their beaver pelts from the spring hunt and for a week it was a busy time in the store, collecting the last of the winter's debts, buying fur and baling up the pelts to get them out for the June or July auction sales.

Since the melting of the snow in April, the airstrip behind the house had been wet and soggy, completely unusable until the frost went out and allowed the water to soak in and dry up. It was often the fifteenth of June before we could use the strip. So that all I could do now in the way of flying was to check over the airplane, wash the oil off the undercarriage and belly, and do odd small repair jobs before the mosquitos got thick.

The month of May has to be the best time of the year to

appreciate the beauty of the lowlands of the Nahanni foothill country. It is before the floods and the heat of the summer. The mosquitos have not hatched in their millions. The goose-grass, wild onions, wild cabbage and many other early plants are springing up. The air is sweet with the damp clinging perfume of new buds and leaves. The frog orchestras are going full blast in the ponds, the returning robins, blackbirds and flickers are calling and filling the air with music. In the evenings mallards and pintails come whistling by and splash down in a quiet place on the river. Vera and I would walk down the airstrip and onto the winter road, that is a swamp now except for a dry spot here and there. We marvel at the beauty of the north coming back to life, and say to one another what a paradise it would be if there were no mosquitos.

When women get together it seems to me that the topic of conversation is people: women, children and men in that order. When men get together the topics are often about things and ideas. When two pilots get together you may be sure that only two subjects are discussed—airplanes and the gathering of the necessary long-green to keep them in the air.

Ted Taylor and I spent many evenings over coffee and other beverages in conversation dealing mainly with each other's flying exploits, experiences and mistakes; all this leading to how we could procure better and faster airplanes, and how we were to make enough money to fly and keep them in the air.

A pet scheme of mine for some time had been to establish a sport fishing lodge at Trout Lake, which was pretty well equi-distant from Fort Nelson, Nahanni and Fort Simpson. At least one float plane would be needed to fly fishermen into the lake as it was over a hundred miles from the nearest road. The idea was well received and Ted in partnership with Ward Keebaugh bought a Cessna 180 equipped with floats. They each got a float endorsement and the three of us set out on this somewhat ill-conceived venture.

At summer's end and after a vast expenditure of money, time and labor we had a very nice log cabin fishing lodge in operation. The lake trout, pickerel and northern pike were plentiful, the largest trout taken being twenty-three pounds. We advertised extensively but could not attract sufficient customers to make the lodge a paying proposition. After two years of financial loss we eventually sold out, lock, stock and barrel to the Northwest Territories Administration, who turned it over to the Indians of Trout Lake for a native-run project. While we had it in operation we did learn some lessons.

My Super Cub was left in Fort Nelson on wheels for a good part of the summer and Ted's 180 was used for transportation into the lake. When I had the cabins near completion, Ted and Ward flew in one day with supplies and the next morning I watched them take off on the small lake behind the cabins. Trout Lake itself is so huge that a wind will create a sea of rough water quickly, so that to avoid damage to the aircraft when moored overnight we used the small lake behind the cabins for landing and take off. This 'pond' as we called it was four thousand feet in length, narrow, well sheltered by trees with a good approach at the north end. All three of us at that time were low-time pilots with Ted and Ward having less than one hundred hours each on floats.

I stood on the dock, pushed them off and watched them taxi to the south end of the lake, do the run-up, turn and begin the take-off to the north. There was no breeze and the lake covering of lily pads shimmered in the early morning sun. The 180 was lightly loaded and it and many others like it had been in and out of the lake many times before.

As FYN came roaring down the lake toward me I felt that something was not quite right with the sound of the engine. It was slow to get up on the step and seemed in no hurry to take to the air. It was still on the water when it passed me and had only about three hundred feet of lake left, and this was fast disappearing. Suddenly Ted 'chopped' the engine and the nose began to drop, then with the echo of the silent engine in my ears it came to life again with a full blast and I had an instant vision of FYN spreading itself over the muskeg and small trees past the end of the lake. Miraculously it lifted off inches from the grass, continued in a gentle climb, turned and faded from sight in the direction of Fort Nelson.

I felt certain that my heart had stopped beating, and I clung to a tree for support at the edge of the wharf until I could regain my breath. I had come closer than I ever hope to in seeing a float plane fail in a take-off from the water. They might have come to a stop safely in the muskeg beyond the lake but there was a chance the floats might have caught up on the humps of ground and bushes at the edge of the lake with results I did not care to contemplate.

As I walked back to the cabins I thought, "Wait till I see those two crazy incompetent stupid partners of mine, I'll give them a 'dressing down' they won't forget for scaring the daylights out of me. I've aged ten years and I know my hair is grey after that shock."

I determined that whenever those two came out to the lake again, when they prepared for take-off I would either stay in bed or go fishing. I wanted no spectator's part in cleaning up after two pilots with homicidal tendencies who make such determined efforts to commit suicide.

A week later when I again met up with those two alleged pilots they both fervently denied they had deliberately tried to scare me to death. They assured me that they had returned to Fort Nelson wiser and humbler than when they had left.

What happened was this: Ted was the pilot in command in the left hand seat; he taxied out to the south end of the lake doing his cockpit check and runup on the way, and turned for the take-off run. As the north end of the lake came dangerously close and they were still on the water, Ted saw that they were not going to get airborne in time and deciding to abort, closed the throttle. Ward had different ideas; thinking it was too late to abort, he jammed the throttle ahead again. Ward was right, they did make it off, just clearing the shoreline. And it was not until they had gained altitude that they discovered the Carb. heat was in the HOT position. Now Carb. heat is an important part of the pre-flight check and it must be in the OFF or COLD position when the take-off run is commenced otherwise the engine will not develop full power. Full power is mandatory for take-off in most aircraft, and the Carb. heat is one of the checks you do NOT forget. There is another way of putting it and that is that those who forget to utilize Carb. heat properly sometimes do not live to try again. Although many light planes are now equipped with fuel injection engines and consequently have no carburetor to heat, it is still an important factor as many light planes have the older conventional engines.

In all the material sent out to pilots in safety bulletins and advice given by competent aviation authorities there is perhaps few things of greater importance than the insistance of developing good habits regarding pre-flight and pre-landing checks. In all heavy and multi-engined aircraft there is an itemized check in the cockpit in view of the flight crew which is read out and checked item by item. This list must be gone through religiously before all take-offs and landings. Pilots have been warned that a hurried or incomplete pre-flight check could be a factor in causing an accident. In some light aircraft there is no placard indicating the necessary checks, which makes it more essential for a pilot of a light aircraft to develop an inflexible habit of always doing a complete pre-flight and pre-landing check.

VERA'S DIARY:
July 15, 1960.
Ross McFee was in, also Gordie Cameron.

What memories crowd in on me now! Both these men were friends who flew Beaver aircraft for oil companies. They were two of many professional bush pilots whose competence I envied and whom I tried to pattern myself after.

Another one of many bush pilots who were in and out of Nahanni that year was Doug Rae. His aircraft, as I recall was CF-JOF, one of the first Beaver aircraft to come off the assembly line. Doug landed one day at Nahanni with a load of groceries for one of the camps. Vera and I were among several who were at the river bank to greet him. Doug got out of the airplane, walked up the hill and loudly announced, "Where the hell is that God damned airplane eating horse?"

Doug had not seen her, but standing behind us was Martha, and when she heard these words she came flying at Doug with all the fury of seven female tigers. "Don't you talk about Honey that way," she cried, her eyes flashing and her fists flailing at him. I do believe she would have driven him into the river if we had not restrained her.

6

Headless Valley

In the fall of 1961 Ted Taylor leased FYN to a group of men who were going to spend some time in the McLeod Creek area of the Flat River filming some placer mining operations and other winter scenes of the Nahanni mountains.

We met them in late October when they made a base camp in our yard at the Butte in order to look the Nahanni over by air. Two of the partners in the venture were John Langdon and Blake Mackenzie. One of the two prospectors hired turned out to be our old friend Jack Mulholland who had trapped with Bill Epler on the Liard River in the 1930s. The fourth member of the crew was Tom Haggerty, an old timer from the Yukon. I had not seen Jack for many years and we had much to talk about. We again went over the tragedy of twenty-five years previously when Jack's brother Joe and Bill Epler were lost without a trace in the Nahanni mountains, one of the more intriguing stories giving rise to the legends of the Headless Valley.

John Langdon was the pilot and he made several trips up into the valley until oncoming winter forced them to return to Fort Nelson to have the floats on FYN replaced with skis for the winter operation. About the middle of December they landed again at Nahanni and stayed at our house for almost two weeks waiting for the weather to improve, to fly supplies into their base camp on Bennett Creek.

Day after day the weather stayed poor, snowing heavily with poor visibility. I had many talks with Langdon and Mackenzie and came to know them very well. John was an experienced bush pilot with some knowledge of photography. Blake Mackenzie had been a navigator in the R.C.A.F. in World War Two, and had some idea of finding a gold mine on Bennett Creek. Both John and Blake I think were in this venture mostly from adventurous spirits. I could see that neither of them thought to get rich at it. Like so many others who were drawn to her embrace the Nahanni had lured them with enchantment and a promise of gold, with no warning or premonition whatever that one of them was to be the next victim of the Headless men or the jealous Gods who guarded those mysterious valleys. What reason could there be that Blake Mackenzie should be picked from among the rest as a sacrifice to the endless Nahanni legends? He survived his plane crash and should be alive today. It is inexplicable to me that his body was never found. Here are some of the events which led up to his disappearance.

Smith River airport on the Alaska Highway is only one hundred miles from Bennett Creek and John Langdon decided to fly their supplies in from there. The four men flew into Micky Lake in December and established themselves in a cabin close by on Bennett Creek. Blake Mackenzie then flew FYN back to Smith River for the next load of supplies and left there bound for Micky Lake, a fifty minute flight, on January 2nd. The aircraft FYN was found six months later but Blake Mackenzie was never seen again.

When we first heard that Blake was missing we hoped that he had only been forced down on a lake somewhere and was waiting for the weather to clear, but when the weather did clear and the R.C.A.F. Search and Rescue teams came into Fort Nelson and started the search, we knew that Blake might be in real trouble.

Up to now LCZ had been equipped with what we termed a 'Micky Mouse' radio transmitter and receiver, which made communication with Radio Ranges at D.O.T. airports difficult if not impossible at any distance over twenty miles.

Early in January I made arrangements to have an expensive high frequency set with a trailing antenna installed in LCZ, as at that time 5680 K.C. was used extensively for long range air to ground communication. The radio was installed in Fort St. John and I left there bound for Fort Nelson and Nahanni on January 15th.

It was a lovely warm day at Fort St. John with a balmy west wind blowing. The weather forecast did not mention any system moving in and I took off thinking I would have a pleasant warm flight at least as far as Fort Nelson 225 miles north. About twenty miles past the Beaton River airstrip I ran into a cold front with the wind changing to the north. The temperature dropped from forty above, to zero in a few minutes. Snow developed and got worse and worse until it was a howling blizzard. By this time I was over the Sikanni River which I knew would take me right into the old town of Fort Nelson.

The visibility ahead had now become so poor that I could see nothing, so I concentrated on the trees and riverbed below. I regretted not turning back to the Beaton River strip while there was yet time, but it was too late now. The Sikanni River valley for its last one hundred miles, is probably two hundred yards wide bordered by hundred foot banks and big spruce timber, and while the valley itself is gently curved the river winds back and forth from one side to the other. I had to stay at treetop level in order to maintain ground contact. All I could do was to stay within the valley and cross the river bed whenever it chose to swing from one side to the other. The wind increased in velocity with gobs of fog mixed in with the snow. When I judged I was about forty miles out of Fort Nelson I wound out the trailing antenna in order to call Fort Nelson radio on 5680. I was unfamiliar with this particular setup and before I knew it the reel had come off in my hand and the antenna had unwound to an alarming extent. With one hand I gathered it up as best I could and folded it under my leg. I picked up the mike and called Fort Nelson but there was of course no answer.

Now I concentrated only on the flying and tried to anticipate what was ahead. A sawmill about twelve miles out

of Nelson should appear, then a few miles farther would be
the bridge and telephone lines. What height would they be
above the bridge and would there be orange markers hung
from the wire? If I was to pull up to a safe altitude to avoid
the lines I would almost certainly lose sight of the ground and
would have to go on instruments momentarily. I had no
instrument training and knew it would be dangerous,
especially as I would be just over a mile from the airport and
there would be other low flying aircraft in the vicinity and
with no radio contact with the Range, this would be
foolhardy.

The other alternative was to land. At a point two miles
below the sawmill I knew the river was straight for a mile and
as soon as I passed the bend below the mill I would set her
down and hope the ice was not rough. There was no way I
could circle to drag the strip; the fog was in the trees and I
was afraid to lose sight of the river.

Now I could just make out the sawdust-burning tower of the
mill and soon ahead a beginning of a bend to the left. I made
the turn, reduced power and let her settle into the snow.
Beautiful. No rough ice and no sweepers and I coasted to a
smooth stop. After tramping down the snow and placing
sticks under the skis I put on my snowshoes and walked back
to the sawmill, got a ride out to the Highway and phoned into
the Range to close my Flight Plan.

An hour later the weather cleared, the wind died and the
sun came out. I went back to the airplane and flew it into the
ski strip at the airport. And that was that. Once again I had
fumbled my way through safely.

Later I checked in at the Search and Rescue headquarters
and got the latest on the search for Blake Mackenzie. I was
informed there were three R.C.A.F. aircraft searching on a
regular basis with civilian aircraft helping from time to time.
The area from Smith River to Mickey Lake had been combed
over and over again day and night without any sign of Blake
or CF-FYN.

"He could have become lost and tried to follow some creek
or river down into the Nahanni," I suggested. "Meilleur
Creek, Jackfish or Mary River would have led him into
Nahanni and down to the Butte. He knew the Nahanni to

some extent and might have tried to go that way."

"We have thought of any and all possibilities," the Search Master replied, "but we will give you an area to search if you would like to."

They gave me the region around Fort Liard, and the Jackfish and Meullier Creeks. For the next week John Brucker who was living at Nahanni Butte then, went with me as an observer and on clear days we combed the area as well as we could, flying low and watching carefully for any sign of a downed airplane. We did see moose, caribou and timber wolves; lynx tracks, fox tracks and even rabbit tracks and marten tracks but nothing else.

After a forty day search the Rescue teams gave up and went home. Local flyers kept looking whenever any of us were in the area we presumed he had gone down in, but without much hope. If Blake were still alive surely he would have a fire going with the smoke to attract attention. At last we had to assume he had run into the side of a mountain and there was nothing left that could be seen from the air.

After an urgent message from Jack Mulholland's wife Daisy, I gathered up some supplies, food and tobacco and flew into Micky Lake where Jack and Tom Haggerty were. I had never been into Mickey and was not sure as to its precise location. Gus Kraus knew the area well and informed me that the lake was on Bennett Creek very near the cabin below the canyon, and said, "You can't miss it."

From that day to this I never say, "You can't miss it." There are many things people can miss, that might seen obvious to others.

On the map I had at the time, the only lake in that immediate area was right on Bennett Creek and seemed to be close to where the canyon should be, but it was not named.

On February 20th when Blake had been missing for forty-nine days I set off on the flight to Mickey Lake. It was a lovely warm clear day and I flew at six thousand feet in a direct line for the lake. All the way in I looked for any sign of smoke or a downed aircraft and found that moose and caribou tracks showed up very well in the bright sunshine from a very great height. When still some miles from the lake I quit looking for Blake and concentrated on my intended destination and landing. The lake was in a narrow, deep valley with mountains to 6000 feet on each side. It was over half a mile long with a good approach at the north end. The surface seemed smooth with no sign of overflow. There were no ski tracks from the landing of other aircraft as there should have been, but a snowstorm with wind could have obliterated them. I circled twice and came in for a landing. All OK, the snow packed some with wind, but it was not rough and not over a foot deep on the lake.

I should have known as soon as I landed that I was on the wrong lake; there were no ski tracks and no sign of a trail to the cabin. But - dammit! I was on the only lake on Bennett Creek and must be close to the cabin. The sun was still high so I unloaded the aircraft, put on my snowshoes and headed down the creek toward the cabin. My snowshoes were small trail shoes and I sank a foot at each step and once I left the lake the snow was deep with many humps and bumps among the willows and small spruce trees near the winding creek. After an hour I had only gone a mile and I returned to the aircraft thinking that Tom and Jack would not have far to come at any rate.

On take-off I followed the creek down to the cabin, circled once and, shutting the power down momentarily, shouted, "Go to the lake. Go to the lake." Then I turned and headed home, going around by McLeod Creek and MacMillan Lake then up and over the hills back to Nahanni.

Weeks later it slowly dawned on me that I had landed on the wrong lake. I learned that Mickey Lake was a large slough which drained into Borden Creek, and was a mile and a half directly west of Bennett Creek. Long afterward I heard that Jack and Tom had heard my shout from the aircraft and went out the well travelled trail to Mickey Lake. There was no sign of the groceries and no indication that I had even landed. They were very puzzled and concluded that Dick Turner must have lost his marbles or was bewitched by the headless men and was going batty. Neither of them were aware that there was another lake on Bennett Creek close by.

It transpired that the supplies I left on Bennett Creek were never picked up. I had piled them on the ice close to the shore and they would have sunk in the water when the ice melted.

And yet there should have been some items which would float and should have drifted into shore with a wind. Some years later I landed on the lake again with floats in the month of August. I thought perhaps something would have drifted into shore that I could see. All along the lake shore on the sand beaches and grassy shallows there was nothing to be seen. It was as if no one had been to the lake for the last forty years.

We gave Blake Mackenzie up for lost and chalked up another black mark against Nahanni. We heard many wierd and silly explanations for Blake's disappearance. Some said it was all done on purpose, he had wanted to escape something or other and had flown to Alaska or South America. Or that John Langdon and he had found a gold mine and Blake had escaped with the money, and that putting the plane down in the bush was only a ploy to further his ends. Others said, "'Find the woman and you will find Blake." There was no basis for these rumors at all; some people just let their imaginations run riot.

Six months later John Langdon and two companions were prospecting in the Bennett Creek area when one of them spotted a shining object across the valley a mile or more away. It was only six miles from Mickey Lake and they didn't think it could be FYN. But on arrival at the site they found that indeed it was. It had come down in a grove of spruce trees at 4500 feet altitude on the inside of a small valley. The airplane was very badly damaged and broken but was right side up and supported by small trees. A quarter of a mile away sat the remains of a camp where Blake had lived for about fifty days. There was a shelter made of canvas, inside which he had set up the two-burner gas stove he had borrowed from me. The BC Heater he had set up close by and had used to cook his food. His bedroll and supplies were all there with a diary with the last date toward the end of February. Nothing was found of Blake himself and all that seemed to be missing from his camp was a rifle and his snowshoes.

The R.C.A.F. Search and Rescue was notified and a search conducted for Blake's remains. Nothing more was ever found and there the case rests to this day. The plane was still loaded with most of the food and supplies he had on board that day of January 2nd, including a chain saw, gas and oil and many other items intended for use at the camp on Bennett Creek.

From the reports of the contents of Blake's diary and what was known about the weather that day I put together what I think must have happened on the day of the crash and following.

When Blake left Smith River airport there was a strong Chinook wind blowing from the west, and at the same time a cold front was moving in from the north for it was snowing at Bennett Creek with an estimated visibility of three miles. So Blake must have encountered a sudden change of weather along the way. Over Clarke Lake and MacMillan Lake he was right on track and must have by then been in a situation of heavy snow and much reduced visibility. On leaving MacMillan Lake instead of continuing on down McLeod Creek and then turning left to follow up Bennett Creek, he turned too soon and went up McLeod Creek to the headwaters.

He would then have found himself in a blind valley that ended at the top of a 6000 foot mountain. He must have now realized that he was in a cul-de-sac for he made a left-hand turn to get out of the valley where he had entered it, but now found there was not enough room to complete the turn and was likely in much reduced visibility when he plowed into the trees. Although the plane was damaged beyond repair Blake said in his diary that he was unhurt and assumed quite confidently that he would be found in a matter of a few days. He did not panic, but set up his camp beside a small creek and waited. He saw many aircraft fly over that he assumed were out looking for him, but no one saw him.

He was only six miles in a straight line from his destination and no one searching for him thought he would be that close to the cabin. To walk to the camp he would have had to climb 2000 feet up a gentle incline then go along the top for four miles, then down through timber onto Bennett Creek. But whether he knew precisely where he was in relation to the cabin is still doubtful to me.

Sometime close to when the diary ended was the day I flew over and landed on Bennett Lake. I must have been directly above him when I passed over. He knew my Super Cub well and might have recognized the registration LCZ. I hate to imagine what he must have thought of me about the time I disappeared over the hill and failed to return.

After Blake was lost and FYN was gone forever, Ward Keebaugh, the third partner in the Trout Lake venture, moved to Australia and Ted and I were left without an airplane to operate our fly-in camp. We resolved to get floats for LCZ and try to operate the lodge for another year, even if it meant chartering a larger aircraft for some trips.

7

Floats and Fishing

On June 4th I left Nahanni for Cooking Lake near Edmonton to have the new floats installed on LCZ. At the float base the undercarriage was removed and a set of CAP 2000 floats were put on. Now what? Up to now I had no float endorsement, which required an hour or two of instruction from a float endorsed commercial pilot with his signature on an application to the Department of Transport. Without this it was illegal to fly a float plane. I knew of no one at Cooking Lake who could do this for me and I was anxious to get back to Nahanni.

"I'll give it one try," I thought. "I'll go into the Industrial Airport in Edmonton and see if there is a pilot I know who can spare an afternoon of his time for me."

Art Spooner, the manager of the float base very kindly drove me to Edmonton and I started making the rounds. Everyone I knew seemed to be busy or away up north flying. At last I went to the Shell Oil hangar and found Gordie Thorne, who was Shell Oil's chief pilot.

I told him my problem, saying, "I would like to get a check-out, but if not, I know I can manage all right, and can get someone up north to check me out later."

"No," he said, "that won't do. You can't go without any float instruction at all. Hop in my car and well go to the lake and I'll give you a couple of circuits anyway."

At the lake Gordie said, "I'll sit behind and do one circuit, then you do a couple, and listen while I talk."

He taxied out into the lake and continued, "The attitude of the aircraft on floats is of the utmost importance while landing and taking off. A nose down attitude will put you into the water. Two of my friends have gone through the windshield of an aircraft. You must remember two things above all else and never forget them. The first is concerning 'glassy' water; always make your touch-down approach nose high with power on and losing altitude at about 200 feet per minute. You might possibly bounce a little but the landing will be safe. If the water has glassy patches, ALWAYS assume the whole surface is glassy and make a glassy water approach. The other thing is this; some float planes are not as forgiving as a Super Cub, so to play safe and live long, as soon as you lift off, climb out straight ahead, level off, build up your airspeed, and then and ONLY then go into your turn."

I then did two circuits under Gordie's supervision. We taxied into shore and he drove off into town. That was fourteen years ago and I feel that I have quoted his instructions verbatum. I have never forgotten his words.

June 14, 1962 - Arrived home with LCZ on floats from Edmonton. Now we were mobile at any season of the year. Floats on the aircraft during the months of open water, skis for the winter snow conditions and wheels for the short periods in between.

To keep the Trout Lake lodge open I was kept busy flying supplies and people to the lake from Nahanni and Fort Nelson. The tug and barge business could not be abandoned, for that revenue was our bread and butter. So it fell upon Don to run the water operation. I see by Vera's diary that Don and Rolf were kept busy during the summer moving freight from Fort Nelson to Wrigley, Norman Wells, and points on the Nahanni River.

Don had recently acquired his pilot's licence and in our spare time I undertook to check him out on floats. This could possibly be a case of the blind leading the blind. We were both low-time pilots who needed to build up our hours. There was no time to sit brooding over our real or imagined short-comings, so day after day we fired up LCZ and made like the birds. I repeated to Don the instructions that Gordie Thorne had given me regarding float training and to keep it fresh in our minds I went over the details of the accident a friend of ours, Ray Crowther had been in some years previously.

Ray had been a pilot on the Lancaster bombers in World War Two and had taken part in the air raids over Germany. When the war was over he and a close friend, Johnny Barasso, another war ace, came back to northern British Columbia. Johnny took a job flying a civilian commercial aircraft and Ray bought a small single engine bush airplane a PA-12 and started a commercial air service out of Fort Nelson.

Ray had the mail contract from Fort Nelson to Fort Liard and would come to Netla River, Nahanni and Fort Simpson taking trappers back and forth and doing whatever charter work he could get. His airplane was CF-FIS and he did some flying for us when we had a trading post at Netla River and Trout Lake.

On March 14, 1948, Ray flew Vera to Fort Simpson two weeks before our last child was due. Martha Ruth was born next day March 15. Ray and I required four or five bottles of home-made beer each, to recover from the shock.

Ray told me that the summer before he and Johnny Barasso were in Yellowknife when another pilot they knew, who had a trip to make into the barren lands with a Bellanca float plane with two prospectors, offered to take Ray and Johnny along for the ride.

Here I must digress for a moment for a few words of explanation as to why aircraft accidents and near accidents play such an important part in the education of a pilot. The present Ministry of Transport documents and sends out to all pilots who ask for them the relevant factors of all aircraft accidents. This is not done out of indulgence, vindictiveness or a sense of the macabre but is solely to enable all other pilots to learn from the mistakes and misfortunes of others. It is perhaps a sad commentary on human nature, but it is a fact that the best teacher is the fright at having made an error, and the next best is the shock induced by thinking of another's error. The M.O.T. people who send out the safety bulletins maintain that a high percentage of aircraft accidents could have been prevented, by better judgment on the part of the pilot concerned.

Accident reports state, "This pilot made an error, take note of the circumstances and avoid any like occurence."
In 'hangar flying' there is mental therapy in discussions with other pilots and we pick up much information on dangerous situations and how they can be avoided.

On the day of the incident that Ray speaks of, the wind was calm, the water was glassy and there was many miles of lake available for the take-off run. All was normal and everyone was looking forward to a pleasant ride. The pilot warmed the engine, did his run-up and cockpit check, opened the tap and started his take-off run. In normal time the airplane was up on the step and lifted off soon after. What Ray remembered was that when the Bellanca had gained about fifty feet of altitude the pilot went into a banking turn and the next thing Ray recalled was coming up out of the water and striking madly for something to hold on to. He and Johnny Barasso were the only ones to come to the surface and they both clung to the part of the fuselage being held up by one float.

The other float had broken loose and was floating nearby. The water was cool but not freezing and as Ray was a good swimmer he announced that he would attempt to swim to the shore which appeared to be fairly close. He struck out but after going some distance he realized that it was farther away than he had thought, and that he could never make it and would have to turn back before he was completely exhausted. Soon he knew he could not even make it back to the wreck and it raced through his mind that he had escaped many imminent dangers of warfare only to come back home and drown in a freak accident. But Johnny now could see that Ray was in trouble and somehow got the loose float pointed in Ray's direction and gave it a mighty heave. It had just enough momentum to reach Ray who, giving fervent thanks, clung to it to get back his breath then slowly kicked his way over to Johnny. By this time they had been spotted and were soon rescued.

I asked, "What do you think was the cause of the accident Ray?"

"Pilot error."

"What time did he have in the air?"

"About 3000 hours with 300 of those on floats."

"What in the world induced him to go into a turn when he was obviously on the point of a stall?"

"Well, you know, Dick, I think it was 'show-off'."

It seems to me that Ray was right in his assessment of the type of error. The pilot in command, had on board two renowned war aces and perhaps wished to impress them. It is one of many human frailties that we wish to impress those whom we admire and respect. In this frame of mind this unfortunate pilot (who might easily have been as competent as many pilots who are living) must have allowed himself to forget that the stalling speed of a heavily loaded aircraft can be doubled if the bank is steep enough. With merely fifty feet of altitude there was no time to recover.

God help me, but I hope that airline pilots are not like bush pilots in this respect: that we are when in the air, either bored to death, scared to death, or feeling so damned exuberant that we are tempted to take off the chimney of a friend's house, stand the plane on its tail in a wing-over or something equally dangerous and silly.

In trying to get a true picture of the habits, attitudes, characteristics and behaviour of bush pilots, I have found an unanimous opinion upon one subject which is exemplified by the remark of one pilot. He is Bill Foote, a typical helicopter pilot with many thousands of hours in the air; a former fixed wing pilot and instructor; and to boot a married man with a family, who is very serious and cool. He says, "Pilots are terrible show-offs; if truck drivers played around with their equipment as pilots do, there would be more accidents. Pilots like to think they are Captains and tend to glorify themselves."

Not many years later we were all saddened to learn that Johnny Barasso had been lost in the Barren Lands on a flight from Baker Lake to Yellowknife. A prolonged search revealed no trace of the plane, but some months later the aircraft was found intact and undamaged on the shore of a lake. He had been many miles off course. After staying with the aircraft for ten days (if I recall correctly) he started out walking and was never found. Fate is indeed "The Hunter".

Due to a lack of customers at the lake, Ted and I found at the end of the season that we were going deeper into the red and regretfully decided to close up the operation and sell out. We gave it up as a bad job and accepted our loss as best we could. It was hard to abandon the lake completely as the fishing was good and the location with the wide white sand beaches and the cabins set among the birches and pines, was a place of natural beauty. The wild berries in the autumn making a red carpet among the trees, coupled with the complete isolation of the camp always gave us a sense of relaxed freedom to spend some days at our 'Shangri La'.

Alas! Aesthetic pleasures will not put bread upon the table, and we do live in a mundane world. In this frame of mind I returned to the Nahanni, where there untold riches yet hidden away in its valleys and mountains and streams.

8

Prospecting

While I was prospecting my brother Stan decided to also relive the good old days. Ever since he and John Norgaard had packed over from Nahanni Butte to the Coal River in July of 1935 he is prone to reminisce about their trip. They had set off with canoe and kicker for the alleged gold fields on McLeod Creek. They made poor time against the flood waters of the Nahanni and they had not gone far when their kicker gave out entirely. Instead of turning back they beached the canoe well above high water, spent a day in sewing canvas into dogpacks for the three dogs and set off in a westerly direction for the high Flat River country and the Yukon border.

Their progress was slow for the first three days as their packs were heavy with flour, beans and other items of what was then called 'white grub'. This term was used by the native meat eaters to designate the type of food the white men ate. Stan said that when the packs became lighter and he and John out of necessity became meat eaters, they made much better time. The dogs could carry about twenty-five or thirty pounds each, and that enabled them to lighten their loads considerably. Stan found that if the dogs could gorge on meat about twice a week they stayed in good shape and it did not seem to bother them to go a day or two without eating.

Their route took them across several mountain ranges to the west, and in this season the woodland caribou and Dall sheep are above timberline and there was no trouble in killing an animal when needed. A camp was then made where there was good timber and water; the meat was brought into camp and for two days they would dry the meat that had to be carried with them on the next leg of the journey. The meat was cut in strips and hung on a rack above the fire where the heat from the sun and from the fire would dry it and the smoke would tend to keep off the flies. Meat that is even partially dried is light in weight and will keep for a week without spoiling. Stan says that they found the diet quite satisfying and they both stayed in the best of health and spirits for the two months they were in the bush.

Once they were clear of the Nahanni, they were pretty well out of the canyons and could bear to the west crossing valleys and ranges of bald hills to a height of 6000 feet. In places there was steep climbing to be done but usually a way could be found up a timbered slope to the top. If it rained they picked a good place to camp and waited out the storm. John refused to travel when the bush was wet. Stan agreed it was just as well: there was no advantage in gaining a few miles at the expense of getting themselves and their packs thoroughly soaked.

One day on approaching the top of a ridge John went on ahead where he would have a better chance of sighting a caribou without the immediate presence of the dogs. Stan came along behind and by voice commands kept the dogs at heel. On one occasion Stan saw John ahead, who shouted back to him, "I've killed a big bull caribou." Just then the caribou in question that had fallen when shot and was thought to be dead, leaped to his feet and took off with John in hot pursuit.

Stan's dog Rusty, who was a strong and willing dog and somewhat of a pet, must have got wind of the caribou and with his pack catching on the bushes and making quite a noise, took off in hot pursuit after said caribou. This only served to hasten the stride of the caribou and to displease John who was attempting to get within rifle shot of the animal.

Soon after this John abandoned the chase obviously annoyed with Rusty to whom he was addressing some uncomplimentary remarks while he walked back toward Stan. Rusty also abandoned the chase; but observing John in his path, checked himself, backtracked slightly and made a wide detour around him, turning his head and looking at John occasionally.

Stan thought the whole performance was very amusing as Rusty knew he had misbehaved and was going to avoid John until he had cooled off.

Later that day they ran into and killed another big bull caribou and found it had a fresh bullet mark on the base of the horn! But this time John waited until the steaks were sizzling in the pan before he announced he had killed a caribou.

They had no problem in fording the Caribou River; the water was warm and they found a crossing that was not over four feet deep so they carried the dog packs across to keep them dry. From on top of the next range they could see the high country of the Yukon border ahead, away across the valley.

They had panned for gold on all the creeks they crossed but so far had not seen a 'color'. After crossing the ridge they came upon a creek and followed it down into the valley. It was obviously no bonanza, but it did produce two small nuggets that went "clunk" when they were dropped back into the pan. But nothing more than these two small chunks were found on that creek.

Three days later they crossed a divide and came to a good sized river flowing south. They knew now that this must be the Coal River and they must be in the Yukon Territory. As the summer was going fast they returned to the divide and down into the Flat River valley and McLeod Creek. At the mouth of McLeod Creek they found old Boo Jodah and Swuft Water Joe, who were waiting for two companions to return from staking claims. Joe had been waiting alone here for some time before Boo had arrived and Stan reported that Joe, who it is presumed was not armed, had devised a rather novel escape method for eluding any grizzly bear that might put in an appearance. At his camp on the river bank there were many large spruce trees and on one of these Swuft Water had used an axe to chop notches for hand holds for twenty feet up the tree, at which point I presume there was a perch of some sort for Joe to sit upon. He had, I suppose tested the operation of this 'bear escape' but had not notified the others if he had found it satisfactory or not. For my part I would rather chance facing a grizzly than to have my friends return to find me perched on a limb like a frightened bird.

Eight miles below McLeod Creek is the Canyon on the Flat. It is not much of a canyon but the river is impassable here and a portage of half a mile is necessary. Below the canyon, John and Stan built their raft. It was well constructed with morticed cross beams. They devised a pair of oars for it and a sweep at the stern for steering. The first fifteen miles to Irvine Creek is a mess of boulders and rapids and to see it from the air you would think it next to impossible to run it with a raft. The summer before Stan's trip, four of us had been up and down here with a twenty foot canoe and I do not recall thinking there was anything exceptional about it. Forty years later I was here again, once with a boat and again with a canoe. If it is not because I am now old and timid, then those forty intervening years have allowed the river bed to change and erode to a marked degree. I wish I knew for sure, I hate to be losing my grip.

Stan said he and John had no problem coming down, Stan manned the oars and John directed the raft with the sweep. They dodged many boulders but did not run into one. Three days later they were at the Butte and Vera and I were at our cabin on the Long Reach when they came by. From their appearance it seemed that a meat diet for the summer had not done them any harm.

From then on as the years passed into decades, Stan would often tell us how he had enjoyed that summer. What a contrast it had been to our abortive Beaver River trip three years previous. In the evenings around the fire he had made up a song about the Nahanni and inflicted it on poor John. As I recall John was tone deaf, which was possibly a blessing in this case. Stan would also recall how they had found those two tiny nuggets of gold. Details of the creek he had forgotten, but we both concluded that where there were two nuggets there might possibly be more. But we had neither the time nor the money to spend a summer walking into that creek for another look.

Years later Stan was living and working at Fort Nelson when I got floats on LCZ and was back in the hills again, looking for that elusive yellow metal. Stan had two weeks holiday coming up in July and it was not hard to persuade him and Ross Clark to come and have another look at Two Nugget Creek. With the aid of modern air photos we found the creek on the map and saw that we had a suitable lake for a float plane landing not far to the south.

After two trips with the Super Cub I had both Stan and Ross with their camp equipment and food in at the lake where we found a good camping place. According to the map it was six miles to the creek through what from the air looked to be small timber and part open country that should be fair walking. On our reconnaissance from the air we found an open slough near the creek that would be a good spot to make a 'drop'. Back at the lake we filled a five gallon oil pail with food, tied it well with rope so that it would not spill the contents on impact, fastened yards of red plastic ribbon to it and set it on Stan's knees in the airplane. We took off and I made one low pass over the slough then went around again for the drop pass. We had the door open and at the right moment Stan heaved the pail overboard. To make sure of finding the drop from the ground we made another pass and threw out a roll of toilet paper. This would hang up on the trees and could be seen more easily than the pail itself which could possibly be in a hollow.

The next day Stan and Ross shouldered their packs and with shovel, axe and rifle set off through the bush for our Two Nugget Creek. Since Stan's brush with the timber wolves twenty years before he refused to take a step without his .303 British rifle.

In a week's time I was back at the lake with the airplane to pick them up. I had told them that I would leave them at the lake and would not land if they did not have a pile of gold I could see from the air. I came over the lake and saw them both at the camp standing on the beach to welcome me. They looked a little thinner and the worse for wear, with their clothes torn and patched but still and all healthy enough. I landed and taxied in.

"Where are all the nuggets?" I enquired.

"Sorry," Stan replied, "no nuggets."

"You dumb apes, you probably didn't find the right creek."

"Oh, yeah? We found the right creek all right," Ross said. "After a day of slogging through the most miserable mess of thick spruce and ground birch you ever saw. All the game trails were going north and south and as we were headed west it didn't do us much good."

"Did you find the grub we dropped?" I asked.

"Yes, without too much trouble," Stan replied. "It was there all right."

"Look, you guys, are you sure you found the right creek?"

"No doubt about it," Stan said, "we found one of the overnight camps John and I made; some of the poles were still up, and after almost thirty years at that."

"We followed the creek back almost to its source," Ross continued. "Then back down to the mouth, digging here and there and panning in a hundred places. We did see a grizzly near the head of the creek in the buck-brush, but he didn't see us and we left the vicinity very quietly so as not to bother him."

"As to gold," said Stan, "we did not get one single color. But we did find a wonderful fishing hole down near the mouth, and we pulled out many speckled trout and had a scrumptious feed."

That night Ross produced a "Micky" of whisky that he had cached away and we all had 'coffee royal' before going to bed.

The next day we moved camp to Mickey Lake and spent several days panning creeks that drained the giant batholith. There was nothing in the pans but black sand and iron pyrites. And for that summer we called it quits. For the time being fortune again had eluded us.

9

Do It Yourself

It seems likely that soon after man's emergence from the thick-necked, humped over stance of the Neanderthal Man, to a more upright position, when the head could be turned to the stars and the wonder of the heavens observed; when he saw the eagle soar, hover and glide there must have been an awakening of man's imaginative mind, an emerging desire to emulate the birds of the air. When they became conscious of their dreams the most daring individuals may have fancied themselves with wings upon their bodies, flying with the birds.

Today we can and do fly. True, we cannot spread our arms, hop into the air and flip around as a sparrow does; but we can, after much painful outlay of time, money and effort coat ourselves with a contraption of metal, wood and fabric, button it up and take to the air much as an eagle does. A sail-plane or a small powered aircraft is as close a mimicry of birds as we will ever get. The thrill and exhilaration experienced in the freedom of the air is likely unsurpassed by any other endeavor attempted by man.

Some men and women who have a desire to fly and to own planes have gone a step further than most and have designed and made their own flying machines. There are clubs and organizations whose members band together to exchange plans and information on the design and construction of many different types of small home-built machines. These aircraft, after being constructed are inspected by the Ministry of Transport and licenced as experimental aircraft. After a number of hours in the air flown by a licenced pilot non-paying passengers may legally be flown.

At the time that Ross Clark and Stan were doing their thing on Two Nugget Creek, Ross had a home-built under construction in his garage at Fort Nelson. He had bought plans for a modified Miranda and was making further modifications on it himself. When completed it would be similar to a PA-14, which is identical to a Super Cub with the exception of the cabin part of the fuselage being wider, thus permitting side by side seating. The PA-14 was classed as a four place machine although the engine power was exactly the same as the two place PA-18 (the Super Cub). I was told there had been only 260 PA-14s made and in these last years they have become as scarce as a two dollar meal. Because they have more room and fly as well as a Super Cub, many small time bush pilots like myself consider them to be one of the best aircraft in their class ever manufactured.

Ross planned on installing a 150 HP Lycoming engine in his Miranda and he would then have an aircraft equal to a PA-14. Up to this time I had considered home-built airplanes poor for bush operation. Around an airport for a Sunday afternoon, to build time in the air, yes, but to be used for landing on rough bush airstrips perhaps they would be less than satisfactory. The Miranda was built out of WOOD and GLUE. "Good Heavens," I asked Ross. "Will the wings stay on?"

Thereupon began what amounted to an education for me. Ross had books and more books on aircraft construction with charts and graphs showing the strength of wood, glue and metals. He made my head swim with more information than I could absorb. I learned that there was a vast store of technical information on the relative stresses, strains and fatigues in woods and metals. I found that wood is not just wood; laminated wood of very thin sheets, bonded with special kinds of glue can be of fantastic strength. The limiting factor, which must be considered when comparing wood with metals is weight.

For two years whenever I overnighted at Fort Nelson I observed the progress of the building of the aircraft and absorbed more knowledge of its construction. Ross's wife Lil must have become fed up with us. She would give us our supper and then would have to listen all evening to Ross and me discuss nothing but flying and airplanes. I have since given much thought to designing a plaque or medal of some exotic and expensive material to be presented to all long suffering wives of pilots. Only of course to those who are not themselves pilots: some wives have had to take up flying out of sheer desperation and self protection. I have not actually constructed one of these medals as yet but when I do I think that after Vera, the next recipient will be Lil Clark.

One day Ross said to me, "My flying lessons will be finished and I will have my licence about the same time as the airplane is completed. The Department of Transport requirement is that the first fifty hours on an experimental aircraft must be flown by a pilot with at least one hundred hours, and I will have to get someone to test fly it. How about you?"

Right then a pleasant glow came over me and I must have had a silly grin on my face for the next three days. Ross became a friend for life. Damon and Pythias had nothing on us. I could hardly believe it. Ross had asked me to fly his beautiful airplane, upon which he had spent 3000 hours of his time and over $ 2,500 in cash.

Light planes are so wonderfully strong and yet so fragile. One mistake such as a bad landing on my part could possibly wreck his machine, or at least cost him time and money to repair it. We both knew of far better bush pilots than I was, who flew out of the Fort Nelson airport and who, I feel sure, would have been proud to test fly the Miranda.

"Ross," I said shaking his hand, "that's a deal. I never in my wildest dreams hoped to test fly an airplane such as this; because of your modifications, nothing quite like it has ever flown before. It will be the biggest day of my life."

"This must surely call for a drink," Ross said. "Let's see what we can find." And we drank a toast to the new airplane and its first successful flight.

In due course the construction was completed, inspected by the D.O.T., marked with the experimental designation, and the flying permit received. It was given its designation CF-XKH. The engine was test run and Ross completed the required hours of taxi time wherein the plane was taxied on the ramp and the operation of the controls was checked and double checked. Then came the big day.

I was a bit tense, mainly I think because I had anticipated this test flight for so long. I had confidence in Ross's work and in Hilton Burry who in his capacity as an aircraft engineer had examined all the components as they were assembled and had given his approval to the completed job. Ross had installed the conventional stick for the control column and had designed a pedestal for throttle, mixture and Carb. heat in place of the push-pull controls which most small planes had. We did not know where the trim tab should be set, so we put it in the middle position knowing that if it was not correct it could be over-ridden by pressure on the elevators. We had been told that on the larger heavy type of aircraft the setting of the trim in the correct position for take-off was essential. It had been reported that a test pilot had been killed when he was unable to over-ride the improper setting of trim, by elevator control. In light aircraft the center of lift can only vary a few inches and if the trim is set to direct the tail downward and if the force of air over the elevators can not be manually overcome, the nose high aircraft will stall and fall out of the air. Large modern aircraft now I understand have automatic compensating equipment.

On a warm day in July I climbed aboard and taxied out to runway 021, put on the brakes, did the run-up and cockpit check, got the all clear from the radio range, taxied to the live runway, lined up with the center line and opened the tap. The little red bird came unstuck from the tarmack just as soon as a Super Cub at forty miles an hour. I leveled off at 500 feet and did a wide circuit. The nose wanted to go to heaven so I wound the trim ahead as far as it would go, but had to keep a light pressure on the elevators to keep the nose down. The left rudder needed some pressure to keep the plane from swinging to the right, but otherwise she flew like the perfect bird she was. I had never seen aileron control so positive and so effortless. Looking out I noticed gas dripping from the port tank. I knew both wing tanks were full and the fuel selector was on BOTH. No problem there. The overflow was probably from an imperfect vent. Anyway one circuit showed that CF-XKH flew like a charm and I went in for a landing to get Ross to repair the Gas tank vent and to adjust the trim. On landing there is a 'lift' given to an aircraft from ground effect that can be felt on the seat of your pants just when you are about to touch down, then the tires squeaked and we were on.

In a few minutes Ross had the gas tank fixed and the trim adjusted and the next flight was as enjoyable as the first. I was impressed with the ease and control of the ailerons. It could have been because of the size of the ailerons and of the wing tips which Ross had designed and built himself. They were shaped in a precise aerodynamic curve which prevented the wing tips from stalling out before the balance of the wing.

Later that fall Don flew CF-XKH down to Nahanni and landed in one hell of a cross wind. It was a north wind of a steady velocity but vicious just the same. I was not home but Vera said Don put it down very nicely on the short strip. When I asked Don about it he said, "No problem, I had good control."

My conclusion after flying CF-XKH is that any man that can build an airplane like that is a blooming bloody artist. Ross went on to become a proficient pilot and put in many hours on the little red bird.

Although constructing a home-built is one sure way to acquire an airplane, it is only for a small minority of people. There cannot be many who have the necessary aptitude and tenacity to complete such a painstaking task. Ross for instance could take a malfunctioning electric fuel pump and in a few minutes have it scattered over the bench in a hundred pieces, then with a remark such as, "This bearing is worn," or, "This bushing should be replaced," he would have it back together and operating in a short time. Or—take the time we salvaged a damaged cowling from a wreck in the bush. It looked like a horrible piece of bent tin to me; but in a week this piece of 'junk' was hammered and cut and reshaped into a cowling for CF-XKH. I would have thought it had been stamped out with a press in a factory. I have heard of some builders who after a year or so of meticulous labor have become discouraged and given up. Home-builts are only for a special kind of person who must be rewarded with a special kind of satisfaction as he skips and doodles among the clouds with the child of his own creation.

10

The Group of Eight

Each summer now I spent many weeks with LCZ exploring the Nahanni mountains, landing on lakes and poking around in the hills. Sometimes I would go alone; often Don and I would go together and at other times I would take Stan or Ted Taylor or Ross Clark. Hilton Burry, who at that time was employed by Gateway Aviation as an aircraft engineer, also joined us on some expeditions. There were eight of us all told in this rather loose association of alleged pilots and prospectors. All but Stan have or have had pilot's licences and four still own airplanes. John Bruckner and George Bayer, who lived at Nahanni for several years, were in on one or two of our rather abortive expeditions. George bought a Luscombe while he was at Nahanni and kept it at our little airstrip. George, Don and I were all learning to fly, and what better place to learn than on short, rough bush strips? George eventually sold his Luscombe to John Bruckner and bought a 180.

About 1965 our gang started to break up, some moving to new jobs and others started businesses on their own. All the leads to riches we thought we had had turned to dust and left us with but memories of back-packing over mountains, wading streams, fighting mosquitos and sometimes standing in wonderment as a caribou, sheep or bear came so close they could have been hit with a stone.

Once on the Redstone River, George Bayer and I were only minutes late in seeing a black bear kill a moose.

Once on the Yukon-N.W.T. border two Dall ewes and a lamb just about ran over Stan, missing him by twenty feet.

One spring we found a quartz vein loaded with galena, and six of us staked 200 mineral claims on a spine of a range of mountains where no self-respecting mountain goat would go. Among the many quartz veins we staked there was only one that bore minerals and that one assayed out to two dollars per ton! so we gave it up. No one complained as we all agreed we had had a lot of fun and got into good physical condition with the mountain climbing and packing.

That summer Don and I chartered a helicopter to set him down in a mountain valley at a spot we hoped was near an exposed vein of silver ore reported thirty years ago. Ten days of searching revealed nothing and Don then walked fifteen miles over a range of hills, across bogs and creeks, to a lake just large enough for me to pick him up with the Super Cub.

In March of 1963 I traded in LCZ for a brand new Super Cub, CF-MTI. The new aircraft had a more complete panel of instruments than did LCZ, which had only an airspeed indicator, rate of climb, ball and needle, and altimeter. It had a magnetic compass also, which is mandatory according to D.O.T. Air Regs. The compass in LCZ did not point east all the time as did the one in HAL; it went round and round while the engine was running, occasionally stopping momentarily at some point, then hurrying on again as if to catch up with itself. It was most annoying, and I had it repaired at Fort Nelson not once but many times. Whereupon it would steady down for a short time, and halfway home the needle would slowly edge to the left in an anti-clockwise motion and gathering speed would whirl madly around in its old accustomed manner. I did eventually find a way to slow it down and to steady it, but for a few moments only. I would put the airplane in a tight turn with one wing high in the air and go round and round. This maneuver was more than the compass could reckon with: it became disoriented, set its horrible distorted face at me with an N or W or S or E tilted at a rakish angle. I would at last have to cease this maneuver as the compass and I were merely outdoing one another in configuration and facial expression. When I did resume straight and level flight it would hesitate, then in frustrated anger would whirl madly for a time before settling down to its usual eccentric turning.

The new bird not only had a magnetic compass that pointed roughly at the magnetic pole, it also had a Gyro compass and a Gyro horizon. With the HF radio I had in LCZ now installed in MTI, I thought I was pretty well equipped and was almost on the point of buying myself a sash and goggles.

It is strictly against Air Regulations for a VFR (Visual Flight Rules) rated pilot to fly an aircraft in IFR (Instrument Flight Rules) conditions without proper instruction, but with my new instruments the temptation was too great and I started out by entering small clouds, then bigger and bigger ones. Needless to say I was not so stupid as to do this in a Control Zone, or anywhere near an airport, where other aircraft could be encountered. This nonsensical practice of mine went on until I was caught in a cloud layer at 4000 feet and set myself to go down through it. It had only been a thousand feet thick when I had come up through it but on the way down I didn't break out into the clear until I was less than 1000 feet above the ground. I had only gone a few miles and the cloud layer had increased from one to three thousand feet. I was sweating and a little scared when at last I saw the ground and right then determined to take IFR training before I ventured into clouds again.

In the late winter of 1963 a Piper Tri-Pacer of American registration was lost on a flight from Fort Nelson to Watson Lake. It is a 250 mile flight through mountain terrain with very few visual guides for a pilot flying VFR, the only ones being the Alaska Highway and the Liard River. Many pilots flying VFR have gone down in this area, some have crashed and some have landed safely. The Tri-Pacer was lost for more than a week. After an extensive search the R.C.A.F. Search and Rescue located the aircraft upside down on the ice surface of the Coal River. The pilot was uninjured and was very happy to be found and rescued. He had become lost and had landed before running completely out of fuel. He found a spot on the Coal River where the overflow was frozen solid and covered only with an inch or so of snow, and made a good job of setting the plane down. During the time he was there the wind turned the plane over on its back doing extensive damage.

After the pilot was rescued he sold the aircraft to Hilton Burry on condition Hilton accept it 'As is, where is'. By now it was April with warm weather expected soon and the aircraft had to be repaired quickly and moved from its location on the river a hundred miles from Watson Lake. Hilton chartered a helicopter to fly in a load of parts, supplies, welding equipment and various other items needed to repair the damaged aircraft.

By twisting my arm and threatening me with dire consequences he enlisted my services with the Super Cub. Another pilot and mutual friend, Art Gordon, who was an expert welder, was also enticed into the salvage operation.

Art became a member of our wild and rather irresponsible bunch of alleged aviators operating out of Fort Nelson and Nahanni Butte. Hilton was our leader, by virtue of the fact that he was the most daring and the most competent of us all. Those in our group did not have to spend all their time flying for a living so we could often find the time to indulge ourselves in some hair-raising and childish pranks. The salvaging of the Tri-Pacer was in no way a childish prank however as it represented a goodly financial investment for Hilton and had to be repaired and flown out of the Coal River on wheels and soon, for the snow was melting and there would soon be water on the ice.

As MTI was now on wheels for the spring of the year, Art and Hilton loaded the skis for MTI with the other supplies into Hilton's van and took off for the 300 mile drive to Watson Lake. I met them there with the Super Cub where we removed the wheels and installed the skis as there was still enough snow left at the edge of the runway for our purpose. I then stuffed Art and Hilton into the back seat of the Cub and pushed bedrolls and grub boxes around them until they complained loudly and impolitely that they could not breathe. "That's fine," I announced, "maybe if you both quit breathing for long enough I won't be bothered with your continual chatter."

Hilton was still breathing and he could talk, for he replied, "Shut up Turner and get in this machine and fire up before I die of cramps. And none of your bumbling and heavy handed flying either. You have two very important passengers on board who would like to be delivered intact within the hour to ----"

The engine roared to life and I was spared any further comments from the back seat.

MTI settled down nicely on the Coal River and Art and Hilton got busy welding the nose gear and the struts, switching propellers and inspecting for all needed repairs. I boiled a pot of coffee for lunch and stood by offering unsolicited criticism and advice.

The sun was high and warm making the snow soft and slushy on the ice by mid afternoon. The plane was repaired and inspected, oil was changed, enough fuel for the flight to Watson Lake was put in the tank, the engine was run-up and all was in readiness for the final test. Art was to fly it to Watson Lake and on to Fort Nelson.

The extent of the frozen overflow was fairly short, possibly 800 feet and there was some doubt that there was sufficient room to attain take-off speed before reaching the deeper snow. We stripped the Tri-Pacer down of all possible excess weight including axe, rifle and emergency gear. Now Art was ready to go. There was no point at which he could abort the take-off safely as he needed every foot of the available surface. If it wouldn't fly, it wouldn't fly and would end up in the deep snow farther down the river and perhaps go over on its back.

Art got in, fired up, warmed the engine, did his pre-flight check, and opened the tap as Hilton and I stood watching, slightly apprehensive. None of us had flown a 'Fly Paper' as we called it and did not know how it would perform. We need not have worried; Art had many feet to spare when he lifted off, climbed out and disappeared over the hills. Hilton and I gathered up the tools and all the odds and ends scattered around, piled them in the Super Cub and followed Art back to Watson Lake.

Back at Watson Lake it did not take Art and Hilton long to

slap the wheels back on the MTI and Art and I took off for Nelson and left Hilton to drive the van home.

That night at Art's house, he and his wife Phyllis told me about their adventures in helping Jimmy Anderson corral some Stone mountain sheep on a high plateau in the mountains. They were to capture them alive and deliver them to a game farm at Edmonton. As I recall Art, Phyllis and Jimmy landed in two Super Cubs on a 5000 foot high alpine plateau where they built a fence corral out of poles and wire mesh, with wings extending in a V. With the help of the airplane to herd them in the right direction, Art and Phyllis on the ground managed to get some ewes and lambs in between the fences, on into the corral and to close the gate. For a time the sheep were in a panic, would dash around, gather in a huddle and then dash around again. Now they had to be caught, tied up and put into the aircraft to be flown out to the Highway. Art and Phyllis both entered the corral and after some rather frantic dashing about they each managed to grab a ewe.

Phyllis said, "I held the poor struggling animal tightly and tried to quiet it by stroking its head and nose. Inside of ten minutes the ewe's heart ceased to pound, it closed its eyes and relaxed in my arms. The little lambs did the same. They were darling little things."

"Yes," Art said. "We were really surprised how quickly they quieted down as we held them in our arms and petted them. We had no trouble at all in getting them in the airplanes and out to the Highway."

I think it was the summer before this that I was told of an attempt to capture some white Dall sheep in the Mackenzie Mountains west of Norman Wells. With the help of many men and a helicopter, again on a high open plateau, a herd was driven into a corral made of netting of some sort. The ewes and lambs submitted to capture and were taken out to the Mackenzie River. The one mature Ram had different ideas and fought them hoof and horn every step of the way. He was eventually tied securely and put into a Beaver aircraft to be taken to Norman Wells. On the way there which possibly was an hour's flight, he fought and struggled so violently that he broke his own neck.

I can't help but feel sympathy for the old fellow, as in order to survive throughout the ages, the rams must have developed an instinct to fight to the death to protect their herd of ewes and lambs, as they are pretty helpless. He was being restrained, and as far as he was concerned he was having no part of it.

In later years I believe it has been shown that if given time a Dall ram can be approached and tamed and learn to submit to handling.

From what I know of wild animals in the north, it seems there is a wide difference in the adaptability of animals to the immediate and constant presence of humans.

Vera and I in our trapping days have had weasels around the house that raised their families with ours and could possibly be termed tame, but they went their own way and really only tolerated us. A wild mink lived in Stan's cabin for many days and another one lived on our boat (the Come Later) for over a week. Some trappers have said that a lynx will submit to domestication to some extent but like all cats are very independent.

There is one wild animal that I feel certain can never be tamed and that is the marten. We had two in cages in our cabin for many months and they fought viciously at any and all attempts to approach them. They never did give an inch to us.

By the time Hilton got the Tri-Pacer repaired, repainted, and back in the air again the total financial outlay was about the same as the price he would have had to pay for a good used one. But as I said, we would not have had the fun of a salvage job.

Hilton went on to take up sky diving, and is now I believe one of the most accomplished divers in Canada, and engages in some of the most fantastic group performances in the air. It frightens me to death to think of it. Do you suppose this man had ever been air sick? AIR SICK? But yes, I made him sick once in the Super Cub and never fail to remind him of it.

We were on an extended flight somewhere in the Nahanni Mountains and were dressed in winter clothing, parkas, moccasins etc. In Super Cubs the passenger sits directly behind the pilot, which in this case could have been fatal for me. This flight was on one of our abortive prospecting schemes and we were to drop some supplies to Don, in a little high mountain valley.

I had to do a bit of circling to find the camp and to check the wind; and another tight turn to come in low and make the drop. Hilton opened the door and let the parcel go, and upon glancing around I noticed he was not his exuberant self, and his face looked like an over ripe musk melon that had been made into a Jack-o-lantern for halloween. After getting back to altitude and setting a course for The Butte I suddenly felt my hat disappear from my head. Looking back I saw poor Hilton in the usual configuration of one who is busily unloading his last meal. When he had recovered to some degree and I could see that he was not going to die, I said to him, "Burry, if you do not wish to die a premature death, do not ever use my hat for that purpose again."

I should have known better than to speak in that tone of voice to Hilton. Nobody, but NOBODY gets ahead of Hilton.

He immediately replied, "One more word out of you Turner, and I'll use your parka hood instead of your cap, which I could just as easily have done. Now, you sit quietly, and fly this machine very gently back to Nahanni, and don't you make one unnecessary turn or maneuver on the way."

He had a hammer lock on me, that's for sure. If he had asked me to loosen my seat belt, stand on my head, and sing MOTHER McREE, I would have done so.

My prolonged periods of northern solitude with nothing much to do but think have induced me to philosophize on many aspects of human nature. The field of normal human relationships has many facets; the main and overpowering one is love for a woman, and the closely related protective love for one's children. Second only to this is a male bond that is manifested when a dangerous situation is encountered. *i.e.* (When men are engaged in mortal combat against a common enemy.) As bush flying can be at times hazardous this leads to a camaraderie among pilots who are good friends that is above price.

A pilot will never broadcast an incident about a friend, if it might be embarrassing and detract from his public image. It is an embarrassment to all pilots to make a poor landing, it detracts from his ego. If you ever make a horrible uncontrolled landing you will soon know who your friends are. A close friend will never mention it, and will never refer to the incident in any way. He will put it out of his mind and never recall it. If a pilot has made a terrible boo-boo, only he is at liberty to let it be known.

A typical case in point happened one winter when Hilton and I went out to an old abandoned airstrip in the mountains. Sometime before Hilton had had the daylights scared out of him by a grizzly bear at a camp in the hills. It became an obsession with him to get this bear and tack his hide to the wall. I was talked into going out to camp in the area in the hope of getting a look at Mr. Grizzly.

We loaded MTI with supplies and camping equipment and flew out to find the strip which was high on a hill and had a slope to the north. The strip was partly obscured with snow and haze when we arrived and the snow appeared to be about eighteen inches deep. I came around to land uphill and touched down too soon. There was a slight breeze from the east which tended to push me to the edge, and down we went careening over the brink and down among the rocks. Fortunately we did not go right over and we were able to get back up onto the strip. Not even the tail-ski was damaged, but we could easily have ended up cart-wheeling down that rocky slope. I should have been more observant on making the approach and touched down farther up the strip. I had no excuse for making such a stupid landing. We stayed for the night at the old camp site and did not get the bear; and Hilton has never told anyone about me running him into those boulders. A month ago I mentioned it to him and he said, "I had forgotten about that. I don't remember it at all."

11

The Search Goes On

Each spring when the snow melted and the wild geese called with their plaintive cry and the distant hills took on the blue haze of summer, the mountain lakes seemed to beckon me to come with my red and white bird to stir their placid waters with the sleek, silver floats.

The loons were calling. The hills had been silent too long, they wanted to hear again the echo of the engine—the roar—the trembling of the air as we circled for a landing. The overhanging spruce with its dry bed of golden needles beneath, needed to feel again the camp-fire's crackling heat. The sandpipers would bob their welcome to me as I dipped a pail of sparkling water from the lake. As twilight fell the tumbling stream would burble and tinkle as it sang me to sleep.

Who could resist the call?

I had to go back. And perhaps when the stars so willed and fate was in the mood, the gods who guarded her secrets would direct my footsteps to Nahanni treasures.

Paul Tesou, the old Indian I had known now for thirty-five years, insisted he had found a quartz vein with gobs of honey colored metal showing in the rock. He knew in his mind exactly where it was and tried to convey the location to me.

He said the vein came out of the bank and was exposed on the creek bed. The flood waters of the spring run-off will often erode banks and change the course of a creek bed over the years. In this process the vein must have been covered up, for no amount of searching could locate it.

On one of the many attempts at locating this prospect I flew Ted Taylor and Glenn Robinson in to a lake where they had a mere twenty miles to walk to the location. A week later when I returned to pick them up, they were tired but jubilant.

"Here, look at this, see this, feel this," they said, as they showed me a gold pan full of mineral as heavy as lead. It was shiny and metallic.

"Hey, man, that sure looks like the real thing," I said. "I wonder what it is? How much is there? Where did you find it?"

"Man, there's tons of it," Robby chortled.

"Just a couple of miles up the creek," Ted said. "It's in little veins all over the hillside."

I hated to dampen them down but it didn't look too good to me. "I don't know about this stuff. It is awfully brittle, I wish it was soft and malleable."

Later on we walked through the pine ridges to the creek and on up to where the mineral had been found. The total knowledge the three of us had of geology and prospecting was, to put it kindly, minimal. And probably because I was the older of the three and had white whiskers Ted and Robby assumed I should know something of what we were doing. The outcrop, if it could be called an outcrop, was on a side-hill. There were four inch veins of mineral dispersed at two foot intervals in the black shale. There was no sign of quartz and no other gauge mineral and the showing did not seem to fit into any pattern of deposit that I had read about.

Back home at Nahanni Butte we got out our books and our enthusiasm was dampened to a hopeless laugh of self deprecation when we learned that the mineral was marcasite, a useless and worthless compound of sulphur and iron.

We were not yet discouraged. Tomorrow, next month or next year we would find the big one.

Each summer whenever we could take time from our barging commitments Don and I would head off into the

mountains, (leaving Vera to tend the trading post) and try to
trace down the different leads we had. Often the walk from
the aircraft was so far that I became exhausted from back-
packing and tended to lose interest in the objective. Then
after a period of resting up and studying geological maps and
reports, off we would go again. We found many quartz veins
entirely barren of mineral content. Many hours were spent in
flying close to the rocks, zigging and zagging and circling,
looking over a gossan or a vein and noting the rock formation.
This was done after we had spent hours studying aerial
photos, which were available for a price from the Geological
Survey of Canada, Department of Mines and Surveys. Then
when something interesting was spotted we would figure out
the best way of getting to it from the ground. Preferably some
way that did not entail a considerable amount of back
packing.

"How far is it from the lake?"

"Oh, perhaps ten or twelve miles."

"Hmmm, nothing to it, we can make that in one good day."

'One good day' turned out to be two damned hard days
of slogging through the bush, climbing hills and getting
down and out of canyons. Also from the ground the
topography looked far different than from the air and we
would muddle around for hours finding a spot that we had
thought would be obvious.

Rolf, who had never taken to trapping or hunting and had
been disgusted with a trapper's life when at the age of twelve
he and I had chased a wounded beaver with our canoe for half
an hour before I managed to kill it, still had a love for the
north woods where he was born and grew up. He was now in
his early twenties and was home each summer after getting a
Ph.D. in Math at Ann Arbor, Michigan. I told him that as he
was over six feet and all muscle and brawn he should come
with me into the mountains and help me pack into that lost
gold mine.

He agreed and we made several gruelling pack trips into the
head of the Flat River. Although our search was fruitless we
did have fun. We saw some of the most beautiful little
mountain valleys, where glaciers towered above, pretty little
alpine flowers grew and the air tasted like wine. We drank

literally gallons of the most pure sparkling water in the world.

Rolf told me that some of the people he met at the university went almost into convulsions when he told them his father was a trapper in the Canadian north.

This aroused my ire immediately as it did when at Nahanni Butte tourists seemed surprised to find that we could read, sat at a table for our meals, lived in a house and not a hole in the ground, and spoke instead of grunted.

"How is that?" I asked Rolf. "Were there not students and teachers there from different parts of the world; Europe, Africa and Asia? Why not someone from northern Canada?"

"Yes," Rolf replied. "There were some from distant parts of the world, but they thought it was a gas to see a trapper's son at University."

"The Americans seem to be a strange people," I said. "I feel sorry for them. Do many of them speak English?"

At this he disdained to reply.

Back at the Flat River we used Don's big freight canoe to go down the river to a lake where we were to be picked up by a float plane. The water was low, the stream was infested with boulders and we had a rough and exciting voyage.

Rolf said, "My friends back at Ann Arbor would never believe the God-awful waves we've come through."

We saw two wolf pups at the edge of the river, and at a lake a mile from there we heard the mother wolf woofing at us from the cover of heavy trees close by. A moose cow with her wee calf stood in the shallows of the Flat River one morning, not thirty feet away.

One evening at dusk on the lake where we camped for two days, a loon came out of the sky in a screaming, high pitched dive and hit the water at a terrific speed.

"Good heavens," I thought, "he must surely have broken his neck." Not so. He popped up to the surface and shook the water from himself as if he did this everyday for a pastime. We saw the bluest bluebird that ever was seen. I think he had escaped from Paradise. And one day we almost stepped upon a tiny mother bird, no more than three inches long that was frightened from her nest. Her eggs were little larger than grains of wheat.

The side-hills were hot where the pine needles lay thick in

the heat of the sun and where the dry twigs snapped under-foot. The bogs and wet places were brilliant with green and yellow lichens where the sweet tang of mountain flowers was in the air.

On examining the air photos I had found a criss-cross pattern of lines which I had hoped were anomalies in the rock formation. In tramping over the land we found that many of the lines that appeared on the photos were in fact veins of quartz which would appear intermittently for half a mile or more. The quartz was what prospectors call "bull quartz" colored brown and white and quite barren of minerals. Some of the adjacent shales were loaded with cubes of iron pyrites, but nothing else.

Our two weeks were now coming to an end and the day before the float plane was due to pick us up we made our way back to the Flat River near the lake where we were to be picked up.

Once again we lifted off the water and left the mountains behind leaving whatever wealth there was still hidden in the rocks.

12

River Running

Albert Faille, the most famous trapper in Canada was now in his seventies and although his spirit was willing he was becoming too feeble to attempt the arduous boat trips into his beloved valley to sate his yet unabated enthusiasm for the search for the McLeods' lost placer gold. I feel sure that after Albert had to give up trapping he used the legend of the McLeods, as an excuse and justification for his boat trips into the Nahanni.

Now that there was a renewed interest in the discovery and development of base metals Albert turned his mind to trying to recall where he had found some promising outcrops of lead and copper when the early days of searching for placer gold had excluded an interest in the more common base metals. Albert had a lot of information of the Nahanni region and I now had an aircraft suitable for exploration of mountain areas, so it was inevitable we would pool our resources and 'get with it'.

In August of 1963 we spent the best part of a month in trying to search out and track down some of the mineral showings that Albert had come across in his wanderings at the heads of the Nahanni and Flat Rivers.

He left his boat and kickers at the Butte and we headed off into the hills with CF-MTI. We made our base camp at Loon Lake on the Flat River where Don had a big game outfitting camp. Although MTI with her thirty gallon fuel capacity had a four hour range, the distance we wished to cover was so great that I had to establish additional fuel caches at two strategic points. MTI could carry five kegs to a load, which was fifty gallons. I put one hundred gallons at Loon Lake, another hundred at the Flat Lakes, and three kegs above the falls. From the Flat Lakes we could reach all points on the Nahanni.

First we flew back and forth in the Irvine Creek valley where Albert had trapped for many years, searching for a creek that Albert thought might be the one marked on a map he had seen which was reported to have been drawn by Frank and Willie McLeod, whose bodies were later found decapitated in Dead Mans Valley—(Later called Headless Valley by Pierre Berton.) The map had shown three small creeks draining three ponds, that ran parallel into a larger river. An ore body was marked near one of the small creeks. The word Liard was marked on the main stream and Albert always maintained that LIARD was the name of the McLeods boat.

After eliminating the Irvine Creek area we flew to Rabbitkettle Lake and set up camp. This was possibly the best wild game and fur region in the whole Nahanni. Albert had trapped here, and this was where a pack of timber wolves had attacked him back in the 1940s. He shot the leader and it dropped and died only four feet from him; the others held their ground and Albert was able to retreat to his camp close by.

Woodland caribou and moose were common here at all times except January, February and March, when they retreated to a higher elevation because the depth of snow at lower levels made it difficult for them to move and find food. Also the deep snow made sitting ducks of them for the wolves.

Albert had picked up some samples on the Broken Skull River to the north-east and we were to try to relocate it from the air and walk into it later if possible.

At Rabbitkettle Lake we found a tent camp established

there. It proved to be a field party of the Geological Survey of Canada, Dept. of Energy, Mines and Resouces, under the supervision of the party chief, H. Gabrielse. We unloaded the aircraft, established our camp nearby and invited ourselves to supper at the cook tent.

We were told that a day or so prior to our arrival, the camp had been visited by three Swiss canoeists who were on their way downstream to Virginia Falls and Nahanni Butte. They had walked into the lake from the Nahanni River, which is separated from the lake by half a mile of low timbered hills which had been burned over two years previously. The three were travelling in a seventeen foot canoe and from what we heard, Albert and I concluded that their expedition had been poorly organized. To begin with, one seventeen foot canoe with the necessary equipment for a month's river travel is not suitable for three men. In this case they travelled with one man in the stern, another in the bow and the third sat on top of the load midships. A child could have seen that the center of gravity was too high. All three were reported to be dressed in what I would charitably term a very odd manner. They were covered from head to toe in buckskin clothing, which might look very woodsy and romantic in a Hollywood Western and might be someone's conception of how Buffalo Bill and his cohorts were dressed, but for fast water canoeists it was nothing less than ludicrous. A buckskin jacket and moccasins yes, but in the event of a mishap a person fully clothed in buckskin would float about as well as a man dressed in armour.

After taking in the situation and seeing the canoeists' attire, apparent lack of experience and noting from their conversation the incompatability of the group, Mr. Gabrielse suggested that it might be advisable for them to abandon the trip of 200 miles and to return to Watson Lake, the starting point of their northern journey. He said there was a Beaver aircraft due in from Watson Lake shortly with supplies and the three would be welcome to return with no charge to themselves. The offer was rejected and the three Swiss continued down the Nahanni to the falls and points below.

The men at the camp wondered how the three had made out. This was the first Albert and I had heard of this so we could throw no light on the fortunes of the party. And it seemed to me at the time a case of premonition on the part of the geological crew that the party of canoeists were facing disaster.

For some reason that I cannot now recall Albert and I returned to the Butte before continuing with our prospecting. While we were at home, two men from Grande Prairie, Alberta returned from a trip to Virginia Falls with a jet boat and reported that they had seen no sign of the three canoeists, but did see a canoe pulled up on a sand beach at the mouth of the Flat River. They assumed the men were off in the bush on a hike. From what the jet boat men said I had no good reason to be alarmed about the safety of the three but our apprehension was heightened and the other members of the household agreed that perhaps I should zip up the river with MTI to make another check.

The next morning I took off and, following the river, saw not a sign of anyone until I came to the mouth of the Flat. At one glance I knew that disaster had struck the unfortunate three. The canoe was upside down on a large sandbar island in the middle of the Nahanni River. On circling low a good look showed the bow of the canoe had been bashed in, with a tarpaulin and a rope trailing from the stern, which was pointed down stream. The upturned, floating canoe had obviously been caught on a root when the level of the water was four feet higher, and was held there as the water receded. I did not land but flew low over the river to the falls, twenty miles upstream, then returned to the Butte, seeing no indication of survivors, and then on to Fort Simpson to inform Corporal Bob Ward of the R.C.M.P.

Bob thought the first thing we should do was to search for survivors, so we took off immediately for a flight up river. This time we landed near the canoe, and found the only item left in the canoe besides the tarp, was a plastic bag of rice, well soaked. The canoe had rammed something solid, had upset and after floating for a distance had been caught up on the sandbar.

To my mind the most likely possibility was that the canoe had rammed the wall at the Figure Eight about seven miles upstream. At this point the river, gathering speed, piles up against a gently turning limestone cliff, not more than twenty feet in height. This points the onrushing current directly at another higher rock cliff. Spilling directly against this wall the water is forced in two directions, to the right upstream, and downstream to the left. Thus is created two whirlpools that vary in speed and intensity with the amount of water coming down. It has been my experience that the lower the water is the less turbulence in the Figure Eight.

We believed that when the three men arrived here the river was in a state of mild flood with some small amount of driftwood in the current. Without life jackets the chance of escaping from an overturned canoe here would be slim indeed. To make matters worse the ages of onrushing waters had worn away a larged curved hollow in the cliff at the low water level, which would tend to hold an object in its grip for some minutes once it was caught here. Not finding any survivors leads me to believe that the Figure Eight had taken three lives.

From the Flat River to the falls we again searched carefully for survivors, flying low over the water and looking for anything that moved. Then back down the river to the Butte with no better results that the last time.

Corporal Ward said that the next item on the agenda would be a search of the river by boat for bodies, and asked me if I would accompany him as a guide. "I should have some one along who knows the river," he said.

"Sure," I replied, "I'll go along with you. If I don't you'll likely run on the first pile of rocks you come to, and wreck the outfit. And while you yourself are expendable I don't like to see my tax money wasted on canoes and kickers for you to wreck."

Bob owned and flew a Cessna 170 aircraft, and in addition to being a very good pilot he was also expert with both river boats and canoes; although I took pains not to let him know I thought so. He also made light of my self-asserted ability as a river man.

"Robert, my boy," I intoned in a stentorious voice, "you will now see how an expert guides a boat up that fearsome Nahanni River, among the rocks and treacherous rapids, without ever grazing a rock or sandbar. We will find and bring back the bodies of the three would-be canoeists. I will do all the work, and you my son, may take all the glory."

We were having supper at the Ward house. Bob turned to his wife Cecile and with a horrible grimace he moaned, "My God, I can hardly stand the wind around here, we sure need a scoop-shovel in the house when this wild Nahanni character is around."

Cecile is such a sweet girl she came to my defense, and Bob who found himself outnumbered, had to beat a retreat.

I flew into Nahanni that evening and Bob brought the Police boat up the next day. At some settlements in the N.W.T., the R.C.M.P. used river scows with high powered outboard motors. At Simpson, for some reason, they had a twenty foot freight canoe with a wide stern, with two 18 HP motors to drive it. It was not a bad outfit for a warm day and rattled right along at a good clip.

Now comes an incident or two that I would like to 'disremember', as a trapper used to say. Painful as it is, it must be told, for if it isn't, when Bob Ward writes his memoirs he might expose me. I had no justification for doing so, but twenty miles into the Splits I ran slam bang onto a pile of rocks covered by a foot of water, in the middle of the river. I was so surprised that I fumbled with the controls of the motors for many seconds before I got them out of gear and shut down, and by that time had ground half an inch off the propellers of both motors.

Bob, sitting in front of the canoe, turned and said, "Look, you don't have to ruin those motors before we are barely out of sight of the Butte, even though they do belong to the government."

For about the second time in my life I had nothing to say. It felt as if all the blood in my body had come to my head. How could I be so clumsy? Instead of feeling fat and happy, I should have been watching the surface for any indication of shallow water ahead. I well knew that the river ice moving out in the spring run-off will often rip out rock bars and pile them in some other place farther down stream. From now on, for the hundred miles to the Flat River I would be more careful.

We steamed along up to the first canyon, making fifteen

miles an hour against the current. A mile or two below the canyon Bob pointed and, "Over there, look, there's one."

Sure enough, there was a body floating spread-eagled and high in the water. We circled around and came up to him on the windward side, or what we hoped was the windward side. It turned out to be NOT the windward side. We got a rope on him anyway and towed him to shore on a sand beach.

"He seems well preserved," Bob announced. "He's only been in the water for two weeks and the water is pretty cold."

"I'm glad he's not much worse," I volunteered, "we're certainly not going to put him in the canoe with us. And there is mud all over him, he must have been resting on the bottom for some time."

"It is said that a body will stay down for nine days," Bob said, "but the water is very cold and in these conditions it could take longer. We'll roll him on shore and pick him up on the way back."

With the paddles and a stick we finally got the body rolled into a tarpaulin and dragged up on shore, where we covered it with brush and logs to keep away the ravens. We both agreed that travellers were not likely to camp in the vicinity while we were gone.

We made good time through the first canyon, saw Dead Mans Valley ahead and the dancing waves of George's Riffle.

"Here is one place," I thought, "that we won't have any trouble. I know this riffle like the back of my hand."

So—shut down the power a little, sneak up into the waves, ease across gently toward the wall, keep to the edge of the waves, just out of the swirls, very good, open up the kickers, only a few feet now, and BANG! The starboard motor struck something, came out of the water, crashed back into position and we were roaring ahead again before I had time to even think about what had happened.

"Well, Turner," I mumbled to myself, "you blithering idiot, will you never remember that big black rock is just where it has always been, twelve feet out from shore and a foot under the surface?" And almost every time I come by I had to take a chip off it.

Bob sat relaxed in the bow and never so much as turned his head, bless him. We were past Stark's Rock before I thought to look down at the transom of the canoe. It had damned near been wrenched off with the jar, and one kicker was hanging on by faith and a sliver. In the quiet water ahead Bob looked around with his shy, quiet smile and I knew by God that I was in for it later on.

At the Forestry cabin at Prairie River we pulled in, to camp for the night. The table in the cabin was a four by eight sheet of plywood. I spotted this and said, "The Lord looks after fools and drunkards, Robert my lad, and here is just what the Doctor ordered to repair our craft."

"You're right about the first part of that statement, Dick, but let's not push our luck too far eh?"

"Tut, tut, what's a little nick in one small rock? A half inch to the side would have missed it entirely."

"Maybe so, maybe so," Bob mumbled, "but do take care please, I would prefer to arrive home IN the canoe and not being dragged behind it as we'll be doing with our friend down the river."

"Have no fear Robert," I said. "I will deliver you back to Nahanni Butte safe and sound if it's the last thing I do."

"If you don't, it will be the last thing you do."

"Oh, my, Corporal Ward, you are sharp today, but I'm starved to death and if you will do the cooking act I will repair the transom of that flimsy craft of yours. And by-the-way," I continued, "why doesn't the R.C.M.P. supply the Simpson detachment with a jet boat? We could travel in comfort and safety then."

"I really don't know," was the answer. "We keep trying."

After we had eaten supper we finished the repair on the transom of the canoe, checked over the motors, got out our sleeping bags and lay awake talking for over an hour. First we talked of airplanes, mountain flying, Albert Faille, the McLeods' lost gold creek, and prospecting generally. Then back to airplanes again and pilots we had known who had crashed or been lost in the Nahanni and Mackenzie mountains: the trappers and prospectors who had spent years in the Nahanni, many of whom had returned safely and some who had not. What could have happened to Bill Epler and Joe Mulholland, who disappeared without a trace? Bob thought as I did that there was no basis for thinking that any of those who had died or disappeared in the Nahanni had met with foul play. Anyone who lived in these mountains for any extended length of time was bound to have some close calls; some were unfortunate and the 'calls' developed into permanency. Then we went back to airplanes and Blake Mackenzie and we both marveled at the fact that he had apparently survived the crash without a scratch, lived and kept a diary for nearly fifty days and then must have met with some unusual accident preventing him from returning to his camp when he had, it seemed, intended to go only a mile or so, perhaps to the top of the mountain and back.

As I lay awake that night composing myself for sleep it passed through my mind that the Nahanni and I had a love-hate relationship: I loved the beauty of its wilderness, the vastness of its almost unexplored regions, the thrill of pitting myself against its dangers, felt the pleasure of being drawn into the magnetic spell of the lonely valleys, as a bird to the call of its mate, but I hated it for taking the lives of my friends and for being so unforgiving to those who made mistakes. I did not particularly enjoy this river travelling any more, and there were many other tasks I would have preferred to do than to look for the bodies of those poor souls who had perished in these icy waters. I was glad to have a companion with me, and our jocular remarks and attitude was to cover our sadness.

Possibly because of our mutual interest in airplanes and flying, Bob and I had become good friends almost as soon as we met. When he was transferred to the Simpson detachment I would come zooming in to town with LCZ and as transportation and accommodation in town at that time was limited I would 'buzz' the barracks to alert them to the fact that the wild Nahanni trapper was in town and needed to be met at the airstrip, brought in and fed. Bob maintains the only reason he put up with me was because of the beautiful little airplane that I flew. All pilots are drawn to Super Cubs as bees are to a flower. Consequently I had many meals at the Wards' home and he at ours. Vera and I became very close to Cecile and Bob and considered their three children as our grandchildren. In March of 1963 Bob and I went together in the Super Cub to Wetaskiwin Alberta where I bought a brand new Super Cub and Bob purchased a Cessna 170 with wheels and skis, and flew it back to Simpson.

Reminiscent dreaming came to an end with, "Get out of the sack you wild trapper, coffee is on and we have to get to the Figure Eight and back to the Butte tonight."

I groaned and opened my eyes and there was Ward, as large as life and as cheerful as if it was the middle of the day. "Your parents must have been night owls," I said.

"It is six o'clock in the morning, man, it'll soon be noon, and nothing done yet."

"It is two hours before any civilized man would be awake, I'm sure glad morning only comes once a day."

A thorough search of the river from the Figure Eight to the Butte revealed no other trace of the two missing bodies. We did find a bedroll and some food in a bag, caught in a pile of driftwood, but nothing more.

Ten miles below the Flat, we pulled into the mouth of Mary River to make a cup of tea and to have lunch. While we were there a little boat came roaring up the river and pulled in. It was Cpl. Bill Craig and his guide Joe Donta from Fort Liard. It was Bill's first trip to the falls and he said he was duly impressed with both the river and the scenery. Bill too was a pilot and the last year he was at Fort Liard he bought a Fleet Canuck.

While we were eating lunch we discussed the present mission that Bob was on and one of us asked Bill if he would like to deliver a cargo we had cached below the canyon, to Nahanni Butte.

Bill replied, "Look you chaps, don't try to get me involved in your nefarious activities. I have no doubt that the Fort Simpson detachment under Corporal Ward is quite capable of carrying out its duties. This," he pointed grandly to himself, "is the Liard detachment and I have other important matters to attend to. We will however, keep an eye out for any items that might interest you."

I believe it is no secret to say that up to the early 1960s a posting for a member of the R.C.M.P. to the Northwest Territories or the Yukon was considered to be a lucky break. Conditions are different now with roads being built and traffic problems to be dealt with, so that some northern towns are not the soft touch they used to be.

In those earlier years Fort Liard was a pleasant little settlement with few serious problems. There were no roads and consequently no vehicles. Summer patrols were made with canoe and kicker, then scows and bigger kickers. Winter patrols were made by dog team. In the 1950's a young constable, John Clark was posted to Fort Liard from some place near Vancouver. He told us it was a happy day when he heard he was being transferred to Liard. He had recently received a bullet through his heart in an incident in the course of duty. It was reported that someone had shot at him with a .22 calibre rifle and that a by-stander who had never driven a car before, loaded the wounded constable in the patrol car and had driven at a hundred miles an hour to the nearest hospital, in time to save his life.

Bill and his wife Marge enjoyed their stay at Liard and when their two years were up hoped to be transferred to another northern settlement. The outcome was in doubt for some time and then the blow fell.

One day when I landed at Liard on the way to Fort Nelson, Bill was away somewhere and I sat and had coffee with Marge. "How did Bill's transfer come out?" I asked. "Did he get any final word on it yet?"

"Did he ever," Marge replied, "let me tell you about it. He was talking with Fort Smith on the radio as he does every day and was told there was a message from the C.O. His posting would be to Ottawa."

"Too bad," I said, "I know Bill will be disappointed."

"He took it with great calm though, I heard no language or comments from the office in the other room, but when he came into the kitchen he aimed a terrific kick at the door. His face was flushed and he was mumbling faintly."

And I am sorry to say we both doubled over with laughter.

Less than three hours after leaving Mary River, Bob and I were back at the Hot Springs at the foot of the first canyon. At an abandoned camp we found a sheet of plywood and with the aid of some slender spruce poles we manufactured a sort of 'travois' on which we transported our cadaver downstream to the Butte.

That evening, at supper, as I had anticipated, Bob said to Vera, "Dick only piled up on the rocks twice on the way up to the Flat River. It was fortunate for me I had an expert riverman for a guide. I tremble to think how we would have made out with a non-expert."

And there was really nothing much I could say in reply.

. The bodies of the other two men were never found. At the Figure Eight there is a quarter mile portage trail cut out through the bush and wise canoeists who are safety conscious will use it. Unless it is carefully observed before entering, the danger of the place is not immediately apparent. The peril for unpowered craft is that the full fury of the river pours itself into an undercut wall.

In May of 1934 John Norgaard and Harry Southard, two experienced trappers, got caught here with their large home-made canvas canoe. They were thrown against the wall and were held there by the force of the water rushing underneath. Although the canoe tended to roll, it was held upright by the two men holding onto the rock wall with their hands. They slowly inched themselves along until they were out of danger. John said that after that experience he always held the Figure Eight in great respect; he and others referred to it as Hell's Gate.

In July of 1959 a Dr. Hohne and his wife attempted to run the Figure Eight with a two-man kayak. Dr. Hohne was not a novice as he had run many streams in Germany, but this was his first trip on the Nahanni. The problem with this place for unpowered craft is that the river must be crossed in a short distance while you are being carried swiftly into the wall. On their first attempt they were caught in the upstream whirl-pool. On the second try they paddled furiously to get across the river before they were carried into the wall; the time for them to cross was too short and they hit the center of the under-cut, swinging the kayak just in time to avoid a head-on collision. The kayak rolled immediately and they found themselves in the water. Their life jackets helped to support them and they clung to the upturned kayak and drifted down through several more sets of rapids before they were able to get to shore. Mrs. Hohne had a bruised shoulder but otherwise they escaped with only a fright. They too, like John Norgaard had more respect for the Nahanni after that.

With a powered boat of good size the maneuverability is

much more positive and the hazard is much less. With a jet boat at 30 mph you can zip up and down through the Figure Eight and hardly notice it.

There is a myth that canoes are made for rivers, even big rivers, and the general public does not realize that in inexperienced hands they are death traps. Canoes were used in the early day exploration and settlement of the north because portaging was necessary. It was essential to utilize a small craft that was light in weight. On the Mackenzie River system, as soon as lumber was available, boats and scows were built. This must have begun when the traders brought in steel whip-saws.

Those engaged in transportation, as well as natives and settlers, then built larger boats that would haul bigger loads and weather more of a storm. Soon after the era of the York boats the outboard motor was invented and small scows and boats came into their own. They were easily constructed and for far less money, would hold a good load and stand far more rough usage than a canoe of comparable size. Canoes were now relegated for use on small lakes and streams in the hunting of beaver, muskrats, water birds and sometimes moose. But—alas—tradition dies hard and the romance of voyageurs in their high-powered canoes speeding down the white water of slick paper magazines and imaginative writers in a very real way tends to brainwash people into thinking that canoes are THE mode of transportation on all northern rivers. Consequently almost every year bodies of canoeists are taken from the rivers, cold, stiff and stinking.

After Bob left for Simpson towing his cargo behind, Albert and I again loaded the Super Cub with food and camping gear and headed off into the Nahanni mountains.

This time we would investigate two places on the Broken Skull River that Albert wanted to check into. Years ago he had picked up rock samples that on later examination proved to contain lead and copper. Twenty-five years had passed since he had been in that part of the valley. Our plan was to map the locality from the air, and establish a base camp on the nearest suitable lake. Albert would stay with the airplane while I, with a pack and a gold pan, would walk into the location panning the streams and checking the outcrops.

The first place and the one Albert thought the most promising, we could not locate at all. It was a hill with a black rock outcrop exposed by stream erosion, and should have been obvious from the air. We flew back and forth and up and down right over the tops of the trees and saw no trace of the hill. We went from there to a lake hidden away in a deep valley where the creeks drained a granite intrusive. The McLeod boys had come this way and Albert wanted me to pan a creek leading from the intrusive.

We heeled in the airplane onto a gentle shale beach and set up the tent. From our camp-fire, the lake seemed like a shining black pool of ebony, from which rose towering granite crags with silver streaks of ice and snow. We seemed to be at the bottom of a deep, dark depression with no way out but straight up. In reality the lake extended into the valley to the left which led down and out to the main Nahanni.

Bright and early in the morning I took off with a pack, over a low pass to a creek five miles to the south. There were many game trails and the walking was easy. I followed the creek for an hour or two, panning here and there but without success. That night, weary and exhausted, I wended my way over the hills and back to camp.

The next lake we landed on was near the Flat River where Albert had trapped in the 1930's. In two different places within a four mile radius he had seen outcrops of galena and copper. Here surely, we thought, we would have better luck. This we knew was a mineralized zone, and a good country for walking, with many game trails.

The first day of hiking I returned to camp, wet, tired and weary. I found the exact place where Albert had seen the galena. I found the old camp site he had described to me. Some fire wood and tent poles he had cut were still in place, thirty years old and still there and recognizable as an Albert Faille camp, but there was absolutely no sign of the galena outcrop. The creek however was big, even by northern standards, with a steep gradient and filled with boulders. The water, ice and rocks moving down the stream throughout the years must have removed all signs of the galena showing.

"It was there," Albert said, on my return to camp. "There

Dick Turner, author of NAHANNI.

Dick, Vera, and Don at our cabin, Nahanni Butte, Aug. 1964.

At Turner's Cabin Nahanni. Gus Kraus, Vera, Mary Kraus, and Don Turner.

At our cabin at Nahanni Butte.
L to R: Ross Clark, Dick Turner, Hilton Burry, Don Turner, Stan Turner. Just returned from staking claims.

Ross Clark with his home-built Aircraft CF-XKH, 1975.

A noon stop on my trapline. The winter road at the Long Reach. March 1969.

Me setting off on prospecting pack trip. CF-UAH in background. MacMillan Lake August 1969.

Stan [and me—out of sight] coming up George's Riffle into Dead Man's Valley, 1963.

Staking claims near Dead Man's Valley at 6000' altitude, May 1963.

Looking into Dead Man's Valley from where we staked claims on mountain tops, May 1963.

Dead Man's Valley, June 1966.

Two Nugget Creek near the source.

Stan Turner at Two Nugget Creek.
Aug. 1964.

Stan. At fishing hole on Two Nugget Creek, July 1962.

Two Nugget Creek near the mouth.

Two Nugget Creek.

Ross Clark on Two Nugget Creek.

Stan Turner. Camp near Two Nugget Creek, Ross taking picture, Aug. 1964.

Stan panning gold on Two Nugget Creek. Aug. 1964.

CF-MTI landing Skinboat Lakes.

Glenn Robinson.   Prospecting.
1965. Skinboat Lakes. N.W.T.

Dick Turner and Ross Clark. Skinboat Lakes, CF-MTI.

Don Turner with MTI. Skinboat Lakes near Flat River, July 1963.

Our camp on Flat River when staking claims on Bennett Creek, May 1974.

Flat River. Near Faille's cabin on Borden Creek, 1974.

Prospecting area. Flat River.

Dick Turner looking for galena. Near the Flat River, May 1974.

Rolf Turner. Prospecting near Flat River, 1973.

Loon Lake, Flat River in 1965. Don's base camp for Dall Sheep and Mountain Goat Hunting.

Dick Turner, Fort Nelson, 1966.

Don's camp on Loon Lake, July 1966.

My first Super Cub LCZ—Fort Nelson, 1962.

CF-RID moored on Mackenzie River at Fort Simpson—July, 1974.

My leased Cessna 185—CF-RID at our camp on Summit Lake, Yukon, 1974.

CF-BZY at McMillan Lake, 1974.

Art Gordon, soon after he purchased CF-JMI at Selkirk Manitoba. Probably 1962.

Cpl. Bill Craig, his wife Marge and their children, with Aeronca Sedan CF-OGP soon after Bill purchased it from Art Gordon. Fort Resolution, N.W.T. Probably March of 1964.

Turner Expediting Truck Fort Simpson 1972. Aircraft Turbo Beaver.

Catching Stone Sheep on Maternity Mountain, for Al Oming, Alberta Game Farm.

CF-UAH, Dead Man's Valley, March 1966.

Dick Turner at Virginia Falls, August 1976. Falls on the Nahanni are twice as high as Niagara.

Art Gordon with aircraft CF-OGP and record Stone Sheep horns.

Dick Turner on trapline with LCZ 1961.

CF-MTM damaged on landing on dirt strip 70 miles south of Watson Lake, Yukon Territory May 1964. George Bayer patched it up and flew it out.

CF-FYN, Ted Taylor's plane that Blake MacKenzie crashed near McMillan Lake, 1963. Blake survived crash but died later.

Bob Ward's Cessna 170 in Mackenzie Mountains.

Plane crashed in Nahanni Mountains, all on board killed.

Cpl. Bob Ward, RCMP, at crash site of Cessna 185 in Nahanni Mountains, September 1965—four men killed.

George Bayer's Cessna 180 at Fantas Strip, northern B.C. Man not identified.

This is CF-XKH — Ross Clark's Homebuilt that I test flew.

Cockpit and instrument panel of CF-XKH.

t Simpson—showing junction of Liard and Mackenzie Rivers.

ne taken from the winter road 150 miles north of Fort Simpson. January 1973.

Albert Faille. Fort Simpson 1968.

The C.N. Telephone line that ran for 800 miles from Fort Simpson to Inuvik. March 1972.

Nahanni Butte.

CF-GGU at Nahanni Butte June 1964.

John Brucker, Hilton Burry, Stan and Dick Turner, leaving Nahanni River & heading up Prairie River & over mountains to stake claims. Packs were about 40 lbs. each. May 1963.

Fairchild 24 in which Chris Van Toole flew the first Diesel Electric Lighting Plants into Nahanni Butte Village. Don Turner sitting there thinks he would like to own it. Yellowknife, May 1964.

At Nahanni Butte 1969. Colleen, Don's wife. Nancy Turner. Edward, Nancy's son. Don, Gina, Nancy's daughter and me.

John Brucker at Nahanni Hot Springs with GGU. March 1963.

A modern trapline. My cabin and snowmobile. March 1969.

Stan and Dick with CF-HAL at Nahanni Butte. April 1959.
The Go-Easy tug and barge in background.

Don's airplane CF-LKL at Nahanni Butte 1973.

Pictures hurriedly snapped of an object thought to be a Sasquatch near our cabin at Nahanni Butte April 1967.

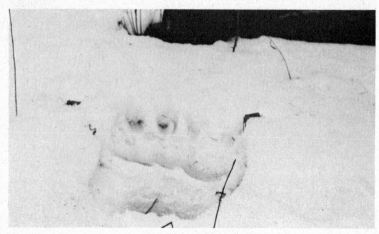

Pictures of alleged Sasquatch tracks. Nahanni Butte 1967.

Vera Turner — 1933.

Vera Turner — 1965.

Vera Turner — 1972.

Dick Turner. Super Cub CF-MTI over Mickey Lake.

Mickey Lake. July 1963.

The former Turner & Taylor Sport Fishing Lodge. Trout Lake, N.W.T. 1970.

Virginia Falls.

Fort Nelson Airport. March 1964.

Don Turner and George Bayer with George's aircraft CF-GGU at Fort Nelson. June 1964.

Dick Turner refueling CF-MTI on the river at Fort Nelson. July 1964.

Stagger Wing Beachcraft, out of gas and lost, made landing in deep snow on Patrie Lake north-west of Fort Nelson. The plane was salvaged by Hilton Burry. Probably March 1963.

Bob Ward, Cecile Ward, Vera Turner, Dick Turner at
Commissioner's Ball. Yellowknife 1972.

Working out way up the mountain to our camp 2 miles farther.

was chunks as big as a kettle scattered all along the creek just above my camp."

"There's no sign of it now Albert, I didn't find one speck of galena anywhere. I can't understand it. It must have been ripped out and covered over."

"It could be. It's such a hell roarin' creek when the snow is melting, it might have washed it away. Did you look into the bank on the other side of the creek?"

"Sure as hell did. It's all flat on that side with moss and big trees, and back against the hill there's no exposure of rock at all."

"There was chunks of galena on the bench where the camp was, did you find them?"

"By God, Albert, there's no galena anywhere on that bench. The waters never been up there because the camp has never been flooded. I must have found the wrong camp."

"I only camped in the one place, Dick, right where the trail hits the creek."

"That's got to be the place I guess, but if there was any lead or silver there, the headless men must have gathered it all up and carried it away."

"It sure is a mystery, I can't understand it. But it was there when I trapped here in '35."

"I may as well have a look for the copper showing tomorrow. Boy, am I tired. That rifle gets heavier every mile, but if I leave it behind, sure as hell that'll be the day a grizzly decides to cross my path."

"That's right Dick, never leave your gun behind, if you ever need it you won't have time to go home to get it."

"I wonder on which side of that little lake I should start looking for copper?"

"I don't know for sure, it was only a small showing in the muskeg and I wasn't too interested in it at the time. I think it must be on the south side of the small lake as that's the way I went most of the time."

I stood up and put some more wood on the fire. "What I want right now Albert is to get some dry socks on and then some supper. Tomorrow I'll charge around in the bush, and see what I can see."

The nights are usually quite cool in the mountains and we

sat around the campfire smoking and talking, getting up once in a while to put a root or a log on the fire. The flames would blaze up as we sat back against the trunk of a tree, and I would glance toward the airplane with its floats heeled up on the sand beach with the three ropes that held it firmly to the shore. The lake seemed like a sheet of silver in the still air. As always in the bush, the air smelled fresh and sweet with an occasional whiff of the pungent perfume of burning willow bark from the fire. A call of a loon echoed from the cliff; two mallards swam through the grass, and little night birds twittered in the trees.

I listened to Albert telling of his first years here, and thought, "This has to be the nicest time of the year in the best place in the world, I'd like to build a cabin here." Aloud I said, "Albert, it's been many years since our first trip up here together. Just how many years I hate to think, but it must be close to thirty-five. Man, there's been a lot of water under the bridge in that time; we're a lot older and very little richer, but, by God we're travelling better anyway." And I motioned to the little red and white bird moored to the shore.

Albert laughed his soft quiet chuckle. "It sure is the rig for getting around, but for me if I was only a bit younger I would be frogging around the rivers with a boat and a kicker."

In the morning after bacon, toast and coffee, I stuffed into the packsack a lunch and tea-billy, prospector's pick, skinning knife and file (from trapper's habit), and shells for the gun, then picking up the rifle, headed up the hill. I had hardly gone more than half a mile when I ran slam bang into a six foot wide quartz vein sticking from the ground.

Quartz veins are evidence of gases and vapors from the region below the earth's crust having worked their way to the surface. These gases and vapors sometimes bring metals in solution and deposit them in or near the quartz. "All we need now is a bit more of a miracle," I thought. "Chunks of gold, copper, silver and lead in big gobs in said quartz."

Nothing of the kind showed up in the outcrop and I went on in the direction in which the vein was pointed, and found that every few hundred yards the vein surfaced for a hundred feet or so then went to ground again. This continued for over a mile. All day I trudged back and forth, digging into the vein and down beside it in the host rock. With the prospector's pick I happily banged away, chipping here and chipping there, examining every piece carefully with the magnifying glass, hoping to see some sign of mineralization. Along the vein I hammered, on this side, that side, the front side and the other side; I hammered on the up side and the down side and the backside, the inside and the outside. Then I sat down and sighed. At least I had found quartz; beautiful grains of quartz; white quartz, blue quartz, brown quartz, pink quartz and purple quartz. Nice quartz, mind you, pretty little crystals, all tucked in so tightly together there was no room left for gold, silver, or copper, or even the teeniest, weeniest bit of lead. The merest glint of calcopyrite would have been a welcome sight.

"To hell with it," I said aloud, and wandered back to camp. What the hell, the sun still shone, the birds sang, and another day we would yet find it.

For the next three days I tramped the hills, banging on the rocks and digging into the moss here and there, on the lookout for Albert's copper. On the fourth day we abandoned the search, concluding the stars had agreed that it was not a propitious time for us to seek our fortunes.

13

Victims and Near Victims

In the lower Liard River area the first good frost often comes in the first week of September. Snow appears on the mountains and by the end of the month they are clothed in a blue-white glistening blanket. Most years severe frosts hold off until October. Ice appears on the small lakes in the first week of October and the big rivers begin to run ice after October 15th. The weather in the mountains is often poor for flying during the latter part of September, because of freezing conditions, low clouds and snow. The elevation of Nahanni Butte is 600 feet above sea level and if in the fall there is cold wind and rain the freezing level could be down to 3000 feet, making flight at these levels extremely hazardous, with the likelihood of ice forming on the aircraft wings and propeller. Experienced northern flyers are usually wary of flying in these conditions, and will turn back or wait for an improvement.

However, it is a rare pilot who will not push his luck from time to time. Sometimes it is the pilot who is impatient, sometimes it is the employer, who for economic reasons is anxious to have the trip completed without delay. Often the customer who is paying the charter wishes to push on and does not realize the danger of VFR mountain flying. It is also true to say that if a pilot waits for a perfect day to make a designated trip, he had better quit flying and take up some more congenial occupation such as lingerie salesman or interior decorating, where his work will not be influenced by the vagaries of the weather.

Bush flying for a private or a commercial pilot can be an interesting and rewarding occupation, and a safe occupation providing a correct mental attitude is maintained. The bush pilots who I know and who have many thousands of hours in the air and who have lived to a mature age have all been proficient flyers who have maintained a serious and professional respect toward flying. The best ones keep their bodies and minds in a healthy condition, have a cheerful personality and are considerate of others. They do not over-indulge in the use of alcohol. Most of us lesser beings cannot hope to attain their proficiency, but I do believe that we can fly and live to a ripe old age if we pattern our flying habits after the true professionals.

The Mackenzie, Nahanni and northern British Columbia mountains have taken the lives of many pilots and their passengers, and in those cases of which I have some knowledge, deteriorating weather has been paramount. In most of these 'pilot error' has been designated as the cause. In many other instances in which a pilot has pressed on, blind luck has kept him from becoming a statistic.

For my part I have always had such a degree of respect for the mountains, with their uncushioned rock surfaces, that I have so far avoided working myself into a position among the rocks in which there was no way out. But on the lowlands east of the hills I have on three different occasions pushed on into deteriorating weather when I knew it was foolhardy to do so. The first instance I have already described.

The next time was when I was flying LCZ to pick up two trappers one winter on December 24th. Their camp was on a small lake at 2700 feet elevation, forty miles east of Nahanni Butte. When I left the Butte soon after sunup there was a light wind from the north and the visibility was good. At the lake the sun was shining. With the two young men, their furs, bedrolls, packsacks and guns, etc. I had a full load with two hours fuel. It was less than a thirty minute flight back to the

Butte and was what we call a dry run, no lakes or creeks to follow. Almost as soon as we left the lake it started to snow, which in itself gave no cause for alarm. Many miles are flown in snow, which is quite normal as visibility rarely gets down below half a mile. In this instance the distance between the snowflakes decreased until I could see absolutely nothing ahead and only the trees directly below. I should have turned at this juncture and gone back to the lake. However I had visions of spending Christmas day in a small tent with nothing to eat but rabbits and bannock while at home we were preparing for a feast and a celebration, so I pressed on. I had zigged and zagged to pick up a creek and when I found it I was not sure if I was heading for the Liard River or back to the source of the creek. The creek was so twisted that it was impossible to follow directly above it. It was however bordered here and there with larger than normal spruce trees, giving a wider corridor to stay within. There was no forward visibility at all and I had to almost brush the tops of the trees to keep them in sight. I did not let myself think of anything but following that creek.

You will recall that LCZ had a paucity of instruments, but it did have a reliable altimeter. Now in the last few minutes it had slowly unwound from 2500 feet to 2000 then 1800 feet and I gave a sigh of relief as I knew then that I was headed in the right direction and must soon come out to the Liard River. Soon I recognized an area where I had trapped and knew that the creek was Scotty Creek. Before long it joined the Blackstone River, then the Liard. We were now over fifty miles below the Netla River where I was to deliver the two trappers. There was still no forward visibility and at no time could I see across the Liard and therefore had to follow every bend and turn in the shoreline right to Netla. There I left my passengers and half an hour later the storm had abated somewhat and I flew back the ten miles to the Butte. When I landed there was enough gas left for about another thirty minutes, and I was very glad that I had left home with at least one full tank of gas.

Another time with MTI, which had better instrumentation than LCZ, when I had just enough hours to be feeling bold, I had left Fort Nelson on the morning of a beautiful warm sunny March day and was headed home to Nahanni. Sixty miles out it started to snow and as it looked dark ahead I swung over to follow one of the many cutlines that criss-cross the north country. Most of the lines were in a north south direction and some went for forty miles in a straight line.

Within the next thirty miles I was brought up short and learned a lesson that was not soon forgotten. I had failed to consider the valley of the Black River which had to be crossed at a point where it is a wide canyon, a quarter of a mile in width and 300 feet deep. I had no excuse for continuing the flight when, within five miles of the crossing, the snow was coming down thicker than I had ever seen it. My gyro compass was holding right on the mark and I felt I would break out into better visibility at any moment. But it did not improve and I held as low as I could right over the cut-line, bringing the nose up once or twice to clear big clumps of poplar trees. Then suddenly I lost sight of the ground, and could see nothing but swirling snow, up, down, ahead and sideways. Without wanting to be or intending to be, I was IFR. I was over the Black River and had to retain my precise altitude or I would plow into the opposite side of the valley, or I would be too high and lose sight of the trees. Right then I decided to do a one-eighty, which in layman's language means to turn and go back. Putting the plane into a sharp bank to the left I kept my eyes glued to the instruments, the turn and bank and the rate-of-climb. I watched the gyro come around to 180 degrees, leveled out, then I was over the trees continuing a gentle turn to the left and soon picked up the cutline again. Back at Fort Nelson I landed, a more humble and a wiser pilot.

Over coffee in the Terminal building I admitted my error to other pilots and told them what I had done. Bill Blake who now flies a Boeing 737 for P.W.A., reached to shake hands and said, "It's been good to know you Dick, if you keep that up you won't be around for long."

With the preceding incidents in mind it can easily be imagined what can happen to a light aircraft in the mountains in similar conditions perhaps worsened by icing or fog. With bush pilots it is known as 'suicide weather'.

In early October one Saturday morning I planned on flying

to Fort Nelson with LCZ on floats. There was a wind from the north-east with intermittent rain and fog. All day the mountain behind the cabin was shrouded in cloud down to the 1500 foot level. I was happy to sit by the fire and look out the window. Once in a while the clouds would break, then close in again. By Monday morning the storm was over and it was clear and sunny.

On arriving at Fort Nelson I heard that Ken Stockall was missing on a flight from Fort Simpson to Virginia Falls and Glacier Lake, with a Cessna 185 on floats and three passengers. There was no big panic as yet, for with floats he could always sit down on a lake or river if he encountered problems. When the R.C.A.F. Search and Rescue arrived in Fort Nelson and started a methodical search I felt that here again those cursed canyons and rocks had perhaps taken another aircraft with more victims; Ken was missing on the flight to Glacier Lake the same day that I sat watching the scudding clouds raise and lower on the Butte.

Ken Stockall was considered to be one of the best bush pilots operating out of Yellowknife. He had many years' experience in flying single engine aircraft for a charter company. He was a favorite pilot of Government employees. I had never met him but Mark Fairbrother told me Ken was an excellent pilot but a bit inclined to push his luck. He had recently started a small company and owned, I think, three small bush planes.

On this day he had taken three passengers from Yellowknife, had stopped at Simpson for fuel, and had then taken off for Virginia Falls and Glacier Lake. After leaving Simpson he had followed the Liard River almost to the Butte where he had apparently swung north to what we call the First Gap, and on into the mountains. Albert Faille had seen the plane go over the Liard rapids and a local trapper Alfred Thomas, had seen the plane over the Liard about eight miles below the Butte. That was all there was to go on, in planning the search. The R.C.A.F. covered the Nahanni area all the way to Glacier Lake and back many times over. We local pilots searched within fifty miles of the Butte. Nothing was found and we were left with another Nahanni mystery. When winter conditions set in the search was abandoned.

The following July a bush pilot named Jim Cox was flying a Beaver aircraft from Watson Lake to a geological camp on Little Doctor Lake. He had crossed the Nahanni at 5000 feet and was in sight of the lake when he happened to glance down and saw two white patches that looked somewhat similar to the wings of an aircraft at the bottom of a canyon on Sundog Creek. He drew it to the attention of his passengers, and on circling as low as was practical they identified the broken wings of a downed aircraft.

On receiving the report in Fort Simpson, Bob Ward flew into the site with a helicopter. It proved to be the remains of Ken Stockall's airplane and all on board had been killed on impact.

Many of the creeks on the North and South Nahanni Rivers start out in wide valleys with high walls often to a height of three or four thousand feet, and there are very few that do not pinch out at the top end in an abrupt mountain slope. The aircraft clock was stopped at 2:30 and the films in the camera of one of the passengers showed pictures that had been taken at the Hot Springs at the entrance to the First Canyon, thirty miles west of the crash. There was evidence that the four men had lunched there also.

Piecing all the parts together my conclusions are these: as Ken approached the mountain front he saw that the clouds were right down on the Butte. As happens so often in these conditions with a north-east wind the first and second gaps were open; seeing this he flew through one of them and was able to get to the Nahanni and follow it to the Hot Springs by staying low. At the Hot Springs the weather must have been right down. If not he could have got into Dead Mans Valley by a low pass of 3000 feet to the west of the canyon. The first canyon is wide enough to let an aircraft through, although there are some sharp jogs in it. With fog low over the water, to fly through you would have to be both brave and foolish. Perhaps there was a wind blowing, or the fog might have been right down on the river. The flying conditions must have been bad for Ken to abandon the river route in favor of going around to the east and trying to get in via a tributary of the North Nahanni. If the weather is down at all it is not possible to reach the main Nahanni by this route. On the Ram or the

North Nahanni the lowest pass to the west is well over 4000 feet; and even then you must know the area like the back of your hand, because you have to be in the right pass, and they are narrow with not enough room to turn. It is not known if Ken had maps in the aircraft or not. Pilots who know a section of the country well, often do not carry maps at all. Some have them tucked away in their brief case. Furthermore the eight miles to the inch maps that are used for navigation are not detailed enough to be of much use in a situation of this kind. Perhaps Ken thought at first he was on the Ram River pass and when he concluded he was not and attempted to turn, there was not enough room. He went into the rock wall under full power. Another few feet to spare and he would have made it. Then again he might have known exactly where he was and tried to get through this way anyway. On a day like that, clouds can move in and out of valleys very quickly.

In talking with George C.F. Dalziel who probably has more hours bush flying than ten average bush pilots and who I know has had his share of scrapes and close calls, I heard some wise counselling. I was admiring his aircraft, an immaculate new Beaver, and discussing the Cessna 185 I was flying. I mentioned that I had only about a hundred hours on this type but was very happy with its performance. Dalziel said, "If you ever have to make a 180 degree turn in a bad situation, Dick, give yourself a mile to make the turn, they do not come around like a Super Cub or a Beaver."

I am at a complete loss to understand why Ken Stockall did not stop at Nahanni Butte that rainy day when he and his passengers could have waited out the weather in a warm cabin enjoying good food and where there was gasoline to refuel his aircraft. Ken knew the Nahanni well and had often stopped at the Kraus cabin in the village. Someone suggested the urgency to complete the trip was because the passengers were reported to have said they had to be back in Yellowknife by Monday morning. If that is so, then the urgency to be back probably contributed to their early demise.

When an aircraft crashes in the bush killing men whom I have known well I sometimes think that it would have been better if airplanes had not been invented and we would all be safer using dogteams and packhorses. But men have been drowned using pack horses, and probably dog teams aren't all that safe either. I suppose from the instant we are born we are all in danger. It still hurts when you hear that a friend is lost with an aircraft and you imagine all sorts of things until he is found.

One of the first Cessna 185 s on floats that was brought into the Nahanni was flown by Hal Cornelius. He was flying for a company that was doing geological exploration in the Mackenzie mountains. We came to know Hal well as Don and I were doing barge work for the same company and Hal was often at our house. I remember him saying he thought the 185 was one of the best bush planes he had ever flown.

Late in the summer the company moved their camp to Wrigley on the Mackenzie River as their work was in the mountains to the west. Not long after the camp was moved, we heard that Hal was missing on a flight into a lake near the Redstone River. He had left Wrigley with a load of groceries and one passenger. The return flight should have taken him three hours flying and he had five hours fuel on board. Again for many days the search revealed nothing. Nearly thirty days later the wreck was found. It seems he had gotten into a blind valley under a layer of fog and with not enough room he had tried to turn. Coming out of the turn, one wing had contacted some obstruction and the plane contacted the ground under full power.

I heard later that the weather had been very poor with rain and fog for several days before the accident, and the last was Hal's fifth attempt to reach his destination.

If someone could only come up with a fool-proof formula for a bush pilot, of when to go and when not to go he could save a good many lives.

When the 1965 election for the Northwest Territories Council was called, John Goodall Sr. who had held the seat for the Simpson, Providence, Liard, Nahanni, Wrigley, Fort Norman and Fort Franklin constituency decided not to run again so I resolved to throw my hat in the ring. Two friends of mine also filed their nomination papers: John Kidd the hotel owner and Bill Berg, who had been an R.C.M.P. constable under Cpl. Ward. Among the contestants there was no official party alignment, and the election resolved itself into a personality contest. I visited all the settlements once to meet the voters but to my knowledge none of the candidates addressed a public meeting.

It turned out that Bill Berg swamped John and me both. We lost our deposits and congratulated Bill for the victory. I took some satisfaction out of the fact that I got all the votes at Nahanni and all but two at Fort Liard. At Fort Simpson I polled exactly eighteen votes out of a total of about 350 votes that were cast, which goes to show how popular I was. I felt that Bill would likely do as good a job on the council as either John or I. The political power from what I could see was still in Ottawa as far as we in the Northwest Territories was concerned, and for a while at least the function of a Council Member would be to act as a sort of unofficial ombudsman for his constituents.

At any rate Bill and his wife had their home in Simpson and he was starting out into business as a Big Game outfitter, with a base at Little Dall Lake on the Redstone River.

In the fall of '65 the first season that Bill was operating at Little Dall, Don ran one of his base camps at Loon Lake near the Yukon border and I was flying and guiding for him. I had traded in MTI for a new Maule Rocket, a four place machine. It was a good little aircraft on wheels and skis but on floats it was what we in the flying fraternity call a 'dog'. But I had bought and paid for it and now I was stuck with it. The floats cut the speed from 135 to 105 miles per hour and it had to be flown with the nose high at all times to maintain altitude. It would not come out of the water at less than 62 mph and in a power-off stall the right wing would drop right off at 60 mph. It held fifteen gallons of fuel in each of the two wing tanks and due to the high angle of attack would burn a bit less than twelve of the fifteen. I think that the name Rocket comes from the airplane wanting to head for the ground when the power was cut. Despite the drawbacks of the Maule, I did a lot of flying for Don that summer. The new plane had a fuel-injection engine of 210 HP and I learned to get in and out of those mountain lakes with a fair load. With the variable pitch propeller full power could be developed for take-off, and 210 horses is a lot on an airplane the size of a Tri-Pacer.

Snow came to stay that year on September 20th in the mountains down to the 3500 foot level. By September 25th the hunters had all left and I was flying the camp equipment and some wild meat back to Nahanni Butte. After one flight the weather would close in and I would wait a day for the ceiling to lift enough to allow me to sneak in under the clouds for another load. On September 30th I turned back from just below the falls because the fog lay low in the hills to the west.

On October 1st conditions were much improved and I got into Loon Lake for the last load of meat without any trouble but I was glad to be finished with that job for the season.

Some days later we heard that a Beaver aircraft from Fort Simpson had flown into Dall Lake to get Bill Berg and three of his guides and had crashed on the return trip about 10 miles from the lake, killing all five men. The plane had come down heavily on a steep rock slope and had burst into flames on impact. It was a sad day for Fort Simpson as all five men were from our area.

Mark Fairbrother was operating a big game hunting business in an adjacent area at this time. He knew everyone who was concerned with this tragedy and I asked him for his comments on the accident. This is what he said: "The pilot was new to the area and had recently made two trips for me. He flew me out from Trench Lake a day or so before and had scared the wits out of me. When I got home I said to Sylvia, 'Never again will I fly with that man, he is an accident waiting to happen'. He would fly through fog and cloud with no forward visibility, and would make a let-down into a valley in fog, without knowing where he was. I tell you he scared the pants right off me."

"What do you think happened in this case, Mark?"

"It must have been very late in the afternoon when they left Dall Lake for Fort Simpson. We know the weather was bad. I think he must have either tried to go up through the clouds or to make a blind let-down into a valley. There must have been icing conditions too at about the 5000 foot line, and in fog he would soon pick up a load of ice. Anyway he piled into the rocks at a high altitude.

"Would that be a case of hurry up, when the obvious thing to do would be to wait till morning?"

"Yes, I think so. Bill and the boys at camp probably had everything packed and were anxious to get home, and the pilot had a supper date that night that he did not want to miss."

One early fall when the leaves had fallen and the first snows were soon to come Leland Wooley and his wife Jean chartered a plane from Fort Simpson into Dead Mans Valley for a holiday and a photographing trip. I think the pilot was new to the area and did not realize how swift the river flowed. The landing was made and the pilot taxied and drifted for a mile looking for a suitable place to unload his passengers. With the current whipping them along they were soon carried down to where the river was very narrow. Looking ahead the pilot could see some rough water with rocks far out from shore and below that the entrance to the first canyon loomed ahead. He resolved to turn immediately. Going upstream against the current he would have control of the aircraft and could take time in choosing a landing spot on the shoreline. Unfortunately there was not sufficient room to turn and the outside float ran up on a protruding outcrop and before anyone could realize what was happening the airplane was upside down in the river. Somehow the pilot and Leland got the door open and the three got out, the two men digging out the life jackets, one for each person. By this time the aircraft was being carried down stream with the floats above the water. Right below them the river widened to about two hundred yards, then narrowed to half that distance. They all three took to the river and swam for the right hand shore which was the south bank. This was a very wise decision as the left shore was closer but had cut walls in places, and when under shock, people do not always make a correct choice. Leland told me that the water was very cold and turbulent. Initially he and his wife Jean were able to stay together as they struggled toward shore. Near shore however there was a shallow rapid with boulders making it impossible to stand in the water. Floating on his back and buoyed by the lifejacket and working his hands and feet, Leland got into shore about half a mile down stream. Jean was having a worse time and was still out in the current. Leland ran down the shore and in a little back eddy on a small sand beach below, Jean was able to make it to shore.

They now looked around to see where their pilot was. There was not a sign of him upstream or down. Shouting was useless as a voice could not be heard above the roar of the waters. They were now at the head of the rock island above George's Riffle and the river current was faster than ever with large waves right below them and a very steep rock cliff on the outside of the curve.

"If he were carried down this far," they thought, "he's a gonner, for he'd be swept right down into the riffle and it would be a miracle if he survived that."

The next thing in Leland's mind was what steps to take to survive before they both died from exposure. They knew there was one shelter in the valley, a cabin built by the Forestry, which was opposite the mouth of Prairie River and two miles up stream. There was no one at the cabin but surely there would be matches and food. It was their only hope, so off they went with due dispatch. They were so cold by now that they were finding it difficult to move their arms and legs, but the exertion of climbing over logs and pushing through thickets brought their body temperature up so that they moved more freely.

An hour later they were at the cabin and had a fire blazing in the stove and while they had lost much of value in cameras, guns and equipment they were thankful and somewhat overwhelmed to be alive. After entering the water, in the shock and excitement of the disaster they had lost sight of Bill, their pilot and hardly dared hope he had survived. He had started for the same shoreline as they had and they could only assume that he had been carried down into the riffle and had drowned.

Stunned by the events of the late afternoon when their high holiday spirits had suddenly been turned to a struggle for survival, they could only dry their clothes, get some heat into their bodies and hope that Bill had somehow survived. There were food and cooking utensils in the cabin and a hot stew and scalding tea helped to revive their spirits.

Well after dark and near to midnight, there was a stirring outside the cabin, the door opened, and there was Bill. With wonderment and unbelief they welcomed him. He was obviously on the point of exhaustion and looked like he had been through hell. After warmth and food had restored him to some semblance of normality, Bill told his story.

He could remember little of his ordeal in the water except that when he found himself being swept into the swirling violent waters of George's Riffle he gave himself up for lost and thought for sure he would drown. In the waves he was more under the water than out, but managed to get a gasp of air whenever his head came up. Without the life jacket he would have had no chance at all of survival. He was so cold and stiff he could not move his limbs. A mile below the riffle there was a long quiet sand beach and there he was washed up onto the shore. Alive, but barely so he knew he had to start moving immediately to get blood circulating and some warmth into his body. With a supreme effort he laboriously dragged himself onto the sand beach and very slowly got to his knees and then to his feet. He knew he must get to the cabin and as near dead as he was, he must at all costs keep moving. He felt that his passengers had survived but was not sure why he knew they had. He thought he might have heard Leland shouting to Jean as he drifted by, farther out in the river.

Bill knew that he was now down into the canyon and was terrified for a time there would be no gap in the wall where he could climb out. A mile upstream just below the riffle, he could see a dip in the wall and although it was a 2000 foot climb the hill was timbered and he was able to struggle up to the top. By now it was dark and he knew he had more than two miles farther to go. There was no trail and in the darkness he made poor time as he stumbled into bogs and thickets, over roots and windfalls and through dense patches of willows. As long as he could keep moving he knew he would win out. His clothes were already drying and he was getting back some body heat.

It took him six hours to make the total of four miles, and was in a daze and a state of shock when he opened the door of the cabin. His voice was quiet and lifeless as he said, "I almost passed the cabin, but happened to look up and see the faint light from the window."

Two days later when they were picked up by friends in a jet boat, Bill was reported to still be in a state of shock. And no bloody wonder. It was bad enough for Leland and Jean but Bill was carried down another mile and survived George's Riffle. When he was washed ashore on the sand beach he must have been more dead than alive.

With much knowledge and experience in float landings on fast rivers he might possibly have avoided this incident. But how is a pilot going to get the experience without starting somewhere? There may be some pilots who have built up say 5000 hours in the air without making a mistake, but I have yet to know of one. When I hear of a pilot who claims he has never made a mistake I know he is either a liar or has flown very little. An odd thing I have found is that fairly big errors have sometimes resulted in no more than a humorous incident.

For instance, I once heard of a pilot who to secure his aircraft overnight, tied the tail to a large wooden crate. Next morning he got in and took off with the crate in tow, made the flight and landed without incident.

Once in the winter time on the Mackenzie River near Fort Wrigley, Slim Jones, a trapper and free trader had a Beaver aircraft bring him in a load of supplies. This aircraft had a thirty foot rope tied to the tail section, and was left there for winter ski operation. In order to help the pilot get turned around in the deep snow, Slim wrapped the rope well around his arm and pulled on the rope to get the plane turned, then found he could not let go. The pilot gunned the engine and went roaring down the strip to make his turn at the other end for take-off, dragging Slim behind in the snow. With an aircraft on skis you don't stop unless you have to, for often the skis will stick and it is hard to get moving again. The pilot made a wide turn and was ready for take-off in his tracks. Then he noticed that instead of two ski tracks which there should have been, there were three. He idled the motor down and got out to look, and there was Slim almost choked to death with snow and a bit bruised up, but otherwise no worse for wear. That was a lesson for both the pilot and Slim. I don't think anyone would care to speculate on what would have happened if the pilot had opened the tap and taken off.

I have it from reliable sources that in two different cases pilots of airline transport planes have made landings at the wrong airstrip, that is, in each case the pilot mistook an unused street for his intended airstrip and landed. In one case the passengers were quite surprised and had to be taken by bus to the proper airport. In the other case there was not enough room for take-off and as far as I know the aircraft is still there.

In another instance, during World War Two, three large transport planes landed in an open meadow in the wilderness of northern British Columbia. One had apparently run out of fuel and the other two followed him in. I think they are still there. It is known as Million Dollar Valley.

I know of one pilot who was reported to have been intoxicated on most every flight he made. A friend who is an excellent pilot himself was once enticed on board for a flight, then was offered a drink in the air by the drunken pilot. My friend was counting his beads, but a perfect landing was made.

Some other poor son of a gun, who is as careful as careful can be, makes one error and BANG, he bends his airplane or kills himself.

Leland Wooley had considerable experience boating on the northern rivers and became interested in boating on the Nahanni. He had previously built an airboat with a plywood hull and powered by an 85 HP aircraft engine mounted on the stern. This boat would go like hell but was too light for the rough water of the Nahanni. My son Don built a heavier one and powered it with a 150 HP Lycoming aircraft engine. It too would really get up and go, but the continual pounding induced cracks in the engine mounts.

Leland at last built himself a 28 foot river scow for the Nahanni powered with two large outboard motors. This boat would carry enough fuel and supplies for an extended trip and Leland had been up the river as far as the Flat one summer before.

This time with the same boat he set off alone from Fort Simpson with the intention of going right to the falls. He had a big load of food and supplies in addition to a hundred gallons of gasoline on board.

It was July with the river in flood and some small amount of driftwood running. By the time he had made his way through the 'splits' and into the first canyon he felt doubtful about running George's Riffle under such conditions. Coming up on the riffle he had almost made up his mind to run back down a mile to a good camping spot and wait for the flood waters to subside before attempting to run the riffle into the valley.

Afterwards he said that what he did next was really against his better judgment, but he thought it would do no harm to run up into the waves at the bottom of the riffle to get a good look at it with the intention of retreating if it looked too dangerous. But as so often happens, getting into a situation is often easier than getting out of it. He had plenty of power to drive up into the rapids and then too late he realized he had come too far. Right away the water came over the bow and the sides; he shut down the engines to drift back out of it, the craft swung sideways and in two seconds the boat had rolled.

Once again he found himself struggling in the cold waters of the Nahanni with his equipment gone and his life in danger. And once again he swam to shore and struggled up the hill as Bill had done before him but as the weather was warm he was in no danger of freezing as he made his way to the Forestry cabin. With many travellers on the river, he was picked up the next day and was once again back in Simpson rather glad he was alive. Somewhat miraculously the boat with the motors intact drifted into shore and got hung up on a rock three miles below, and when Leland salvaged the boat he found the motors undamaged. His cameras and equipment were never recovered. The boat itself had taken no harm as it was solid and well built.

I had thought of suggesting to Leland that as he was now becoming experienced in running the river at the lower end of Dead Mans Valley, he might recoup his financial losses and perhaps turn a small profit by charging a fee from spectators to watch him run George's Riffle on a barrel or a wooden box or perhaps just swimming through like a porpoise. But I thought better than to mention this to him as I did not want to get my head bashed in.

14

Barge Out — Charter In

By 1965 our small barging business had just about come to an end. The oil exploration of the region was being completed and heavy equipment was being moved into the north to drill experimental or 'wild cat' holes. Large barges and tugs were in demand to move loads of 150 tons or more. It was now the era of steel hulls for barges and tugs which required a heavy investment of funds to build or to purchase. Others in the barging business were giving up wooden vessels in favor of steel. After due consideration I concluded I had had enough of fighting flood waters, driftwood, ice, sandbars, rock piles and the general adversity that one must cope with on northern streams.

Good river pilots were difficult to find and well nigh impossible to hire, and I could not face the interminable hours on the river and day after day and night after night at the wheel of a tug creeping upstream at five miles an hour trying to keep the eyes propped open with an unending intake of coffee and cigarettes. I had my belly full of that and was happy to leave the barging business to others. One by one I sold our tugs and barges and by 1970 we owned only a small river scow and a 40 HP kicker.

Airplanes were in a different class than tugs; you were not apt to fall asleep while struggling past a driftwood pile at the head of an island, and besides there was that lost placer creek that had yet to be found, to say nothing of the lead and silver deposits that were defying discovery. While CF-UAH had its disadvantages as a float plane, with care and persistence I was able to get in and out of mountain lakes to an elevation of 4500 feet. I did sweat sometimes in taking big loads of passengers and supplies to Don's hunting camps. I always hated hauling passengers rather than the equivalent weight of supplies.

Don had a camp for one season at Lucky Lake on the Territory-Yukon border, at 4500 feet altitude. On settling down on this narrow lake for the first time I wondered if I would ever get off with a load. Fortunately I found it was much cooler here than at a lower altitude, which resulted in the wings having more lift and the engine being less likely to overheat. Even in July and August in the mornings the temperature was down to freezing which was a wonderful help on take-off. The aircraft performed better here than it did on Loon Lake which was 2000 feet lower.

It was at Loon Lake one hot day that I came as close as I ever wanted to, to stalling on take-off into the hill at the south end of the lake. I had a flight to make to Nahanni Butte with two guides who were going home for their week off. It was on a day when at 75 degrees there were little warm zephyrs blowing in everywhich direction. At the south end of the lake there was a fifty foot hill to overcome on take-off which meant a fairly steep climb upon leaving the water. What wind there was seemed to be from the south.

Most people except pilots and aircraft engineers seem to think that an aircraft is similar to a truck in respect to the loading: you simply pile in freight to the roof, jump in, start up the engine and go. On one occasion in my early flying days I chartered to two hunters for a few days trip.

In the morning, a stack of supplies that would strain the chassis of a three ton truck was on the dock ready to unload. With the two passengers there were two bedrolls weighing forty pounds each, two packsacks loaded with air mattresses, ground sheets, coats, jackets and waders; two suitcases of toilet articles which must have contained enough towels, soap and hair brushes for six troops of boy scouts; two duffle bags filled with boots, hand guns, coils of rope, tent pegs and half a case of ammunition, which when moved, gave off a clanking sound as of cowbells and horse-shoes; cases of canned food enough to last an army for a campaign; two boxes of cooking utensils which all must have been made of cast iron; four rifles, each in heavy cases; and at last two wooden boxes that certainly must have held an extra suit of armor for every man that King Richard had with him on the Crusades. The last two items were just too much and I turned a flushed face to the innocently smiling hunters and snarled, "What the hell you got in these, two collapsable grand pianos?"

"Oh, no," was the surprised answer, "just some cameras and a few things."

"Oh, I see. Well, we'll have to leave a lot of this junk behind and I'll make another trip out for it. We don't happen to be loading a battleship or a box car."

The reproachful looks now directed at me were those of a child whose candy had been snatched away. It was as if I had suggested murdering their mothers.

Some people see a mile long line of passengers boarding a modern jet aircraft and conclude that any aircraft can take a similar load. They do not see that a float plane is nothing more than a flying boat which has the friction and drag of the water to overcome in attaining flying speed, and has the drag of the floats while in the air. Bush pilots get prematurely white haired and go around talking to themselves when contemplating the ignorance of their customers in regard to the simple facts of thrust, drag, lift and weight as applied to aircraft.

The passengers on this day were no different than most others in that they were completely ignorant of the dangers involved in loading the aircraft with suitcases and packsacks filled with lead and heavy boulders. I had assumed I would have two averaged size men with one bag each to take back to Nahanni for their week off. After we arrived at the Butte I discovered they had filled every available suitcase, packsack and bedroll with fresh meat from the camp for their families at home.

It was only by the grace of God that the three of us were not killed that day. I had not supervised the loading and the displacement of the floats indicated the plane had no more than an all up gross load, but when taxiing for take-off I had a feeling of uneasiness that I couldn't account for. It was an error of judgment on my part at this time not to go back to the dock and leave part of the load for another trip as I well knew there were three factors against attempting a take-off with a gross load at this time; the available distance for a take-off run was limited; the day was warm, giving poor lift to the wings, and the wind was variable and intermittent.

It is a notorious fact that most bush pilots both commercial and private do overload their aircraft from time to time. Most often they get away with it, but once in a while it will kill a pilot and his passengers. An important factor in this is that what constitutes a normal load under some conditions would be an overload under adverse conditions. The onus is on the pilot to exercise his judgment and to take appropriate action.

As so often happens in aviation, a tight situation can be compounded by additional factors which in themselves may not be of crucial importance. On this day my Guardian Angel with the help of the 210 horses of the engine held off the Grim Reaper for yet another day. When I started the run from the north end of the lake the wind was from the south and when I was about to lift off it was directly on my tail. The end of the lake was coming up fast and I was going to chop the power and abort; but noticing the airspeed needle was at 60 mph I hauled back on the stick instead. She came loose from the water with the stall warning sounding and the airspeed dangerously low. I could not lower the nose as the hill was right ahead and I had to keep the nose high with the wings at a high 'angle of attack'. We were now doing what pilots term 'hanging on the prop', on the point of a stall and very near to the stumps and felled trees on the hillside. I felt for a moment that the three of us were very near to our last few seconds on this earth. Miraculously we cleared the top of the hill and I was able to dump the stick ahead to get some airspeed. The two passengers did not know what danger we had escaped and I did not inform them; but I did calculate on the way home that if I had nine lives I had now used up about seven of them.

That was lesson No. 143, which I was not about to forget.

After lesson No. 144 which took place in September, I felt for a time that perhaps I should renounce flying and take up stevedoring, or be a brick-layer's assistant, some occupation more suitable to my qualifications. It did not amount to a resolve; it was only a passing thought brought on by a moment of weakness.

Don had a hunting camp near Blue Lakes where he landed on a high plateau with CF-LKL, his Super Cub. The largest of the lakes is exactly 2560 feet in length, which is much too short to operate from in safety. However one can get off the lake with a very light load. One day with CF-UAH I took in a guide for Don and spent a day in prospecting near the lakes. The next day when I was ready to leave there was a strong Chinook wind from the west. The cross wind for take-off was coming down off the mountain which rose to 3000 feet right off the lake shore. To reduce weight I drained the fuel from the starboard tank leaving ten gallons in the port tank which would be ample to get me home. At the north end of the lake I turned, headed into wind and opened the tap. Before I was halfway down the lake a gust of wind booted me into the air and for the next few minutes my attention was directed to keeping the aircraft right side up. With the almost empty plane I was soon above the hills at 7000 feet, went into a gentle banking turn and headed north. Then for some reason I glanced down at the fuel selector and discovered that it was selected to the empty tank. I instantly thought, "I must be destined to continue flying, and am being saved for some fated purpose, because this engine does not run on air alone and right now I should be spread out on the hill between the lakes, with the nose high, it should have stalled on take-off."

There must have been a gallon of fuel left in the tank I had drained, which normally would not have reached the outlet to get to the engine, but due to the turbulence the gas was sloshing around enough to keep the little 'header' tank filled.

I had failed to do a proper pre-flight check, which is inexcusable. I should have been made to sit in a corner with my face to the wall and write out a hundred times, "I will never again fail to do my pre-flight check."

Sometime later the engine of the Maule developed a habit of

stopping in the air at odd times. For seemingly no reason at all there would suddenly be silence. When the 'booster' pump was switched on the engine would roar into action again. It was agreed by the various mechanics consulted that it was most likely a fuel problem; and we checked over the complete fuel system from gas tank to fuel injectors. The lines were running free, the screens were cleaned, the injectors replaced and still there was no change; at anything less than full throttle it was apt to quit at any time. At the annual C of A inspection nothing was found wrong with the fuel system and I headed home again from Dawson Creek. From Fort St. John to Fort Nelson the engine quit three times, the last was on final approach to the airstrip at Fort Nelson. "That's it," I said to myself, "enough is enough, the trouble will have to be remedied before I take this machine into the air again."

I taxied over to my 'lease' near the hangar and roped the plane to the tie-downs. Then I went over to the hangar where Bill Foote was working on his Bell 206 Helicopter. He listened with patience to my picturesque criticism of the Maule and its problem. "You should know something about aircraft engines Bill," I said. "Have you had any experience with fuel injection gas engines? I'm completely baffled, have you heard of anything like this before?"

"I've run across many strange fuel problems," Bill replied, "but nothing quite like yours. I'll go over and have a look at it anyway."

After disconnecting the fuel line and testing the fuel pressure visually, Bill said, "It must be in the pressure system somewhere, there's an engineer working for Steve Villers now, his name is Dave Hall and he is a top-notch man with fuel injection. See if he will have a look at it for you."

Inside the hangar I found Dave who said, in answer to my questions, "Just a minute till I get this job finished and I'll have a look at it. I think that's an IO-360-A Continental, and I've done some work on them in the Mix Master." (We refer to the Cessna Sky Master as a Mix Master.)

Dave asked some questions, went "Ahhh" and "Ummm", looked the engine over with a critical eye and announced, "I think I can find the trouble, but I'm busy as hell right now. If you leave the plane here for a week I think I can have it fixed by that time."

"You're on, Mr. Hall," I replied. "If you can fix that flying machine so that it will not quit in the air, I'll dance at your wedding and sing at your funeral."

"You'll get an invitation for the one, but not for the other," he smiled. "And don't call me Mr. Hall, it's Dave."

"Roger, dodger, you old codger," I laughed, "and I'll see you in a week."

Now I was afoot and needed an aircraft to get back to Nahanni. "Where can I borrow one for a week?" I thought. You have to be very good friends indeed with the owner of an aircraft to ask and get permission to borrow his airplane: it is almost like asking him to loan you his wife.

Art Gordon owned a Super Cub, CF-JMI, and said, "Sure take it away Turner, and don't bend it eh?"

"Don't you worry," I replied, "I'll not put a scratch on it, and when I bring it back it will be a much improved airplane for having been flown by an expert, bless your soul, you big clumsy ape."

"That's enough out of you Turner, get out of here before I dust your crop for you."

A week later I was back in Fort Nelson and Dave said, "There were two things wrong with the engine, the mixture was set 'way too lean and the engine driven fuel pump was putting out only three pounds pressure instead of eight. It should be all right now."

I paid him for his work and from then on the Maule didn't miss a beat. Well, that's not quite right. It missed several beats but not from the cause Dave had remedied.

The missing of the beats, of my heart as well as the engine occurred later that summer. I had Gus and Mary Kraus on board; we were bound for Loon Lake where Gus was to work for Don. We were past Dead Mans Valley at 5500 feet headed up Meullier Creek, which was almost a straight shot to Loon Lake via Clark Lake and the Flat River Valley. All at once the engine started to run rough and to lose power slightly. The dials were all normal with the exception of the fuel pressure gauge which indicated a drop. Right then I turned and headed back for the Nahanni River where I would have water underneath if an emergency landing had to be made. The motor continued its uneven beat but became no worse. There was enough power to maintain altitude. As soon as I had made the turn back to the river and had taken stock of the situation I turned the radio transmitter to 126.7 on VHF and something like this ensued.

"Calling all aircraft, this is Uniform Alpha Hotel."

"UAH, this is Mach 00700, go ahead."

"Mach 00700, UAH, have you a minute to spare?"

"Sure have, go ahead."

"Would you contact Fort Nelson Radio and relay message as follows. Am at 5000 feet over Nahanni River, estimating the Butte in 25 minutes. Engine running rough with reduced power. Am able to maintain altitude. Please ask Hilton Burry to come Nahanni soonest with his tool box."

"Roger, UAH, will read back to you." He did so and I replied, "Roger, Roger, Mach 00700, this is UAH, thanks a lot."

I had often heard the CP Air flights, the Mach flights and other jets calling ground stations from their high altitudes and I knew they were always in contact with some ground station on 126.7. These men always took time to help us little guys nearer the ground when we had trouble contacting a station.

Near the Butte the dials were all indicating normal operation with the booster pump on. Oil pressure and temp OK, Cylinder temp normal, Fuel pressure somewhat less than normal, but still the roughness in the engine. I made a straight in landing on the river and we taxied into the dock.

Soon after supper that evening we heard a hum from the south and in a minute or two we saw Hilton's little green bird in the sky. We saw the CF-SRS on his wings as he went over, circled and touched down on our little grass strip.

Hilton had no sooner stepped from his airplane when he opened fire on me with, "When you ask me to Nahanni, Dick Turner, you should first get rid of these blessed mosquitos; it's a wonder they don't plug the screen of the carburetor. And all the message I got was to come and bring my tool box, so I brought a sledge hammer to work on your head."

"All right Burry," I replied, "I'll explain to you as a father to his three year old son, but first with this hat pin here, I will have to let some air out of you." And as he jumped around a bit when I made a jab or two at him, I continued, "I've no more idea than you do what tools are needed. I was just nicely into the hills when the engine lost power and started to sound like Jack Benny's Maxwell. We made it back all right so maybe there is not too much wrong."

We had walked down to the river and were now standing on the dock. Hilton said, "Let's nose it into the wharf and we'll take off the cowlings and have a look see." The cowlings were no sooner taken off when Hilton said, "You're lucky it didn't catch on fire Turner, the fuel line to No. 6 cylinder has broken off and gasoline had been pouring onto the engine. Here, have a look." Sure enough, the fuel line was hanging loose and a green stain from the 100/130 fuel had spread over the port cylinders. Fortunately the exhaust stacks were below and on the starboard side and the gasoline squirting from the broken line was not able to reach the red hot exhaust pipe.

"Well, Burry, there's one thing," I remarked, "if we had all been killed, there's one accident that couldn't be put down to pilot error."

Hilton put a new connector on the line to No. 6 cylinder, checked the other five lines and found them all in good condition. The next day we made the flight to Loon Lake without incident.

Sometime after this a small oil leak developed in the engine, for I noticed that after each flight there was oil on the firewall with some blown back onto the belly of the fuselage. I could not see where it was coming from and put it down to a leaking gasket. If I had known where the oil leak was I would not have taken that plane in the air for all the oil in Arabia and a million dollars in cash to boot. But ignorance is bliss and one day I set off for Loon Lake with two guides for Don. There was nothing unusual about the behaviour of the airplane on the way in. We landed and I prepared to take off on a sixty mile trip to the Flat Lakes at the head of Little Nahanni near Cantung where Don was waiting for me with a ton of groceries to shuttle to the camp.

I took off to the south over the little hill and as I made the turn to head north I suddenly had a very uneasy feeling that something was wrong. All the dials were GO and the engine sounded normal; but the feeling of uneasiness persisted. When only a mile past the north end of the lake I turned and came around for a landing.

The camp cook and the two guides were on the dock to help me tie up and as I didn't quite know the reason I had turned back I only said, "I want to check over the engine before I go on, I'll have a cup of coffee while it's cooling off."

On removing the cowlings I noticed more oil than ever smeared over the rear of the engine and the firewall and when the top cowling was removed, there it was, a ten inch crack in the top of the crank-case, and just below that the No. 1 jug was holding on by only two stud bolts, the others had broken off. It was only a matter of a very short time until the jug would have come off with the resulting complete engine failure. From Loon Lake to the Flat Lakes there was no landings en route and I would be sitting in the bush somewhere with a broken wing and perhaps worse.

I could hardly believe my good fortune. I had narrowly escaped a complete write-off of the aircraft and perhaps a write-off of me also. Now I would have to buy a new engine and have it flown in here and exchanged for the broken one. The expense would be terrific, but as the man said when his friend was run over with a car, "It could have been worse. It could have been me."

In the meantime nothing could be done but to sit and wait for Don. The following afternoon we heard the hum of an engine and soon a plane came in from the north and landed. It was Don with a Beaver he had chartered from Watson Lake. Bob Harrison was the pilot. As Don stepped out of the plane he said, "She has finally quit for good eh? I've been looking for you all the way down from Cantung, I expected to see you sitting in the bush some place."

I told him what had happened to the engine and asked, "What did you do when I didn't show up yesterday?"

"I knew something was up when you didn't come by dark, so I drove back to the mine and phoned in for a Beaver."

"I don't know exactly what to do now," I said. "But after you get the freight down from the lake, I'd better get Bob to fly me to Nahanni with the Beaver and I'll get busy and order a new engine. I'll have it come to Watson Lake by CP Air and get Bob to fly it out here with an engineer."

"How long do you think it will take to get the engine, Dad?"

"Possibly with luck about two weeks."

"It could be longer than that, and I'll have to charter all the flying until you get going again."

It turned out that the Maule did not fly again for over three weeks. The engine happened to be one that was used in Viet Nam, with a consequent shortage of them on the continent. After phoning all over Canada and the USA we at last found a new one in some city in the States. I sent out four thousand dollars to pay for the engine and when at last it arrived in Watson Lake there was a COD attached to it for another $1661.00. I had thought that the original four thousand would have been more than enough to cover the cost of the engine and the COD took me by surprise. I knew that I was getting 'taken', but what could I do? I didn't have $1661 with me and it was a week end and the bank was closed. The Agent let me take the engine when I said I would have the money to him within a week. At the B.C. Yukon float base we loaded the new engine on a Beaver and were able to get an aircraft engineer to come out to install it for me.

Before the week was out I was in Fort Nelson with UAH, but found the money I was expecting from the fur auction sales had not yet arrived. I had about a thousand dollars in my pocket, which was not enough for the COD, when I went to have coffee at the Muskwa Cafe that my friends Ray and Norman King owned and operated. I was contemplating going to the bank to inveigle the manager out of the needed funds when Jim McArthur walked in. Jim operated the butcher shop in Sam Leigh's Super Market. He and I differed a bit in politics and we had many good arguments. "Sit your fat beam down here Jim," I said, "and I'll buy you a coffee." After exchanging greetings I continued, "You don't happen to have a thousand dollars on you that I can borrow for a week or so?"

Without batting an eye he replied, "You sure can, I happen to have a thousand right here in my pocket." And he hauled out a bundle of money and handed it to me. I stuffed it in my pocket, then told him about the COD that I had promised to pay in Watson Lake.

That night I flew back to Nahanni and the following day I was in Watson Lake to give the agent the $1661.00. I gave him the cash because I did not want him to have to phone the bank to find out if my cheque was good.

It must have been more than two weeks after this when I was back in Fort Nelson. First I went to the bank and withdrew a thousand in twenty dollar bills, making the same size bundle that I had borrowed from Jim, and as it was coffee time I went over to the Muskwa Cafe where everybody gathered for social reasons as well as to enjoy the best coffee in town. There was Jim McArthur sipping coffee and he opened up on me right away with his usual political dissertation. I sat down, ordered coffee and a sandwich, pulled out the bundle of money and handed it to him. He stuffed it in his pocket without missing a word of his political comment about why he was right and I was wrong.

"Aren't you going to count it?" I asked.

"Why should I, you didn't count what I gave you?"

"I guess that's right," I answered. "You said it was a thousand, so why should I count it?" And we both laughed at the rather unorthodox way we had conducted the transaction.

15

Aerial Antics

When a group of pilots get together and talk of flying I have noted with interest that most will admit to having performed some very foolish maneuvers in their student days. The truthful ones will admit to errors well past their student days. For instance most pilots get bored with hours of flying at high altitudes where there is no sensation of speed and you seem to be floating motionless in the air. It naturally follows that when a pilot is flying alone he will indulge in some low flying, close to the tree tops, over a lake or river water, or some frozen surface. This type of flying is interesting and exciting for it induces a satisfying sensation of speed; it is obviously dangerous which adds to the thrill.

Officially, students are never taught extensive low flying, but I believe that to attain a high level of proficiency a bush pilot must put in many hours of low and consequently dangerous flying. If he is careful and wide awake at all times, he will learn much that will be of great assistance to him if he ever gets in a 'bind' which he will assuredly do if he continues to fly. One advantage he will have is a familiarity with ground terrain which he will never get from any great height. At high altitudes, small hills, ridges and humps cannot be distinguished, and there is sure to come a time when inclement weather will force him near ground level where IFR flight is impossible and VFR is difficult. He will have to detour around fogged in hills and sneak in and out of shallow valleys. If he has flown at this level before in good weather he will be more likely to recognize landmarks from time to time such as an odd looking hilltop, or a towering clump of trees or whatever; and he will be less likely to become lost. Prolonged anxiety from being lost and worried will leave a pilot less able to cope with other problems that might arise. In flying above the snow covered surface of a large river or lake he will see that on a dull or snowy day there would be no reference to the ground for depth perception and would realize the very great danger of making a turn over such a surface in reduced visibility.

A flight of even a very short duration or a 180 degree turn should never be made over an obscured surface when flying VFR. If you must turn, go on instruments until you have visual contact with the ground again. Many a pilot has peered outside for a ground reference and before he realizes there is no ground reference he has plunged into the ice or snow covered surface in a descending spiral. The D. O. T. accident reports have listed many cases of this kind. For my part I will NEVER make a 180 degree turn in such a situation and will rarely fly over a snow covered surface in a low overcast or snowing condition.

A disaster occurred some years ago when an inexperienced pilot was on a flight with three passengers in a Cessna 180. While flying near a large lake the cloud layer began to lower and close in on him. Although it was early in the winter and the ice was newly formed, the only possible decision to make was to land on the frozen lake surface and to hope the ice was thick enough to support the aircraft. The fog was closing in fast and there was no other alternative. But then the pilot make a deadly error: instead of making a turn over the trees where he would have visual reference, he went out over the lake to make the turn. He never did complete it; in a sinking spiral the aircraft drove right through the ice and into the water with a loss of all on board. An experienced pilot would have turned over the trees, then lining himself with the shoreline, staying as close as possible to the shore where he would have a constant reference in making his letdown, touched the ice surface gently at high speed and kept moving until he was near shore. Even with the four inches of new ice which there was at that time, he might have got away with it, for if the plane had broken through, the wings would most likely to have held up the aircraft long enough for everyone to get out.

Another thing to be learned from deliberate low flying in good weather is the time and distance factor in response to a movement of the controls. In making a turn an aircraft with a high wing loading will take longer to come around in a turn than one with a low wing loading. In a Cessna 185 for instance if you make a 180 degree turn within the confines of say a river a mile wide, you might be surprised to find that you had used the complete width to make the turn. This experience would serve you well the next time you were caught in a lowering ceiling over the Mackenzie River, and considered making a 180 to get out of it.

Another lesson that can be learned from low flying regarding the time and distance factor is the ability of your airplane to clear an obstacle in a given distance. For instance if there are eighty foot trees half a mile away and you are flying at ice level, at what point do you activate the controls to bring the aircraft up and over the trees without touching the trees or stalling the airplane? You must know when to pull up to clear an object in the distance. Much time spent in low flying, and at different speeds, will impress upon a person the fact that an aircraft takes a perceptible amount of time to overcome the inertia of straight and level flight plus an additional few seconds to attain the necessary altitude. After a few close brushes with a hill or tree a pilot will be sufficiently impressed and will avoid a situation where he leaves himself insufficient time to clear an obstacle.

There is nothing like an actual experience to impress a person with the facts of life, as this incident will signify. One March day when on a flight to Simpson with two passengers we spied a timber wolf out on a lake. "Let's scare him a bit," I said, as I throttled back for a shallow dive over the lake. The wolf took off in a northerly direction with the aircraft right behind him, a few feet off the ice. Before we caught him I looked up and saw the tall burned timber of a brule ahead. Without thinking I yanked the stick back and we zoomed over the tops of the trees, missing them by only a very few feet. I was a pretty sober boy all the way to Simpson and have resisted buzzing an animal every since. Another incident similar to this took place on a large lake near by, again on a fine day in March.

A pilot of a Cessna 185 delivered some people with a load of freight to a village, and on the way they spotted a pack of wolves out on a lake eating some rotten fish. The pilot said, "On my way home, I'll get one or two of them." He did indeed kill one, but was killed himself in the process. From the aircraft's ski marks on the snow, the dead wolf, and the position of the wrecked airplane we assumed the following had taken place.

The wolves were some distance from shore and the pilot made his approach toward the trees instead of from the shoreline. One of the plane's skis had evidently hit the wolf and the opposite ski had left a mark in the snow. The pilot then had observed the trees on the shoreline ahead coming up fast. He must have pulled up sharply to avoid the trees, then failed to recover flying speed. The aircraft stalled in a nose up attitude, for it fell out of the air on one wing with very little forward motion. The pilot was killed instantly.

The very first thing that is taught in flying school is that an aircraft wing is an airfoil, that when moved through the air at sufficient speed will create 'lift'. It is amazing that pilots can ever forget that airspeed is their life blood. Of secondary importance is the fact that light airplanes can also only withstand a limited airspeed, and excessive velocity will cause a wing to part company from the fuselage. When I was taking instruction in doing stall turns I was warned that there was a danger in recovering from a wing over, of letting the airspeed build to a critical point.

The idea is, at all times to keep your airspeed within the safe limits for your particular aircraft.

As mentioned earlier not all aircraft accidents end in tragedy. Some foolish maneuvers and some errors end in a humorous situation and some induce merriment in the pilot while the victim gets very annoyed. Jim Burroughs once had an engine failure of a Norseman on floats when he was delivering a crew of fire-fighters to a bush camp. The engine quit at a time when there was no water anywhere in sight. Jim picked out an open area in the bush and simply flew the airplane into the spot he had chosen and made a normal power-off approach and landing. He is an old hand at bush flying and did not become excited. He knew that a float plane can usually be landed safely on land and would come to a stop without going over on its back. The landing area was an old 'burn' and the Norseman bumped along over the windfalls and came to a stop. Jim then turned around to assure his passengers that all was well and found that while he was landing the seven natives he had on board had all bailed out and were nowhere to be seen. For a time he thought that they had vacated the aircraft while still in the air, when the engine had quit. But one by one they came out of the woods and all were accounted for.

Many pilots love to 'buzz' people on the ground. One man in particular was renowned for this; he would get low over the ground and come straight at someone and would laugh at them diving for cover. This is something we are all tempted to do, but the impulse should be checked as someone could get hurt. The pilot mentioned, in order to stop a man on a skidoo from getting his aircraft's identification came right at the skidoo with the aircraft skis almost touching the ground. The skidoo driver baled out and dived into the snow.

Often when I spot a friend on the river in a boat, if I think he has not spotted me, I will come up behind him as low as I dare to give him a bit of a shock. If the man in the boat has been unaware of the presence of the aircraft he will be very surprised to suddenly hear it zoom over. For a split second because of the sudden noise he will think that his boat engine has blown up and come apart and will be quite perturbed and is apt to refer to his tormentor in some well chosen and uncomplimentary words.

I was boating once on the Liard River in a swift shallow rocky part of the stream, steaming along downstream at a good clip and keeping my ears atuned for the slight sound of a 'click' that would indicate the propeller had touched a gravel bar, when Telif Vassjo came up behind and zoomed over me with his helicopter. I had no idea an aircraft was within fifty miles; my hair turned gray and I aged ten years in two seconds. He still laughs about it when I see him and the incident is thirty years ago. But it is a long road that doesn't end in a slough and one day I'll catch him in the air and dive on him at 200 miles an hour and dust his crop a little.

There is a good thing about all this foolishness and that is that 99 per cent of pilots will avoid all deliberate horse play whenever they are carrying passengers.

There are two aircraft incidents I know of that ended without loss of life and are so rare and unique and so totally unreal that although I know they are facts, I do not expect anyone to believe either of them.

One February a Beaver aircraft from Watson Lake came into Nahanni Butte with a crew of three men to do some Water Survey work on the Nahanni River. After several days work they finished up at Fort Liard which was their last station before returning to Watson Lake 200 miles westward across mountain terrain rising to no more than 6000 feet. On the day of the flight the weather was within VFR limits at both Liard and Watson Lake with some of the hills in between shrouded in cloud. The pilot who was new to the area, on climbing out at Fort Liard and penetrating the first range of mountains could see that ahead his vision was obscured. He trimmed out the aircraft in a climbing attitude and entered the fog with all reference to the ground obscured. He was IFR and felt confident he would soon break out on top. After possibly ten minutes had elapsed and they were still in cloud, a bump or two was felt, and looking out the side windows the pilot and passengers noticed snowcovered ground and small bushes slipping by. The pilot reduced power and they bumped along and came to a stop.

There are no words to describe the shock and surprise of all on board to discover they had inadvertently landed on a gently sloping top of a mountain at an altitude of close to 5000 feet. Fate had chosen one of the very few spots in the whole area where a landing could be safely made. It was indeed a miracle. Ordinarily the aircraft would have struck a rock wall or a tree or some obstruction that would have at the very least damaged the airplane severely. After a time the fog cleared away and the flight was resumed to their destination. It was told, and I can readily believe that the pilot meditated quietly for two days on his good fortune feeling that he would awake to find it all a dream.

The passengers on the flight say the episode is the entire truth. Who can believe it?

Now hang on tight, for the next story is harder yet to credit. Pat Carey is an experienced bush pilot who flew out of Fort Smith, N.W.T. for many years.

One day he was alone on a flight in a single engine Otter when he had an engine failure. He was in a mountainous terrain with no possible safe landing in view. He was without power and going down and had to find some place in a hurry to put the aircraft. Right ahead was a narrow crack in the rock wall, a sort of canyon-like crevass which the fuselage of the airplane just might fit into. With uncanny coolness and presence of mind Pat flew the Otter right into the crack in the wall. On impact, the wings of course, as he had anticipated, came off and folded back nicely and the Otter came to a stop jammed tightly into the opening high on the cliff. Pat stepped out onto a shelf and being unable to go anywhere, up, down, or sideways, stayed where he was, and was eventually taken off with a helicopter.

How can anyone be expected to believe this? But Mark Fairbrother assures me that Pat is still alive as ever, and the Otter eventually came loose from the cliff and fell to the bottom.

I have found that in talking with other pilots on the foregoing incidents most shake their heads in disbelief and start mumbling to themselves.

To illustrate how chance happenings can influence the fortunes of a flight, Mark Fairbrother tells of the first time he flew a 180 fully loaded out of Fort Simpson. He said that he never felt comfortable in the 180, and was convinced that it would try to kill him every time he took it up. Here is Mark telling the story.

"It was November sometime and the ice was running in the Mackenzie. Fred Sibbeston wanted to go trapping and to be flown down to an old airstrip on the Mackenzie. John Kidd, who owned the plane said, 'Sure, OK, Mark will fly you down with the 180.' The 180 was on skis and I had never landed on skis. Peter Cowie had checked me out, but I had never flown it loaded, always empty. So I put Fred and his dogs and all his camp gear in the airplane, and it was jammed full. So I gassed up and checked over the airplane, got in and went rarin' down the strip. And the damned tail wouldn't come off the ground. I didn't realize the trim was set for an empty plane. Finally I got the tail up and just off the end of the strip when the bloody cowl door on the side of the cowling flopped open and began banging away in the wind.

If I had just ignored it, it would have been all right. But I felt I would have to get back to the runway. There was no wind and I had taken off over the river. By the time I was off I was over the river and climbing out and looking to see if all was clear to make a turn when the airplane started to buffet and I looked up and saw the airspeed needle was coming off the clock. (In pilot jargon that means he was about to stall.) I hadn't wound the trim far enough ahead, and when I was looking around I had relaxed the pressure on the stick and the nose came up and it was just starting to stall, and by that time I was out over the river. I was only up 300 feet and with that airplane it took a minimum of 700 feet to recover from a stall. Fortunately I was still in fine pitch and I jammed the stick as far ahead as it would go and down over the river we went. If there had been anything in the way, anything at all, we never would have made it.

Bill Berg was down at the dump at the end of the island. He saw me and couldn't figure out what the hell I was doing. He said I'd got to be crazy. I never told anybody about that. I'll tell you how scared I was: I went back and landed, fixed the cowl door, took off again and flew with two notches of flap all the way to that airstrip. I was so damned scared I didn't know what I was doing. I was almost at the airstrip when I got to thinking again, By God, that airplane was flying awful slow, 90 mph with a 180? And I got to checking around and found I had forgotten to let off the flaps."

16

The Polaris

By the fall of 1968 trapping as a full time occupation was fast becoming a rarity in the Liard River area, except perhaps for Fort Liard where some natives were going to the bush and staying all winter. Near Nahanni there were few traplines of any length that were still being used. Most men who wanted work were employed at various winter works projects such as seismograph work, road construction etc. Generally speaking traplines were getting shorter each year and the young men were spending less time in the bush.

During the month of September I noticed from the air that my old trapline south of the Long Reach had grown up amazingly since the fire of 1942. Much of the burned off area was covered with a healthy growth of poplar and birch, with the new growth of spruce and jackpine reaching a height of twenty feet. There were bulldozed cutlines everywhere you looked; lines as straight as an arrow, thirty feet wide and ending on the horizon. They had been made by the oil exploration companies within the last ten years. Most were at right angles to the geological structure, but some were parallel to it.

Mostly from curiosity to look over my old trapline and to see if the beaver population had increased since my dogteam trapping days, I flew south from our old home cabin on the Long Reach, following the cutlines here and there, crossed the Blackstone River and on out to the high marten country near Island Lake. The old line cabins had either been burned by the forest fire or had fallen in, for I could see nothing of them from the air. Nostalgic memories flooded over me as I relived my early trapping days. There was Teepee Creek, where the wolves had given me a fright, and where I had encountered one of the few mad bull moose I had ever seen. There was the Big Muskeg where Vera and I had shared four only small slices of bacon for a noonday lunch when she was carrying our first child. There were the jack pine ridges where the rabbits were always thick and where we had caught many lynx. There was the little pothole in the muskeg where I had gone through the ice in September the second winter trapping. And there was the beaver creek that my brother Fred and I followed in May of '37 when we packed over to the head of Birch River on a beaver hunt. And as to beaver—well, bless my soul, there were beaver lodges where I had never seen them before, on creeks grown up with poplar and willows where previously there had only been evergreen trees. There was more than double the amount of beaver than in former years, due to the burning off of the old coniferous trees and their replacement by more edible deciduous species. I could see dams and lodges one after the other on all creeks where food was available. The tips of the food caches could be seen in the clear water near the lodges.

In my mind's eye I mapped out a projected trapline from the Liard River south to Blackstone Lake. By jogging east occasionally I would be able to follow cutlines all the way south to the lake. The rabbits were on the increase and I knew a lynx 'run' was on the way. The prices should be good, perhaps fifty dollars each; a hundred lynx would be five thousand dollars. There would also be mink along the beaver creeks, and marten in the high country, and with very few who were trapping any more I would have the whole country all to myself. But I would need a snowmobile and that I did not have. Those cutlines were made for a skidoo; there would be no trail cutting to be done, and I would not need to shoot moose for dog food. The energy giving material this time would be gasoline. There were no line cabins but with a powerful snowmobile I might be able to haul a tent and stove along.

I could already smell the tang of the muskeg in the late fall, hear the water gurgling under ice in shallow streams, the grouse and partridge go whirring from the snow off into a thicket of pine. I could smell the spruce boughs in the cabin warmth; see the moon through the tree tops in the night and listen to the silence of the pines, the ice-bound lakes and distant hills. The past tumbled in on me.

At home, Vera was very dubious about my plan for going trapping again and anyway it was too late in the season to get a snowmobile shipped in before winter, and I reluctantly abandoned my project for the time.

In January while at Fort Nelson on one of my regular trips for mail, groceries etc., I was in the Sime hardware store for supplies. Jack Sime was fresh out from Scotland when in 1930 Stan and I had met him at Fort Liard. He was then an apprentice for the Hudson's Bay Company and has been in the merchandising business ever since. Jack owned and operated a trading post at Fort Liard when I was trading at Netla and Trout Lake. At one time he owned a share in an aircraft; made very good beer while at Liard and it was said he had never turned a trapper down for credit, which I can well believe. He and I had one hell of a tough boat trip on the Fort Nelson River one fall in early October. We often had to get out into the water and push and pull the boat over rocks and shallows. The water was very cold, and between the two of us we had one pair of waders, one of which leaked badly. And years before when Vera and I trapped on the Long Reach, Jack had arrived at our cabin in an open boat one very cold day, when the ice was running in the Liard. He was so cold, he was more dead than alive.

Now, at Fort Nelson I never missed a chance to go into his store to exchange some banter. This day he had a new Polaris Mustang snowmobile in the showroom and I could not take my eyes off it. It had a twenty inch track and a 26 HP motor. The price was $ 1450.00 I peered here and there; I ran my hands over its shiny surface; I sat on the soft seat cushion and with my hands on the steering wheel I imagined myself whistling along the trapline at 30 mph. Thirty lynx at fifty dollars each would pay for it. I was sold. How nice it would be now that we had no dog team, to have a skidoo at Nahanni for hauling firewood and for going across to the village. I told Jack I would take the machine and would be back in a few days to pick it up. A scheme was already forming in my mind for getting it down to Nahanni.

The winter road from Fort Nelson to Simpson went by Trout Lake and at that point was about eighty miles south east of the Long Reach. I would go out the winter road that far, then follow the cutlines to the Liard River, pulling a toboggan with fuel and supplies behind, then follow the Liard River on the ice the thirty-five miles to Nahanni. The snow was less than two feet deep in the bush and some of the cutlines had been broken open by the oil companies.

To avoid getting lost in the maze of cutlines I would map them carefully from the air so that I would know exactly where I was at all times. Besides it was mostly my old trapping area anyway and I would remember most of the landmarks. On the way back to Nahanni I picked out the route I would follow with the skidoo and from the air marked the cutlines on the map.

At home Vera said that if I went trapping again and caught any amount of fur, the prices would be sure to drop.

"The rabbits are thick," I said, "we might easily get a 'run' of lynx that will last for two or three years. The price should be good, these are prosperous times and women will be buying fur coats."

It was the first days of February when I loaded CF-UAH with tent, campstove, rifle, axe, winter bedroll and much spare clothing and took off for Fort Nelson, telling Vera I would be home with the skidoo in two weeks.

In Fort Nelson I made a two foot wide toboggan to pull behind the snowmobile and made arrangements to have a pick-up take everything out via the Simpson winter road to Trout Lake.

While at Fort Nelson I spent a lot of time with Hilton Burry at his house at the airport. One day I said to him, "Hilton, why not fix up that broken down Skidoo of yours, and come with me to break out the trail to Nahanni?"

"I don't know about that Turner, you would most likely get us lost, and besides that is not a broken down Skidoo that I have. It is almost brand new and will run a lot better than that thing you have."

"Maybe so Burry, but quit your quibbling, are you going to back out of this trip or not? I know you haven't much stamina and I'd probably end up having to carry you most of the way."

"Hey man," moaned Hilton, "hold on. How can I back out when I haven't yet agreed to go? How long will it take us? I don't know if I can afford to be away very long."

"Excuses, excuses," I answered, "that's all I get. You would never be missed from your job for all you do, and anyway we'll be back in five days."

"Dick, you old buzzard, I would like to get away from town for awhile, I think you've talked me into it."

"OK, Burry, now you're talking, we'll send your skiddo out with the truck and get George Bayer to fly us out as soon as you're ready."

"Do you know where you are going Turner? Can we find our way among that maze of cutlines going in all directions?"

"Not to worry man. Here is the map I have with the cutlines all marked out, and besides I've trapped in that country off and on for twenty years, I know it like the back of my hand."

"And how will I get back from Nahanni?" Hilton enquired.

"We'll get someone to fly the Maule down in five days, and I'll bring you back. No problem there. You won't need your Skidoo again this winter and I will bring it back on the barge after breakup."

So it was all arranged and by late the next day we were landed at an airstrip on the winter road where our skidoos and supplies had been left off.

We had a good camp that night as the fire inside made the tent warm and comfortable. In the morning it took some time to get organized but by ten o'clock we were off and away. The new Polaris Mustang ran perfectly as did Hilton's Skidoo. We found the turnoff road at Island Lake and while the snow was deep in the bush this cutline had been used earlier and there was only six inches of snow on it. My toboggan was piled high with supplies and the new machine handled the load well, even up the hills. Hilton was pulling a smaller toboggan behind with no effort.

The cross roads checked out well with the map until we made a turn at the west end of Island Lake to head north. Here we came onto a mixture of cutlines: some had been made in the last few days and some a month previously. I had planned on turning west again at the fifth cross road, but now I was all fouled up as I realized that some roads had been plowed out since I had flown over and made the map. After passing the fourth cross road I turned off and found I was lost. We went back a mile or two and started again, with no better luck. We had hit the middle of a seismograph program area, with fresh lines going in every direction. We went up and down and back and forth until poor Hilton was about ready to shoot me. I am sure the only reason he didn't was because the ammunition for his rifle cost fifty cents per round, and he didn't want to waste the money on me.

At last we spied a lake about a mile across, off a ways in the bush. I unhooked my load and with the Polaris I made a tour of the lake and discovered it was a lake on my trapline I had trapped years ago, which gave me some idea of where we were. Then we met two trucks on their way to the seismic camp. One of the drivers knew in what direction his cook shack was and how far but aside from that he was as lost as we were.

Hilton seemed about to explode, so I said to him, "Burry, it is indeed fortunate for you that you have such a good guide as I am, otherwise if you were left to your own devices you would undoubtedly get yourself lost. As your face is getting flushed and you seem a little worried let me hasten to assure you that somewhere south of this lake there is a road going north-west and about ten miles out on that there is a trail branching off at a slight angle to the left. That cutline should eventually take us to the road on top of the ridge, and from there it's a piece of cake."

"I don't believe a word you say Turner, and I have no choice but to follow you, but you had better deliver or I'll have your gizzard out with a dull spoon."

"Burry, how could you say such a thing? I've never failed

you yet have I?" And I continued in a hurry, "Don't answer that."

By this time night was fast approaching and camp had to be made. Scooping away the snow with our snowshoes used as shovels, we put down a good layer of spruce boughs, erected the 8x10 canvas tent with its four foot walls, folded the edges under a foot, laid a tarpaulin inside and set up the camp stove on two green logs, with one length of pipe up and two going out through a hole rimmed with tin. We cut a pile of dry spruce wood for the night and soon had a roaring fire, making the tent warm and comfortable. Granulated snow in a large frypan quickly melted into water for coffee and for washing dishes. After a supper of steaks, coffee, biscuits, butter and jam, with two candles throwing a good light off the white canvas walls, we settled back on our eiderdowns and spun yarns of our flying days.

When it came time for bed there was a prolonged argument as to who would sleep next to the stove, as he would be the candidate for stoking the fire during the night. After only two hours of argument I had to give in as Hilton wouldn't budge an inch from his place against the wall. I fooled him though for I filled the stove with green wood and only had to stoke it once during the night. When I awoke to stoke the fire I did think of putting some snow on his head or dumping some water in his sleeping robe but was somewhat apprehensive as to the repercussions that may have ensued, so I contented myself with tying his mocassins in knots.

After an early breakfast we had the tent down and everything loaded and were away by nine o'clock. West of the lake we picked up the road we had in mind and found it was being used by a seismic crew with their wheeled vehicles. The surface was good and we barreled right along. At the turn-off trail that angled to the left we found that it had not been used all winter and the snow lay two feet deep. After a conference we decided we would make better time by staying on the well travelled road and then cutting west to intersect our original intended route. So far all was well and we were making good time but after turning west we missed the intersection and continued on ending up on some creeks close to the Blackstone River. Now we were lost again and what is more, the cutlines came to an end at a small lake.

It was getting late in the afternoon and we must make camp. The weather was nice; bright and sunny all day and perhaps 20 below. To cheer Hilton up I pointed toward the mountains far to the west. "Look, Burry," I said, "see that pale blue rounded rock gleaming in the setting sun 80 miles away? That my friend is Nahanni Butte. That, my boy is our destination and therefore you cannot accuse me of being lost."

Dick Turner," Hilton came back, "there is only one thing I would accuse you of right now and that is being a liar. I do not believe you ever were a trapper, you must be from the city. No real trapper could ever get so lost and muddled on his own trapline."

"Hilton," I replied. "Listen, I think I hear a strange noise. It is either a sick duck quacking or some early frogs croaking. Spring must be coming; let us hurry to get the tent up before it rains."

All day long I had been sneezing and that night I lay awake with a fever and aching bones. In the morning I was so weak that travelling was out of the question. I had evidently caught the influenza 'bug' that was going around and we would just have to hole up for the day.

To the northwest of the lake there was a large open area of muskeg and small spruce with sloughs and pot-holes scattered here and there. It was a nice clear day and Hilton said he would take the big skidoo by itself and head off to the top of the ridge northward where I assured him there would be a good cutline that would take us out to the Liard River. Once we found that trail I really would know my way home.

Later in the day Hilton returned and announced that he had found the trail and had followed it for five miles or so to give us a start in the morning. Hilton said the snow on top of the ridge was very deep and it was all the snowmobile could do to struggle along by itself. As it always is in the north as winter advances and the snow gets deep, the top half is hard and crusty while the bottom is loose and crystallized. The rear of the machine would sink into the loose snow, lose its traction and bury itself to the ground. Once a trail of any sort was made it would freeze overnight and a skidoo could easily pull a load over it the next day.

We stayed at the lake for two days waiting for me to recover from the bout with the flu. The second day about noon we heard an aircraft coming and soon the little blue Maule appeared. The boys from Fort Nelson had come to check up on us. It was good to see them. They landed and taxied over to the tent. It was two helicopter pilots and I said, "It's sure good to see you big apes, we're lost. How the hell did you find us in all this maze of roads?"

"Nothing to it boy, we flew to the Butte, then down the Liard thirty miles and then southeast until we picked up your skidoo trail; it's easy to see with the sun shining."

When they were leaving we said, "Give us about three days to get home and then come in and I'll fly you and Hilton back to Fort Nelson."

The next morning I still felt weak and dizzy but we broke camp and set off with Hilton going ahead with the small skidoo. We made fast time as far as he had gone the day before and from there on the snow was so deep that neither of the machines could break out the trail and pull a load. We piled all the traps and any odd thing we did not need off to the side with Hilton's little tobaggan, put all the load on the Polaris toboggan and with the small machine ahead we were able to struggle along very slowly. On some of the upgrades we had to walk ahead on snowshoes to break down the snow so that the machines could climb the hill. By late afternoon we were off the ridge and were headed down into the valley of the Liard River. I was so weak and shivery I suggested we camp for the night. About here we came across a narrow dogteam toboggan trail that I knew was Alfred Thomas' trapline. I started to make camp while Hilton went on a ways to reconnoiter. In an hour he was back and reported that although the dogteam trail was narrow he was able to make fair time. But balancing the skidoo upon it was a problem. He said it was very much like walking a high board fence.

When he came back I caught hell for not having the tent erected. By this time I could hardly stand on my feet, let alone shovel snow and cut down trees. While Hilton set up the tent I got some dry poles to cut into firewood for the night. I made one or two cuts then had to go to my knees to finish the job. I felt almost like I had been hit over the head with a crowbar.

Hilton's only comment was, "If you're not better in the morning Turner, I guess I'll have to shoot you after all. I wouldn't like to leave you here to starve and I know I couldn't kill you with an axe, your head's too solid for that."

"Look, Burry," I replied, in a croaking raspy voice, "tomorrow when I'm a little better I'll tie that obnoxious face of yours down around your ankles with a couple of half hitches in between and fling you in the bushes for the wolves."

In spite of Hilton's rough words he must have been a little concerned for as soon as the tent was up and the fire was lit he insisted I get into the eiderdown right away and he finished the camp chores and cooked supper without a whimper and even insisted on sleeping near the stove to keep the fire stoked as he said I might die during the night.

In the morning I felt much better and told Hilton he could put the shells for his gun back in his packsack as I thought he would not have to use one on me after all. And studying the map carefully I said, "Very soon now we should come to a trail branching to the right that will take us to the Liard River. The snow there should be drifted enough to support the skidoos and we should make the thirty miles to Nahanni in two hours."

We left the tent set up as this would be our last night out and I would need it here when I came back to set up the line.

We were a bit concerned about our supply of fuel for the skidoos but felt we had enough for one more day's travel. As we headed west I was very surprised to find there was no trail forking off the the north. Furthermore we found that the big toboggan would not stay up on the narrow dog trail even though by now the load was very light. After struggling on a mile or two we decided to pile what we could on the machines and abandon the toboggan, and in this way we proceeded by carefully balancing the skidoos on the trail by judiciously shifing our weight.

Our troubles were not yet over. After going about eight miles we could see that the cutline made a turn and I thought it was strange for the map showed no turn here. On coming up to it we discovered there was no turn at all. The road simply came to an end. The bulldozers had piled the trees to one side for a space to turn around and had gone back the way they had come.

I got out the map and sat puzzling over it for some time. "Burrry," I said, "I don't know where we went wrong, this cutline should have taken us out to the river, it can't be far, with the timber so big here we must be near the Liard. Anyway let's make a cup of tea while we think about it."

This was likely the second time since I had known Hilton that he was really annoyed with me.

"OK, Turner, let's make a cup of tea. What the hell good will that do? A cup of tea will not show us out of this mess. We're lost, let's face it. Why the hell don't you take that map and start the fire with it for all the good it is?" Burry was so mad I thought he was going to stamp his foot. In spite of my air reconnaissance and careful mapping of our route we had been lost continuously since we had left the Simpson trail. And he was right about the map. We could have made out no worse if we had burned the map the first day out.

I thought it was wise at this time not to talk when I should be listening. In a few minutes we had a pot of tea on the boil and were eating lunch, and a plan of action was hatched. "Let's go back a mile or so to where Alfred's dog-team trail branched off and follow that. Even if we have to cut some trees here and there to get through the thickets, eventually the trail will have to bring us out to the Liard."

And that is what we did. The trail was so narrow and crooked that the skidoos would fall off on a sharp turn and it took some heaving and lifting to get them back upon the trail again. The Polaris weighed 375 lbs. and was a little too much for me to man-handle in my weakened condition; so Hilton took the big machine and went ahead and I followed with the little skidoo. In this manner we made out very well and were able to progress at about five miles an hour. There were not more than half a dozen places where we had to cut out trees to widen the trail to get through.

About three in the afternoon we started to go downhill and I knew we were only a mile or two from the Liard River. As always we smelled the smoke from the cabin long before we came to it, and there at last it was: Alfred's home cabin and he came out when his dog team started to bark, and stood amazed to see us come out of the wood, as it were.

The sun was not yet down so we said we would grab a quick cup of tea before setting off the twenty miles home to Nahanni Butte.

Alfred said, "I thought you were flying around with your airplane Dick, I sure never expected to see you in the bush with a skidoo. Where did you come from?"

"Fort Nelson, around by the Simpson road. I'm going to set out my line and trap for a year or two. How are the lynx? You catching any?"

"Yeah, a few, they seem to be coming back." And he looked at me and smiled. "I thought you made lots of money trading Dick, you shouldn't have to trap for a living any more."

"Alfred," I replied, "I guess once a trapper, always a trapper, I like the bush, that's all. And besides I'm not as rich as you think, a lot of money goes to buying gas for that little blue airplane of mine."

Alfred smiled and shook his head. It was obvious that he could not make out the behaviour of these crazy white men.

"How's the snow on the river Alfred? Is there any rough ice?"

"No, there's only about a foot of snow on the ice and you can miss all the rough ice around Swan Point by crossing the bar."

"Thanks Alfred, and thanks for the tea, see you lad." And he stood on the bank and waved good-by as we set off.

Hilton said, "You take the big machine Dick, and go ahead and I'll come along behind."

The sun was just going down behind the mountains twenty miles to the west when we sped down the hill onto the river. The snow as Alfred had said, was little over a foot deep and pretty well packed with the wind in most places. Going at a good clip the machines only settled in the snow about six inches. The rough chunks of ice could be plainly seen and I was able to open up the Mustang and let her rip. With no load behind she was running free and I crouched behind the windshield to stay out of the wind. I looked back and old Hilton was right behind, just out of the flying snow. Whenever we hit a drift the machines would leap in the air as if alive. In smooth places I opened the throttle wide and tried to leave Hilton behind, but he stuck tight and we were soon around Swan Point and headed into the homeward stretch.

It was still light when we pulled up the hill into the yard at Nahanni. That big log house looked good to us, as did the rugs on the shiny floor, the bright varnished logs of the walls, Don's trophies, the piano and book cases, the warm kitchen and the smell of food. And Vera as always was ready with a wonderful meal. I went over to the power house, cranked over the diesel and the place lit up with a flood of lights from the windows. I felt I had been away for a year instead of twenty days.

Due to several unavoidable factors it was nearly the end of February before I was able to get down to the Long Reach with the skidoo, and as the open season on lynx would soon be over I picked up the tent and toboggan and left the setting out of traps until the next season.

17

Trapping

Soon after open water appeared I got the floats on the aircraft again for the summer. To prepare for the next season I landed at the Long Reach and picked a spot eight miles above the old cabin where there was good timber to build a small cabin as a base for the trapline. I planned it to be about ten by twelve feet with two windows, plywood floor and six inch trees split with the chain saw for the roof. On weekends and spare days I would fly down with UAH and work on the cabin until by August it was finished. Then on one of the barge trips to Simpson we brought up fifty kegs of gasoline with ten cases of oil for the Polaris. We left off thirty kegs at the Long Reach cabin and with the airplane I put ten kegs of gasoline with a bunch of traps on a lake at the end of the line, to avoid having to haul it out with the skidoo.

Next I set to work making a twenty-four inch wide toboggan with three oak toboggan boards purchased from my old friend Johnny Ross, of the Hudson's Bay Raw Fur Department in Edmonton. Toboggan boards were getting to be a thing of the past and the Bay were the only ones that handled them. Instead of a 'carry-all' made of moose skin, I used plywood for the sides and put narrow steel runners on the bottom. Much time and thought went into designing and making a flexible hitch for the sleigh which would allow a positive connection with the skidoo and which would be flexible in all directions. With steel tubing and tough rubber belting I at last constructed a bridle and hitch that was light in weight, very strong and could be quickly removed.

In September after the tugs and barges were winched from the river to high ground and Don had left to work on the oil rigs, Vera and I set to work making a thirty foot scow for the 40 HP kicker. With the aid of a skill saw I made the frame of ribs from 2x4 spruce lumber with half inch fir plywood for the hull. On Vera's advice I made the sides thirty inches high and gave the bow an eight inch extra turnup. The inside was strengthened with solid sides and the transom was made of three layers of three-quarter inch fir plywood, glued and strengthened with steel rod supports, Vera gave it two coats of paint and it was ready to go.

By October fifteenth, ice was starting to form on the rivers and I loaded the Polaris into the boat with all the supplies and equipment I would need as well as food for the best part of the winter. Trapping season opened on November 1st and I planned on coming home with the skidoo as soon as the river froze over and the ice was safe for travelling. Then I would cross the river at the trapping cabin and use the old Simpson Nahnni winter road to get back and forth to the line, a distance of thirty-five miles.

It is always very cold travelling on the river in October and I had a chilly two hour trip down to the cabin. It was like old times getting set up for the winter: getting the cabin ship shape, planning each day's work, lighting the gas lamp in the evening, cooking supper then stretching out on the bunk (with a spring mattress yet) dozing or reading as the mood took me. While missing Vera a lot (she still thought I was a bit daffy to go trapping again) and the kids who were out at school, there was still something that was extremely satisfying about being alone and isolated in the bush. You are many miles from human habitation and contact. All your decisions are completely independent from interference in any way from your fellow man. It is more than a feeling of euphoria, there is a deep contentment that stems from situations where the choice of direction of any plan or enterprise, and the expediting of such plans are entirely your own. With nothing more than the surmounting of the almost daily battle with the elements in a world of your own there comes a peace and contentment that is deeply rewarding.

But there is a price to pay. If you drink too deeply from this cup of nectar the dregs at the bottom are bitter and damaging. Without a woman of your choice, the one you love, to share and partake of this primitive way of life, the pleasure will wither and waste away; and if you stubbornly continue on your solitary way while rationalizing that you need no one beside you, you will I think become warped and twisted within, and come to live behind a wall, a soft flowing translucent curtain that will prevent you from ever completely entering the world of your fellow men. Strong willed men may fight against and delay the building of the curtain, but even strong men are but flesh and blood and can never win against nature.

Being anything but a strong man, and well aware of the implications of my actions I felt that a month or so in the bush alone would hurt me in no way. Or perhaps I could not resist the call of the woods and lonely trails. Or most frightening of all, perhaps over the years little by little the curtain of isolation was already building and I was slipping into the protection of the sweet drug of loneliness.

Every minute of every day now was taken up with a necessary task. First a hand winch had to be devised for pulling the boat from the river to a shelving bank where it would not be crushed with the break-up of the ice in the spring. In the cabin there were shelves to be built, window and door frames to set in place and an insulated door constructed which would let in no cold. There was over a mile of trail to cut, for access to the cutline to the south; and always there was dry wood to bring in, cut and pile for the winter's fuel.

That first winter trapping with the snowmobile from the cabin on the Long Reach gave me an opportunity to begin a project which I had been contemplating for some years. It was to write an account of trapping and other aspects of life in the northern bush. There seemed to be an interest building in the reading public for information on the life of early settlers in the Canadian north. From what I could see the available material was for the most part prejudiced, trivial or uninformed and some was a combination of all three. An exception was *Dangerous River* by R.M. Patterson which was authentic and stood by itself. After waiting for years for additional authentic material to be written on the Nahanni nothing much but junk appeared.

I was stung by trappers, almost always without exception being portrayed along with Indians and half-breeds as the villains of the piece. Someone in most cases had to be made to appear in a bad light and so the authors chose those who were most unable to defend themselves, the poor maligned Indian, Metis and trapper. They were people who lived in the bush, hunting, trapping and killing innocent animals for a living and must surely be brutal and coarse creatures easily depicted as savages. In later years natives and Metis have been gathering writers to champion their cause, but with few exceptions the 'trapper' still remains the villain. Being a trapper myself and feeling qualified to write about a trapper's life, I at last resolved to 'pick up the glove' and accept the challenge.

I could see there were many obstacles in setting out upon a career as a writer. Many publishing firms in Canada were reported to be in severe financial straits. Books generally were not selling well. Many Canadian writers were starving and having difficulty in finding a publisher. Many writers seemed to start out by taking a course in a school of journalism, writing for the news media, then progressing to short stories and articles and finally perhaps to a full length book, historical or fiction.

Knowing full well that 'Fools walk in where angels fear to tread', I countered this adage with something my mother often told me, 'faint heart ne'er won fair lady'. I decided to plunge right in with both feet and write a full length book right off the bat.

When we loaded the boat at Nahanni Butte in 1969 with supplies for the trapline, I also stuffed into the packsack along with, I think it was Goren, Bradlaugh and Galbraith—Webster, Devlin's Synonyms, some scribblers and a pencil.

Goodness knows in the little cabin among the timber back from the river on the Long Reach there were no diversions, interruptions or noise to distract me from writing. But for all that, the original manuscript of *NAHANNI* was the hardest task I had ever attempted. Evening after evening I would laboriously scribble a few pages, then crumble them and stuff them in the stove until I was afraid if I kept that up the paper would soon be gone and I would be reduced to using birch-bark and charcoal.

One night I thought, "I must stop throwing my writing away; I will save all I write, good, bad and indifferent and at some future date go over it and whip it into shape." This I did, yet nothing ever emerged quite like I had first envisaged.

Where was I to start? I meditated on what had impressed me most in the first years of trapping; the first years of the struggle to survive after Vera and I were married, and upon that I would write. Here is what was written with pencil in a scribbler one of those first nights in that little cabin. It was never included in the book *NAHANNI*.

It was 1936, Vera and I had been married for two years. Our two roomed cabin on the Liard River contained only the barest essentials of a household, all home-made except the stove, clothes and a few scanty dishes. Aside from my brother Stan who trapped across the river from us, our nearest neighbors were twenty one miles away. Dog teams were the only mode of winter travel, and wild fur trapping was the only means of livelihood. Though small, our cabin was warm and cozy and Vera kept it spotless with shining floor and walls.

Our first child, a girl, had been born in May at the hospital in Fort Simpson, and we called her Nancy Jane. Although fur prices were poor, lynx and fox had been plentiful the last two years and we had hopes of another winter's fur catch which would with the help of garden produce and wild meat, help us to better our standard of living to the essentials of food, clothing and shelter.

It was late in January and the days were still quite short. Crossing the last jackpine ridge the dogs had stopped for a moment and I turned to look back and saw the sun sink

behind the mountains that were blue and cold in the distance.
A light fog hung over the dogteam, my parka hood was stiff
with ice and frost where my hot breath had froze and hung in
many tiny icicles that matted the fur hood of my parka. My
mitts were damp and stiff with frozen moisture. It must be
close to fifty below and it would be good to see the 2nd
Blackstone cabin in the deep valley of the river two miles
ahead. We had come twenty miles and that was enough for
one day. The dogs were tired from pulling the heavily loaded
sleigh which resisted movement through the snow that was
more like white powdered glass that cut and held the bottom
of the sleigh. Across the big muskeg to Teepee Creek I had
walked ahead of the team to find the trail which had been
obliterated by a recent storm. In the timber I had walked
behind, shaking up the traps and hurrying on to keep up with
the team. The exertion had kept me warm all day, except the
hands taken from my mitts often now to warm my face, were
getting chilly.

At the cabin, darkness was fast closing in. The dogs were
taken from the harness and spruce boughs were laid for their
beds. Next, a fire was lit in the campstove in the tiny cabin,
chunks of snared moose meat were set by the stove to thaw for
the dogs. Tea pail and frypan filled with crystal snow dug
from the ice on the frozen creek was put to melt for supper.
With the candles lit and the cabin warming with the snap and
crackle of burning wood, thoughts of food assailed me. Fresh
frozen buns (with deep brown crust from Vera's oven at home)
and the can of butter were set beside the stove to thaw. Parka
and mitts, 'duffle' and mocassins were hung to dry. Out of the
grub box came a white flour sack with frozen meat stew and
another one with frozen potato cakes; into the frypan with a
chunk of butter I ladled a portion from each sack. In a few
minutes a steaming pot of tea with the hot food in the frypan
was placed on the diminutive box board table. With buns,
butter and jam I made a hearty meal, thinking all the while
how much better Vera's cooking was than my own poor
efforts.

After the dogs were fed and firewood placed inside the
cabin for the night, the one lynx and red fox were skinned and
put in a bag on the roof to freeze. As I stepped out I could

hear my breath crackle and I knew it would be very cold by morning. The stars were so bright they looked like glass and you could almost hear them snap.

With the cabin warm and snug I climbed into the bedroll and was soon off to the land of Nod. Sometime later I awoke from a horrible vision-like dream, and for the longest time I lay only partially awake fighting off the sudden mental depression that had overcome me. I felt or dreamed that I was looking into our bedroom in our cabin at home. Our baby daughter was seven months old and Vera had taken her into bed with her as we often did when the baby woke up wet and cold. But there was something terribly wrong. Vera was not moving. Her body was cold. Nancy had the bedclothes kicked off and had turned on her stomach and with only her undershirt on her body, had her rump in the air in an effort to rise to her hands and knees. The cabin was cold and she was whimpering unhappily.

Struggling to regain my composure I rationalized there was in fact no such thing as a vision: my concern with leaving the family at home for several days, coupled with the intense cold, had produced a nightmare, that was all. While not normally given to bad dreams, once or twice a year I would awake in a terrible sweat and fear, from a dream where animals, and guns and my family were all mixed up in a completely unreal situation.

By this time I was in such a state that I could not get back to sleep. I lit the candle and stoked the fire and had a very early breakfast. It was two o'clock in the morning. Now what should I do? If I started home immediately it would take me ten hours travelling at least to reach the cabin. And if something had happened to my wife, both she and the baby would be frozen stiff by that time. And it MUST have been only a dream. Neither Vera nor I believed in premonitions. I still had another ten miles of line to check; the traps needed to be shaken up and fur meant food on the table.

Thus trying to console myself I put the dogs in the harness and long before daylight I set out for the end of the line. I had two martens in the traps and well before noon I was back at the cabin. After a hasty lunch and a cup of tea I headed north on the homeward journey. I thanked all the gods that ever were that I had Laddie and Skukum, the two pups that Vera had raised, with the other three dogs, and that I had been able to feed them meat all winter. I never failed to marvel at the speed, strength and energy of those two black pups. As long as I had fat meat to feed them they would strain in the harness for miles and miles and never seem to tire. If they ever slowed down it was because they were exhausted, and a short rest would refresh them. The mixture of Husky and German Shepherd gave them size, a nervous noisy disposition and tremendous energy. The other dogs in the team seemed to take heart from them and do their part.

We had done twenty miles already that day and still had thirty more to go. The load was light and I ran behind for twenty miles, through the jackpine and spruce thickets, across small lakes, down into the Blackstone valley again, on up and across the Big Muskeg to the top of the ridge. The last ten miles was down hill and I rode the tailboard home. It had clouded up, the weather had warmed and we sped along in the dark with the dogs picking up speed as we neared the cabin. I smelled smoke from the cabin fire; there was the soft light from the window and there my two girls warm and happy to see me. As I held them in my arms I kept back hot tears and have never to this day told Vera of that awful dream I had.

I think perhaps the reason I did not include the foregoing in the original manuscript of *NAHANNI* was because I felt it revealed too much of my innermost self and would tend to make me appear sentimental and weak. Now after those eight intervening years I know I am, and why try to hide it?

Every evening I would work on the manuscript and November 1st I started setting out traps and was soon catching lynx, marten and mink. By November tenth the depth of snow was sufficient to load up and head south to the far end of the line. On top of the ridge ten miles south I found the cache of traps Hilton and I had left there eight months before. I set up three winter camp tents fifteen miles apart, the last one near the gasoline cache at Blackstone Lake.

On the lowlands there were rabbit tracks everywhere, and they could often be seen scampering across the cutlines. And with the rabbits there were lynx tracks amounting to trails in some places. There were mink trails along some of the creeks and near the beaver lodges. Out on the high lands thirty miles from the Liard marten were more plentiful than I had ever seen then in the north. On that first trip in November for twenty miles there was at least one marten track on the cutline all the way. Going out I broke out the trail and set up the camps. Coming back to the river I built the pens and set the traps. For most fur bearing animals a small pen of sticks must be built to direct the animal into the trap, and a partial shelter constructed overhead so that a snow storm will not plug the trap.

By November fifteenth the river was still open although the ice had been running for almost two weeks. At the cabin on cold clear nights I could hear the ice grinding and snapping as it swept along, often sounding like the tinkling of bells as brittle bits of thin clear ice broke off and fell against a larger chunk. Often the quietness of the night would be broken with the grinding and crushing of the ice, which would then subside and die away.

Every night now I had two or three lynx to skin, with the high country producing marten and mink. I did not take time to stretch and dry the pelts but froze them after skinning to take to Nahanni. On November 20 the temperature fell to 35 below and in the morning the big river was silent. The ice had jammed and would now freeze quickly if it stayed cold. Two days later the ice was better than three inches thick and I loaded the toboggan with the thirty frozen pelts, gas, grub box, rifle and bedroll and set off for home. It took me a day and a half to get to Nahanni as the river ice was rough and the bush trail poor.

It seemed a waste of time going back and forth with the snowmobile from the Butte to the line, and as soon as conditions permitted I marked out a sandbar near the trapping cabin on the Long Reach and used the aircraft for commuting. This worked out very well as I could run the trapline in five or six days and get back home in fifteen minutes flying time. And the lynx had really come in. Not even in the balmy days of 1934 had I ever seen them so plentiful. On the line down to Birch River which took a day to run I would always pick up from two to six lynx. At one place where three cutlines met, two miles out on the main line I could always expect to catch one. The Birch River line I named 'Lynx Avenue', the three line junction I called 'Kitty Kat Korners'. There were one too many corners to call it simply Kitty Korners. And out on top of the ridge where the cutline wound in curves through thick willows and jackpine, was obviously 'Tom Cat Road.'

As was to be expected my old 'pals' the timber wolves appeared and made more trips over my lines than I did. This was the year they killed and ate a black bear on my line, which I recounted in *NAHANNI*. During the winter the wolves killed and ate from my traps twenty-five lynx, one fox and several marten. I suppose I should not complain as they left me 215 pelts all told, that winter, including 115 lynx. I set out twenty-four double spring No. 4 Victor traps for them as cleverly as I could, but nary a one did I nip in those big traps. But on two different occasions one got caught in a No. 2 trap set for lynx. The first one was held for about fifteen minutes as he sat down and chewed the trap into bits of steel; then took off along the cutline in a straight shot, not stopping to zig and zag and trickle here and there as they usually do. I hope he had something to think about with a sore mouth and broken teeth, besides eating the fur out of my traps. The next one was caught on top of the ridge, again in a lynx set. He dragged the toggle for over a mile before becoming caught up in a spruce thicket. From observing the tracks I think his friends came and chewed off the toggle and he got away with the trap on his foot. They all took off in a southerly direction and I presume they decided to visit Alfred Thomas and his trapline.

Most of my flying friends in the north thought it was a bit droll for me to be using an aircraft to assist me in my trapping activities. I would point out that in no way was I setting a precedent. There was at least one other man who had used an aircraft for this purpose for thirty years, dating from the 1930's. This was George C.F. Dalziel of Watson Lake, Yukon Territory. As a young man he had trapped only with a packsack and packdogs in the Yukon and the Mackenzie mountains. One winter I know of he left Lower Post (near the present town of Watson Lake) on the upper Liard River on snowshoes, with packdogs. He trapped marten all winter and came out in late March at Fort Norman on the Mackenzie. He has to be the toughest man I ever knew. When Stan MacMillan was flying into MacMillan Lake on the pseudo gold rush of 1934, Dalziel was already there, having walked over from the Yukon. Those who saw him then said he was travelling light with but a canvas tarpaulin and one blanket, food, rifle and axe. Soon after this with the proceeds of his fur catch he took flying lessons and bought a Curtiss Robin airplane. With this aircraft equipped with skis Dal operated for many years in the Yukon and the Mackenzie mountains. He would base wherever he could land and set out marten traps on snowshoes. Albert Faille told me he often ran into Dalziel in the most isolated mountain valleys. After World War Two he owned and operated B.C. Yukon Flying Services at Watson Lake. He still flies a Beaver and on it is written, 'Eat Moose meat. Ten thousand wolves can't be wrong'. A typical trapper's viewpoint.

He has the most complete and fantastic collection of Big Game trophies at his house in Watson Lake that you would ever hope to see. There are full mounts, head mounts and half mounts of everything from a Himalayan mountain sheep to a polar bear. He had some record trophies including one of the largest Dall Sheep heads ever taken.

I did not do a beaver hunt that spring, and the total land fur catch amounted to 215 pelts. I took the pelts home frozen and Vera stretched and dried most of them. I had made ten lynx stretchers, six marten stretchers and three mink boards. Stretching and drying the pelt entails much work as they must be turned on the stretcher when half dry, and when turned fur side out will finish drying in two or three days.

There were some wolverine on the trapline that winter and I caught three of them. Not once did they kill or eat a lynx or a marten out of my traps.

If I remember correctly we sold the fur at the fur auction sales in Regina and Edmonton for an average of twenty-two dollars, much less than we had expected to get.

I still thought the price of fur would go much higher and I set out the line again the following winter. The wolves ate about twenty pelts and I was able to bring home 125 lynx.

This time the average price was thirty-three dollars, and I was at last convinced that fur would never go up, and I sold my traps and shut down the trapping operation for good.

Vera's prediction came true. As soon as we quit trapping the price of lynx went to an average of a hundred dollars. C'est la vie.

18

Northern Development

Up to the late 1960's I had always maintained that the vast areas of muskeg and permafrost would make it next to impossible to construct roads in the Northwest Territories. How wrong I was. One fall I flew into Fort Simpson and there was the road right to the edge of the river across from the airport. The road was soft in places to be sure and difficult for cars that first fall. A year later the road from Hay River to Simpson was a pleasure to behold. The crushed gravel surface made it, aside from dust problems, as nice to drive as a hard surface. Then came the Prime Minister's announcement that the Mackenzie Highway would be continued on down the Mackenzie River to the Arctic coast.

Fort Simpson was to be one of the main supply centers for the survey and construction camps. The news of this forthcoming development coincided with our decision to sell our property at Nahanni Butte and move out. And why not to Fort Simpson where we had started from forty years ago? With the exciting developments taking place in the north there would be oil and drilling companies, caterers and contractors operating from their offices in the south. They would need someone in the field to act as their agent and to transport their goods. Vera and I would move to Simpson, establish an office, buy some vehicles and advertise an expediting business. We would call it Turner Expediting.

This move would mean leaving our log cabin with its many memories and ties that held us to the old days. The children were grown and gone but the shelves were lined with their books. Toys and dolls were stashed away in boxes. Picture albums showed the children as babies, there were snaps of dog teams and our old cabins at Netla and the Long Reach and our first boat and barge. In Martha's room she had two white dishes cached away from the set I had bought for Vera for two dollars, before we were married. The memories must be left behind some day and the longer we left it, the harder it would be to make the break.

It was hardest for Vera to leave the cabin at Nahanni. Her roots were there. This beautiful log house contained a part of the smaller cabins we had built when we were young. From each of them we had brought not only household items but with them the memories of hardship, privation, joy and love that culminated at our house at Nahanni. It was almost as hard for me to leave. A sadness seemed to rip through my heart as we gathered our things to leave the cabin. And I was sad too to be leaving the Nahanni, with its treasures still hidden in the silent hills and valleys. Along with Albert Faille I would add my name to those whom the mysterious and jealous gods had failed to divulge their treasure. And insult of insults I would have to part with my little blue bird CF-UAH. It would not be needed now. In Simpson there were roads, telephones and regular air service. The funds from the sale of UAH would go to buy trucks for the expediting business.

The break was made and when Vera got into the airplane for the flight to Simpson she tearfully exclaimed, "I don't want to ever come back. I don't want to ever see my cabin again. I want to remember it as it is, for ever."

At Fort Simpson our new life began. Stan and I had landed here as boys after a canoe trip of 800 miles from Waterways; fresh from the city and never dreaming we would end up here forty years later. Vera had first seen it as a small trading post thirty-seven years before. Now it was a bustling little town which surely had a bright future and might soon be a thriving northern city.

Stan too had been pulled back to our starting point. He and Kay had moved in from Fort Smith in the early summer and had bought a thriving retail grocery business. We laughed at the peculiarity of fate which seemed determined that we both should end up in Fort Simpson. I must write something on "How to go from trapper to business man in forty easy yearly lessons."

Besides merchandising Stan went into raw fur buying. Now the snowshoe was in a different drift; instead of selling lynx pelts he was buying them. He was handling dynamite, for lynx had gone to a hundred dollars and more. In laying out thousands of dollars in cash, a sudden drop in price at the fur auction sales could leave him holding an empty bag. But lynx went up and up and four years later Stan came out of it unscathed.

Over in the expediting corner of the town Vera and I exchanged our dog team, axe and rifle, for trucks, telephone and Telex machine. Now we were slaves to the telephone. When some customer phoned from Calgary at midnight, I would say to Vera, "Who the hell is calling now? Why can't they let a man sleep? We have freight coming in tomorrow and two trips to make to the bush." Then I would pick up the phone and say, "Hello, yes Charlie, how are you Charlie? Yes, just a minute while I get a pencil; OK, go ahead. Sure, Charlie, will do. Yes those six drill bits that were to go out Wednesday, and whatever freight is here, no problem Charlie. Sure, I can get away by six o'clock and should be at the rig by ten. Sure thing, no trouble at all, Charlie, we'll get right after it." And hang up.

Vera always said how amusing it was to hear my voice change to being so pleasant when talking to my customers. And I would reply, "If they have the money, honey, I have the time. They always pay well and it's up to us to deliver, morning, noon or night."

My strategy paid off. By next winter I had Don driving for me as well as a third man. We had a girl in the office eight hours a day and Vera answering the phone when I was away driving. All our trips were on the winter roads to bush camps such as Department of Public Works, Seismic camps and oil rigs, some as far as 200 miles north.

When the ice crossings went out of the big rivers in April, most activity came to a shuddering halt and we were able to catch up on half a winter's lost sleep.

As early as the spring of 1973 I could see that some changes were taking place affecting our anticipated 'boom'. Due to a variety of causes both political and economical the construction of the Mackenzie Highway and projected gas pipeline were being slowly abandoned. The native organizations were quickly adopting the white man's ways in that they were out to get all they could while the getting was good and wanting a settlement of their land claims before the construction of the pipeline.

'Ecology' too was on a big 'kick' in the Northwest Territories; Environment Canada was sending in hundreds of young people from universities to see that we northerners did not pollute and destroy our land. The Department of Water Resources was sending men to outlying areas with airplanes and helicopters measuring and recording the flow of waters in many northern streams. They were gathering information and establishing complicated graphs with lines going up and down and crossways which were supposed to indicate the average volume of flow in cubic feet per second, the time of year of least flow and the time and volume of flood levels. From this information the university educated engineers would know for instance what type of bridge to construct over the northern rivers. And here is the way it turned out.

A bridge was to be built over a northern river to service a gas field nearby. Engineers came in to look over the proposed site. They measured this and they measured that, and bored into the soil at the bottom and sides of the stream. They presumably added all this to the mountain of data that had been collected over the years regarding the volume of water and the height of flood level. Then they set about designing a bridge over this innocent looking stream. Eventually a fine solid bridge was constructed, well above high water, with supporting pilings every hundred feet or so.

When the bridge was completed many oldtimers looked and shook their heads in disbelief and amazement. The bridge was reported to have cost three hundred thousand dollars, and we knew it could not last for long; it was a matter of time that was all. I think that the first summer the Highway people saw where the mistake had been made. During the normal flood period of July, driftwood started to jam up on the pilings. A tug was hired to pull the trees loose as one tree tended to catch any others that went by. This worked fine and soon the flood subsided and all was again well.

The following year the flood was delayed for some time. And then one day it came. The river rose at the rate of six inches an hour and at night a murmuring swirl of speeding waters could be heard that rose to a deep throated roar of a distant avalanche. The water became almost black with silt, sand, muddy foam and small sticks. It started to heave and groan with increasing speed as the headwater mountain streams each poured their roaring spouts into the confines of this one river bed. The driftwood increased from small branches and sticks to logs and trees lifted from sandbars and others torn from the banks by the raging waters. There were cottonwood trees three feet through, jammed together with green spruce of tremendous size. By morning it was too late to take remedial action. The massive trees were piling against the bridge and blocking the flow of the flood waters until the bridge was in effect acting as a dam. Soon the whole massive structure came tumbling down in a twisted mass of wood and steel. It was ground into the bottom of the river and half buried in the sand and silt. Now who was spoiling the ecology? Now who was wasting the tax-payers' money with expensive consultant and engineering fees? Any old Indian for the price of a bottle of whisky could have informed the builders of the bridge of the rare floods on all northern rivers that can carry whole islands of driftwood with them that only a well-designed concrete pier can withstand.

The Federal Fisheries people were on a northern 'kick' at this time too. They had young people travelling up and down the Mackenzie River in expensive high speed boats, and using helicopters at two and three hundred dollars an hour to get to the more distant lakes and rivers. They would net fish in small creeks, tag them and let them go, hoping perhaps to catch them the following year to see if they had migrated upstream, or downstream or had stayed in the same place. Leo Norwegian of Fort Simpson told me of a case where he had seen a very small fish struggling through the grass and willows dragging a large metal tag half his size, that was continually impeding his progress. The old bush Indians know more about the spawning fields, range and life habits of lake trout, whitefish, northern pike and ling cod than kids fresh from southern schools will ever know. But it apparently would never do to solicit information on subjects relevant to the north from northern residents for it would lower the dignity of so-called academics and save the taxpayers' money. I have seen six southern youngsters who were employed by the Federal Department of Fisheries sitting in a heated Government vehicle one cool day in September, on the bank of the Mackenzie River in Fort Simpson, observing with binoculars the placid surface of the river. I was given to understand that they were counting the birds that happened by, mostly ravens and gulls, and tabulating the bits of flotsam and jetsam seen floating on the river, and noting carefully in which direction the river flowed, north, east, south or west. The information thus gathered must I assume be of great benefit to the Fisheries people and could not possibly be procured from northern residents.

If these young men had driven their vehicle about a mile down stream they could have observed a phenomenon which would have been worthy of their energies and might have noted a factor that was far more likely to influence the present and future supply of fish in the Mackenzie River, than bird droppings and bits of sticks seen floating in the river. If their eyes did not tell them their noses would, that here, raw sewage was entering the river, directly from the sewer pipes of Fort Simpson.

It is a fact that for several years we had noticed a marked decrease in the amount of blue-fish (grayling) being caught in sport fly fishing in the Mackenzie River. It seemed obvious to residents such as myself that the dumping of raw sewage from the settlements into the river, coupled with the increased traffic of diesel tugs and oil barges on the river might be a prime factor in the lessening supply of fish. Possibly to placate and pacify critics of the pollution of the Mackenzie River a regulation came into force compelling the tugs operating on the Mackenzie to save their sewage in a holding tank and empty it when they came into port. When I was a member of the village council of Fort Simpson I put a question concerning this matter to the Chairman of the Council and was informed that the said regulation was indeed in force, and that the tugs would pull into Simpson and pump sewage from their holding tank directly into our sewage line in Fort Simpson which ran directly into the Mackenzie River. Big Deal! Who was fooling who? Was it the fish or was it the taxpayer being fooled? Or was it the Government creating regulations for regulations sake?

Our village council here tried to raise the money from the Federal Government to build a sewage lagoon which would purify the effluent before it entered the Mackenzie River, but we didn't get to first base. But helicopters at $ 250 per hour still fly environment personnel around on what I term as joy rides.

It has been said that ours is a civilized society, and judging from the back-handed way in which we attempt to attain our objectives it often seems as if ours is the antithesis of a civilized and enlightened society. Instead of doing something constructive to prevent environmental damage to our country, we pass senseless legislation, establish a bureaucracy of legions of busy, well-meaning, ill-informed people, dashing around on paid holidays, then hope the problem will go away.

On the first few miles of the Mackenzie Highway north of Fort Simpson, a temporary bridge was constructed across a small river. Our council was told that the environment people were raising hell because the vehicles crossing the bridge were spilling sand and dirt from the wheels and chassis of the vehicles onto the ice below. With eyes wide in disbelief and wonder we heard that the sand and soil falling from the vehicles would kill fish in the stream below. For thousands of years before we were invaded by these do-gooder know-it-alls, northern streams have carried literally thousands of tons of gravel, sand, soil and trees in their flood waters and dumped their load into the Mackenzie each year; the sun still shone, the waters flowed and the fish survived quite well. Now we are informed that a few pounds of dust from the road will kill the fish. Phooey!

As we heard this, I felt then that we were in room 101 of the building in George Orwell's *1984*, where people who contradicted the authorities were 'treated' until they were convinced that two plus two equalled one.

Starting north from Fort Simpson on the Mackenzie Highway, Environment Canada was going to make the road to Inuvik a joy and beauty forever: the sides of the cleared right-of-way as it wound in gentle curves through the hills and valleys they said was much too drab and uninteresting for future tourists. So to add more aesthetic value to the scenery, at intervals of every two or three miles the small bushes and trees were removed in an area comprising about half an acre at each site. The Project Manager for Hire North said the cost of clearing each and every one of these sites was about $ 2,000.00. The workers cut and carried out to the right-of-way each stick, without disturbing the moss or leaves upon the ground. Unbelievable? Yes, but true. John Goodall Jr. was the foreman in charge of the crews clearing these 'beauty spots' and he told me that in one instance he was instructed to, quote: "Clear all the underbrush and other trees out and leave only those eleven spruce trees." Unquote.

John replied, "There are nine spruce trees there, the other two are tamrack trees."

"Oh. Well in that case cut out the spruce and leave the tamrack." And this was done.

When my camp was clearing the right-of-way for the Highway north of Fort Wrigley, I was employed by Hire North, under the jurisdiction of the Federal Department of Indian Affairs and Northern Development. Our clearing operations had to conform to regulations laid down by Environment Canada. In the course of our duties there were many creeks and rivers to be crossed including little trickles of a foot or two in width that had water in them only during the run-off periods in the spring. Many of these creeks had banks of from two to ten feet high and had to be crossed with our trucks and Caterpillar tractors etc. Our camps had to be supplied with many tons of fuel, food etc. and the men had to travel back and forth to work, consequently we needed a tote road for the vehicles. The depressions of the creek beds had to be filled in and we were not allowed to use any material except snow for the fill. In very rare cases we were allowed to use logs that had been trimmed of all branches. All of these fills whether of snow or not had to be removed each spring before the run-off. Spruce needles would kill the fish we were informed, thus the ban on using trees with branches for fill. And there would be all sorts of terrifying results from the damming of the spring waters if the snow fills were not removed! I had to assume that the snow in the fills must have had some special quality which would inhibit them from melting in the heat of the sun as the surrounding ice and snow did. This would dam up the creeks which would then rise to the tops of the mountains. At this elevation the air would be cool, the dammed waters would freeze and perhaps another glacial age would be brought on. We workers would then freeze to death and there would be no one left to pay the salaries of environmentalists. Heaven forbid. Not wishing to be instrumental in causing a catastrophe of such alarming proportions, more in sorrow than in anger, each spring I gave instructions to have the snow-fills removed. After all my workers and I had only lived here for forty years. It was only our home. What would we know of snow and ice and creeks and rivers and fish and game?

By 1973 the oil companies were becoming fed up to the gills with the very great extra and needless expense they were put to in conforming to the environmental regulations and to the harrassment. They simply shut down their operations and pulled out.

One oil company executive said to me, "Do they take us for fools? We know as well as anyone that there have been mistakes made in the past. We are more than willing to conform to any and all sensible land use regulations. Our children too will inherit what we leave them. But, by God, enough is enough and we will no longer submit to this foolishness."

"We northerners feel exactly the same as you do," I replied. "I cannot understand the thinking of the authorities on this matter."

Certainly the concept of environmental control in many

parts of our country was long overdue. But like the French Revolution when it did take place, in some cases we went to the opposite extreme. Greed can and does often blind people to some extent but it is useless for a Government to assume their citizens are all ignorant and selfish and with self assumed righteous indignation to blindly impose regulations which are impractical. The harm is twofold: it is firstly a collosal waste of money and manpower, and secondly it tends to destroy people's faith in a true concept of sensible environmental control.

I believe that the money spent on some of the more senseless environmental programs in the Northwest Territories, could, in five years time have built a Sewage Lagoon in each of the principal settlements along the Mackenzie River which would bring the waters back to an acceptable level of pollution and re-establish the fish and bird life of the area.

With the oil companies pulling out of the north, the need for our business came to an end, and I was able to devote my thoughts again to the Nahanni. Fort Simpson gradually began to regress; small business moved out; the operation of Hire North was cut to a minimum and hundreds of native who had been employed had jobs denied them and some were forced back on welfare.

19

Courting Hunters and Courting Hunted

In May of 1973 Don flew in to Fort Simpson with his Super Cub CF-LKL, with the request, "Dad, do you want to fly a Super Cub for me this summer? I have a lot of hunters coming in and I'm renting JMI from Bob McBride and I need a pilot to fly it."

"You'd better believe I'd like to fly it. Have you got the big wheels for it?"

"Oh, yes, and I think I'll put on the 42x82 inch prop. I find that the low pitch gives better performance on take-off in the mountains."

"Does it cut down the cruising speed much?"

"Surprisingly I get about the same cruising speed as I did with the coarser pitch."

"OK, you had better put me on the insurance policy for both LKL and JMI. It will be like old times, JMI is the plane I borrowed from Art Gordon when we lived at Nahanni."

And so it was arranged. Early in July I flew JMI to Don's hunting headquarters at Nahanni Butte, and we got set up to fly Don's hunters into his bush camps. Both aircraft were equipped with 24 inch low pressure tires which facilitated landing on rough ground. Don had a mountain plateau for a landing strip at one camp, a 1000 foot strip of cutline at another and a couple of old abandoned oil exploration bush strips. There were no landing strips of any kind in my prospecting area 200 miles north, so I would have to put prospecting out of my mind for this summer anyway. But that didn't mean I couldn't look back into the distant white peaks and dream of tramping those high alpine valleys in search of riches.

Before the season opened for Dall sheep and grizzlies, camps must be set up and guides taken out in preparation for the arrival of the first hunters, who were picked up off the jets and brought to Nahanni by a commercial air service. Then one at a time Don and I flew them out with the Super Cubs to the bush camps. Two weeks later, when their hunt was over they were brought back. Don gave me mostly the easy trips and took the most difficult ones himself.

Occasionally our flights would be delayed because of rain and fog especially when clouds lay low in the hills. This was not a matter of much concern; if you couldn't see, you couldn't go, it was as simple as that. But if the wind blew that was a different matter. If the wind was light, there was no problem, but if the black clouds were forming over the mountain front and the main lodge shook with the gusts of wind and the trees in the yard were bent double then you made sure the airplane was tied down securely and went back to bed or whatever.

The west winds were the bad ones. North winds brought rain and snow with the wind velocity being consistent. While the Chinook winds during the day were often violent, toward sundown they would decrease enough to allow us to get into the hills. Sometimes we would give it a try and if the wing struts started to snap and your teeth came loose then it was time to turn around and try again later. Most of the landing places were narrow and rough and all too short. An error in landing induced by a gust of wind could mean damaging the aircraft even if there was little danger of injury to the pilot or passengers. The whole hunting operation was dependent on the continued functioning of the two Super Cubs. The consideration uppermost in my mind at all times was NOT TO BEND THE AIRCRAFT.

One day when we both had hunters to bring out of the mountains the Chinook raged all day. By nightfall it had eased and the trees were moving gently but there was still a roar in the Butte. This mountain rose up across the river to a height of 5000 feet and caught the upper winds when all was quiet below.

Don said, "Let's give it a try. I'll go to the Blue Lakes and you to the Kotaneelee. And make sure you turn back if you don't like the look of it."

I lifted off and headed south to gain altitude until I was well above the peaks before going over the two ranges and down into the valley. I was well above the first range at 7000 feet when I crossed the peaks. The turbulence was mild and I thought, "The wind must be down, there should be no problem in getting to the camp tonight."

On approaching the last range I started to make my let-down and what a mistake that was! I was just level with the tops of the hills at 5500 feet when the airplane dropped out from beneath me and my left hand which had been resting on the throttle flew to the top of the cockpit receiving a cut across the back on a projecting piece of metal. Then back up we went just as fast with one wing behaving as if it had been tied to the ground. Right then I lost all desire to land at the Kotaneelee that night; what I wanted to do right then was to get the hell out of there and back to the lowlands. By the time I got turned and headed east the altimeter was unwinding and the plane was flipping around like a drunken rooster in a wind tunnel. "If the wind wants to take me down, all right, we'll go down," I thought and dumped the stick ahead until we were over the main Kotaneelee at tree top level. Here the airplane allowed itself to be coaxed into a more conventional flying attitude and I took the pass into Fisherman's Lake and out over the Liard, landing on the airstrip there.

The next morning the sky had cleared off and all was still. I approached the airstrip at Kotaneelee this time from a great height, spiralling down to check the wind socks. They were both stretched out and pointing due east, and there were little vertical columns of dust crossing the strip from west to east. "This had to be the only place in the whole blessed country the wind is blowing this morning," I thought. "But I'm not going back now, I'll put it on tail high and keep the power on to control direction."

I made the approach from the north and let the airspeed drop off well back. When I was very low I poured on the coal for a tail up landing. I could now see that it wasn't going to be that easy. I was drifting to the left at an alarming rate and to stay lined up with the airstrip I was pointed more west than south. I waited until the last possible second then straightened out, chopped the power and braked to a stop.

The guides were there with the hunter who was ready to go. "Good morning Dick," the hunter said.

"What the hell's good about it?" I snarled.

"At my age, every morning is a good morning," he replied smilingly.

"You're probably right, but I've seen better."

"You know, I haven't been around small planes that much, but that is the first time I have ever seen a plane land sideways."

I was going to say, "Oh, I always land like that, or backwards," but I didn't. He was a nice guy and meant no harm. He didn't know that pilots are often irascible.

While the sheep horns and cape, bedroll, packsack and rifles were being loaded into the aircraft, I sat and puffed on a cigar for a few minutes to let the nicotine re-strengthen me.

At Nahanni, Don was back with his hunter and he too had waited until morning to get into the hills. He said that he had not been worried when I hadn't shown up the previous night as he knew I would not bend the airplane. And the season ended with not a scratch on either LKL or JMI.

That summer at the lodge at Nahanni Butte, Don's cook was a beautiful girl named Martha McLeod. Her husband Mac, guided for Don. Mac was the guide at the Kotaneelee camp when I landed there sideways. Today Vera and I count Mac and Martha among our very dear friends, and I think it possibly all started when Mac failed to comment on my landing that windy day.

Martha's culinary qualifications, her pleasing personality, and her visual attributes made the camp a pleasant place. There was also an American girl staying in a cabin close by who was studying the local Indian population for her thesis in anthropology. Her name was Holly and she also was a very pleasant addition to the scenery. As if this was not enough there was a young man and his wife staying in the school residence for the summer. They were Brian and Sandy Gallup. Brian was a Social Worker for the Dept. of I. A. & N. D. Sandy has to be the most gorgeous blond that ever was created.

One day I was sitting in the cabin kibitzing with the three girls when some of Don's hunters came in for coffee. They could hardly take their eyes off the three girls to glace at the old trapper with white whiskers. When the hunters went to go home a week later they asked me, "Turner, how do you succeed in surrounding yourself with beautiful women all the time?"

"It is a habit I have had all my life," I answered. "Besides I'm young, handsome, have a charming personality, and am suave and debonair." (Only I pronounced it *salve* and *debohner*.)

The groans were unbearable. "Well, you asked me a question and I gave you an honest answer."

Brian Gallup and I inevitably got into lengthy discussions about the problems of young people in our society: those in the north and especially young natives. Brian was all fired up and attacking his job with a great deal of enthusiasm.

In Fort Simpson that fall Brian was established as the Welfare and Probation Officer. He settled into his job with determination to help the young people of Fort Simpson over some of the problems they were encountering.

As it is in this world, among all the people whom you meet and like, there are a few who are what Anne of Green Gables called 'kindred souls'. Brian and Sandy Gallup were of these and Vera and I visited much with them.

In talking with Brian about Nahanni Butte village, the river, the fascination and beauty of the mountains with the mineral wealth that lay hidden and untapped in the vast wilderness, I deplored the fact that in my ignorance I had perhaps walked over promising mineral occurrences without knowing it. "If only I had a better knowledge of geology," I lamented, "I would be rich by now."

"My father is a geologist," Brian volunteered. "Why don't

you get together? It might be mutually advantageous."

"Tell me about him."

"He lives in Calgary, and had been involved in the oil development of Alberta since the early days of Turner Valley. He has also done considerable work in the Mackenzie River area."

"I'm interested in hard rock geology and your father's interest has been with the sediments, but for all that he has probably forgotten more about general geology than I can ever hope to know. Sounds like a good idea."

"He and Lena, his second wife, are coming up for a visit this fall and I'll bring them up to your house."

Thus began a relationship that was finally to result in the discovery of a promising body of ore. The glittering metal did not rear up out of the bowels of the earth and with a blare of trumpets proclaim its whereabouts to us as we flew with searching eyes up and down the alpine valleys and over the endless rock ridges searching for gossans and contact zones. There were many intervening months of effort in raising money for exploration work; many hours of mountain flying when I lost some weight through concern and apprehension. (My male ego restrains me from using the word 'fear'.) Some pedantic son of a gun suggested I was suffering from ergophobia. A month later I found it meant a 'fear of work'.

Fear of work or not there were many hills to be climbed, and many rock and soil samples to be taken. Where I least suspected it, suddenly there it was. Don and I had tramped over it years before as its secret lay hidden in the ground. But we had to wait for a certain day that was yet to come.

One day in Simpson, Brian said to me, "Dick, another Justice of the Peace is needed here in Fort Simpson, if you were asked, would you take the job?"

"I've never thought about it Brian, I've no training for the job and I just don't know."

"J.P.s handle a lot of cases where young people are concerned," Brian continued, "and I thought that we might be able to work together to straighten up some of these kids and keep them out of jail."

"I know what you mean. There is a growing problem with alcohol and young people in our towns, and there is a need for cooperation between the R.C.M.P., the lower courts, your department and concerned citizens: a need to do everything in our power to direct youngsters who are in trouble into some other channel than jail."

"They are often caught in a web of petty infractions, not always of their own making that will lead to their destruction," Brian said, "unless some of us take a hand in helping them."

"Brian, I'll at least say this, if I am approached by the Department of Public Services, for an appointment as a Justice of the Peace, I will give it serious attention."

Corporal Blaine Price of the R.C.M.P. and I later had further discussion on the matter and I said I would agree.

Later that month my appointment arrived from the Dept. of Public Services, signed by Commissioner Hodgson.

My preparation for the job consisted of taking the oath of office, receiving a copy of the Criminal Code along with the Liquor Ordinance and the Vehicle Ordinance of the Northwest Territories, literature on court procedure and a listing of the details of the last year's lower courts' decisions in the N.W.T. that had been appealed to the higher courts.

I knew beforehand that a Justice of the Peace court had jurisdiction to try only those cases designated in the Criminal Code under Summary Convictions, where the greatest penalty was 500 dollars fine and 6 months in jail or both. I found that the majority of cases I would be sitting on would be impaired driving, assault, and offences under the Liquor Ordinance.

First I sat in as an observer at several court sessions held by other J.P.s. Then I went to Yellowknife and sat in on a court session presided over by Magistrate Smith. Then I had a long talk with Mr. Smith about my future work as a J.P. "This is going to be a serious business," I thought. "I'm sure as hell not going to send anyone to jail unless there is no way out." But I kept my thoughts to myself.

On my first session in court, under the gun, I was as nervous as a bridegroom on his wedding night, with not quite the same anticipations. My biggest worry was having to make a fairly quick decision on the merits of the evidence presented. The court never at any time had any knowledge of who would appear in court or on what charges.

Everyone would take their place, the court would be called to order, and the first accused person on the docket would be called. The charge was laid (usually though not always by the R.C.M.P.), a plea of guilty or not guilty was taken, then the evidence and counter evidence was presented. I was given the number of convictions of the accused for the past five years. I often thought in many cases before me, "Here but for the grace of God, go I." But the Criminal Code was there, for all of us, and if guilt was established beyond a reasonable doubt, then a penalty must be handed down. With young people charged under the Liquor Ordinance, a suspended sentence could be considered, and a period of probation given. I was a little surprised to find that many of those charged often had almost regular appearances in court, perhaps two to six convictions in the last year or so.

Before a verdict was given a report from the probation officer would be useful in determining what effect a period of probation was likely to have on a specific individual. In my first case, I thought, "Good, this will serve two purposes, it will give information I would like to have about the accused and it will give me time to consider the verdict." So I called for a report from the probation officer. Except there was now no probation officer; he had been transferred and there was no replacement as yet. Oh, fine. Great help Irvin. Now what the hell do I do? No use in looking around for help in making a decision. There were others waiting their turn. The girl was guilty, in all justice what penalty should be handed down? She was standing there waiting for the blow to fall. I could not see that a jail sentence was warranted; there was only one way she could get the money for a fine, and I couldn't see myself contributing toward that, so, it would be one month's suspended sentence and a month on probation. It wasn't my fault or her fault that the government was short one probation officer. They should damn well have one.

One of the few areas where I was inclined to be tough was in impaired driving charges where the accused was an adult. If guilt was established, I laid it on as heavy as I could, keeping in mind that heavy fines had been successfully appealed to the higher courts, and had been reduced. Other J.P.s were handing out 250 and 300 dollar fines. I handed out

400 dollar fines and prohibited the offender from driving for a month or more.

I will admit that with girls charged under the Liquor Ordinance I was soft. These 'children' as I termed them had often been influenced by older people into partaking of alcohol. I could not see that they were bad, in any sense of the word. What good would it do these kids, or society to send them to jail for 30 days or 60 days?

Regarding fines: there was a policy that I believe all courts adhered to, and that was to always give time to pay. There would be an exceptional case come up occasionally where the court felt an immediate payment was called for.

If the accused was found guilty and a fine was adjudicated, the question was usually asked,

"Have you a job? How much are you making?"

"I'm working for Joe Blow," was the reply. (Or D.P.W. or Dene Mat, or whoever) and I get such and such a month."

"Will you be able to pay this fine within thirty days, or will you require more time?"

When the time factor was agreed to, I would say, "Then you must pay this full amount no later than thirty days from now. But if you experience real difficulty in making payment within the specified time, you must get in touch with me and I will extend the time for payment. If you do not pay on time and do NOT contact me, the R.C.M.P. will pick you up and you could be facing an additional charge."

With the court bending over backwards to accommodate these individuals it was surprising and it made me furious to find that on occasion some did not pay on time and did not approach me for an extension. Later I would get a warrant in the mail from the Court Services in Yellowknife to sign and deliver to the R.C.M.P. for action. On the appearance of the warrant the money would miraculously appear. I consider the police were very lenient on this type of delinquency. But I guess they felt the same as I would; what the hell good would it do to lay a charge for being a few days late in paying a fine?

As a J.P. carrying out his duties, I was involved to some extent with the R.C.M.P. in having to discuss related court matters. I would often have occasion to go to their office with a warrant for them to serve, or they would come to my residence with papers to sign. I considered it my duty to let it be known, without having to say so directly, that any and all decisions made in my court were mine and mine alone, and were in no way influenced by the police except by direct evidence given in court under oath. I think I succeeded in this. I have good reason to believe that the R.C.M.P. were as concerned as I was that the court must make a completely independent adjudication.

In some cases the apprehending of men and women under the influence of alcohol must be one of the most difficult and disagreeable tasks that a policeman has to face. I am constantly amazed at the self control that the members of the R.C.M.P. exhibit in the face of exceptionally rude behavior.

There were three Justices of the Peace in Fort Simpson while I was there and we could take turns holding court, week and week about. Dick Kushko one week, Jim Cumming the next and me the week following. We were all concerned with upgrading ourselves and learning all we could to enable us to function in an informed and humane manner. We supported the program of holding yearly seminars at Yellowknife, and when one was held in March we gladly went.

In the course of many discussions we had and lectures we were given by different experts concerned with the law, I learned much which was of great benefit in carrying out my duties as a Justice of the Peace. For instance, Justice Davey Fulton of the Supreme Court of British Columbia, told us that as Justices of the Peace we were often able to dispense justice, whereas he as a judge must be concerned primarily with law. I felt that this was a vindication of some decisions of mine where I had avoided handing down jail sentences, when perhaps strictly speaking, the law called for such.

Another enlightening comment from a senior probation officer was to the effect that jail sentences of under a year were pretty well useless as far as rehabilitation was concerned: as the services provided to get people back on the right track were often ineffective over short periods of time. I had rather suspected this.

In all directions which we received from officials at our conference I heard nothing to contradict my basic philosophy on crime: which is that incorrigible people must be confined where they cannot harm society, but that a helping hand should be extended to those who run afoul of the law through weakness or misfortune, when there is any hope for them at all.

I know as well as anyone that in our society we must have laws and regulations and penalties for those who break them. But I also believe that an ounce of prevention is more effective than a pound of cure. In part, the answer must be in keeping young people out of court if at all possible. Was there any way I could in my capacity as a Justice of the Peace help in some small way to bring this about? I could but try.

Any fool could sit and hand out fines and jail terms to the weak, the poor and unfortunate who appeared before them, and go home in a self righteous frame of mind thinking that the law had been upheld and that justice was done.

My basic philosophy was to temper justice with reason (keeping in mind our peculiar problems in the North), and always to maintain close contact with the R.C.M.P. and probation officers such as Brian Gallup. This is not a soft-headed philosophy. Cold scientific reasoning indicates that we are indeed 'our Brother's Keeper'.

20

The Quest I

It turned out that Brian's father, Bill Gallup had done field geology in the Mackenzie Mountain area as well as the Barren Lands and the Fort McMurray tar sands. I told him of the various prospects and leads I knew of in the Nahanni area and showed him samples of stuff I had picked up over the years. The upshot was that we entered into an arrangement whereby we would try to raise some capital and carry out a mineral expedition program in the summer months of the coming years.

Bill noted that one interesting qualification we had was that our combined ages amounted to 120 years of experience, which should be impressive. However, I said, "I'm not sure my experience of skinning beaver and chewing frozen bannock added to yours of riding bucking horses and killing caribou with an axe on the Barren Lands, would be an inducement for those with capital."

"Turner," he replied, "let's not get too pedantic about this matter. Let's just say we have 120 years' experience and let it go at that."

Between us Bill and I put together a resume with what information we had on prospects in the Nahanni. Bill took this to Calgary to help persuade potential investors to put up some long green for an exploration program.

By March, Bill came up with a deal with the Mineral Section of Imperial Oil Limited. While they could not be talked into investigating our prospects, they did wish us to carry out a summer's geological program for them. They would provide a budget for us to carry out geological, geochemical, and magnetometer work in designated sections of the Northwest Territories and the Yukon. Bill was to superintend the geological work and I would handle the logistics of the campaign. We would need a helicopter with crew, a fixed wing support and two helpers for the geochemical sampling. Bill and I would each be paid a salary with a bonus for anything of value found in certain areas.

I was more than satisfied with the arrangements for the summer as it would be a good start and opened up possibilities for the future.

To begin with we decided that a Cessna 180 or 185 would be suitable for fixed wing support. We would lease one for the summer and I would fly it, thus giving the operation more flexibility having the aircraft with us at all times. I was getting paid twice what I was worth, plus a chance of a bonus. And being a confirmed optimist I thought that if we had a successful season's operation we might talk the company into doing some exploration work in our own areas the following summer.

Most of the arrangements were made by the end of April and we planned to start work in a high mountain region near Summit Lake in the Yukon. We thought July 1st would be time enough to get started as the snow would be late in going at the altitude of 5000 and 6000 feet.

Before we started on the Imperial Oil Ltd. project in July, I wanted to go to MacMillan Lake and stake some claims on three creeks that had been staked for placer gold in 1934. Bill had done a geological investigation of the area and with the aid of air photos, had found several locations suitable for staking. These creeks were at a low elevation and I could go in by helicopter in May and have the job done in three weeks. This would give Gallup and Turner something tangible to start with and we would call ourselves "NAHANNI PLACERS".

It would be a lot of work cutting lines for the staking of the claims and would also entail considerable back packing. I would need someone to help me and who was I to get? Someone preferably with a strong back. Immediately my youngest son came to mind. Rolf by now had his Ph.D. in Math and was doing research work at the University of Alberta. He said yes, he would come as he knew his Dad could not be trusted alone in the hills anymore and would need supervision in finding the way back to camp and in lighting a campfire. He hoped that I did NOT plan on killing any animals as he had had quite enough of that thank you when he went on a beaver hunt with me when he was twelve years old. I said the work would offer no challenge in his chosen field of Mathematics, but the food would be good; bannock for instance of the finest quality and all the purest sparkling drinking water he wanted.

We chartered a Hughes 500 helicopter out of Fort Simpson and on May 15 flew into Bennett Creek, leaving a cache of grub at MacMillan Lake on the way in. The nights were still cold in the hills in May so we took along an 8x10 wall tent and a wood burning stove so that we would at least have a comfortable camp.

We planned on staking eight claims on Bennett Creek, which embraced about 400 acres of land. Since the borders of each claim must be straight and well marked this meant cutting over six miles of line through the bush so that the claim borders could be marked with blazes and ribboned sticks. The ground was heavily timbered and had recently been burned over, with many of the trees standing, charred and black. There were some hills and the creek had to be crossed and recrossed on felled trees.

Most of the dry trees were like rock-hard frozen rubber and our axes had to be kept razor sharp. At night we would return to camp covered with burned charcoal from the trees, looking for all the world like two bug eyed coal miners. This brought to mind the recording of, "Beyond the Fringe" and to keep me entertained Rolf would at least once a day recite Peter Cook's soliloquy which started with, "Yes, Oy could have been a judge, but Oy didn't have the Latin for it. Oy didn't have the

Latin for it so I became a miner instead." He did a very good mimicry of the whole blessed thing.

There was some snow left in the bush and the creek had 'overflow' ice built up on the edges so we didn't spend much time in diggin into the gravel and panning for gold. Our claims were on an ancient estuary and if there was placer gold here it would likely be at depth.

After ten days we left our comfortable tent camp to pack the fifteen miles over to MacMillan Lake through the bush. We were carrying heavy packs and it took us two days, climbing up and down hills and pushing through thick brush. From now on we had our meals around a camp fire and slept in a small mosquito proof tent that we carried with us. It was too early in the season for the mosquitos to be plentiful and they bothered us very little. We always had a comfortable sleep at night for Rolf had worked on a survey crew during his student days at the University of Victoria and his boss had been an old trapper, George New, who had shown him how to make a fine soft bed of spruce boughs. Rolf always insisted on taking time and great pains to make a bed of the finest quality; a great amount of spruce bough tips must be cut and with meticulous care laid just so.

McLeod Creek and Grizzly Creek had not burned and consequently the claim staking on them was less work than it had been on Bennett. Our four claims on McLeod Creek were just down stream from Lloyd Tyreman's claims and we visited his abandoned cabin where both Rolf and I had camped at different times several years before. We talked of an episode three years previously.

One afternoon when Lloyd was working the claims half a mile from the cabin, his wife Pat who was resting on the bed after washing and baking heard a noise and looking up saw a grizzly bear climbing in the window. The window was small but the bear already had his head and shoulders inside. The door of the cabin was standing open and the first thing Pat thought of was to jump and close the door and then shoo the bear back out of the window. Lloyd's six-gun was hanging on the wall near the door but she had no time to think of it. The grizzly on discovering he had disturbed the cabin's occupant and noting that she did not have enough meat on her ribs to make a proper meal, or perhaps the window was a mite too small to let him through, decided to withdraw. Hastily extracting himself he beat a retreat into the surrounding woods and was not seen again. If I recall rightly, Lloyd told his wife that one look at her was enough to scare the bear to death. Tony Mokry and I, two years before had dinner with the Tyremans here in the cabin and I don't know what the bear might have thought, but in his place I would have regarded her as a dish of honey.

It was on Lloyd's claims here on McLeod Creek the year before Tony and I came by that I had panned half an ounce of gold from a tub of semi-concentrate from an hour's sluicing. Consequently if anyone asks me if there is any gold on McLeod Creek I can truthfully say, "Yes, there is, I have had half an ounce of gold in a pan."

By June seventh we had four claims staked on McLeod Creek and four on Grizzly Creek and we were ready to go home. The aircraft from Simpson was due to pick us up on the eighth. On that morning we looked out from the tent, a fog lay heavy on the lake.

We had finished breakfast and the fog was still heavy in the air when Rolf announced that the airplane would not be along today, they were always late, so he would go to McLeod Creek and hour's walk away on a good game trail and cut out some staking lines a bit more. He had no sooner spoken when we heard a 'humm' in the distance and soon a 185 came zooming over above the fog. "He sure can't land in this fog," we thought. "He'll probably go back to Simpson and we won't see him again for a week."

But we were wrong. The airplane circled once then went to the northwest in the direction of McLeod Lake. An hour later the fog lifted, we again heard the engine and soon the plane came gliding in, touched down and we waved him into the dock we had made of spruce trees. "Thought you might have forgotten us," I said as the pilot got out of the aircraft.

"No danger of that," he replied. "Your niece Linda works for Arctic Air you know and there is no way she would let us forget about her Uncle Dick."

"Bless her dear sweet soul," I said.

We now had all of June to rest up from back packing and

line cutting. I could sleep in, relax and gain back some weight; or so I thought.

The claims had to be recorded within forty days of staking and when I phoned Peter Cowie to borrow some application forms he replied, "Yes, we have quite a bunch of forms left, but Oh, my, your work is only half done my lad. The filling out of the forms to comply with the mining regulations is more work than staking the claims."

"You're joking Peter."

"You'll see," he replied.

In talking later to Betha, Peter's wife she said, "After staking those claims in the mountains last winter, Peter and John Koopman were about driven to distraction before they had all the forms filled out and the paper work done."

For my part if I ever stake and record any more claims I will hire a bookkeeper, a firm of chartered accountants and a lawyer to do the filing of the claims for me. Maps had to be made showing the location of each claim with the adjacent claims bordering. Forms must be made in triplicate of this and that, the number of your licence on each and every claim filing application form with the information that was written on each post; the hour and minute of staking each claim; how many guests there were at your grandmother's wedding, what she wore (in triplicate) with the hour and minute of the time of the consummation of the marriage properly recorded (in triplicate).

For an old trapper turned prospector, who could hardly spell his own name, it was surely a chore. At last it was done. The days had slipped by and now it was time to go flying again.

Before I left for Prince George to pick up the 185 I knew I should get a 'check-out' by another pilot who was proficient on them. Bill Granley's 185 was in town and he said he would get his pilot Wayne Eng to give me a couple of hours flying time. We made a few touch-and-gos on the Mackenzie then went to a small lake nearby for a couple of landings. The only noticeable difference I found between the 185 and the Maule was that the 185 had more torque and care was needed to keep it from swinging to the left when the tap was opened. I found that on a narrow lake or river, when the water rudders were up, the throttle must be advanced very gently so that the plane would not swing to the left. It was also like the Maule in that it could not be 'horsed' out of the water until it was ready to fly. When sufficient airspeed was attained it would leave the water with a slight back pressure.

It turned out that the aircraft we had leased was at Kamloops and it was there I would have to pick it up. At Fort St. John I persuaded my old friend Hank Kepke, an aircraft engineer to come along with me. At Kamloops Hank spent two days in checking over the aircraft until he was satisfied it was ready for a summer's work.

The registration was CF-RID. Its colors were red, white and blue. It had CAP 3000 floats which were said by some to be inferior to the Edo floats, but I found the 3000 floats quite satisfactory. The 185 had the 300 HP fuel injection Continental engine, good instrumentation and a 300 channel VHF radio.

On the way north from Fort St. John I thought, "Man, is this ever a nice airplane. When I get rich and famous I'm going to ask Mama to buy me one of these." But in a more somber frame of mind I knew that the years were slipping away and I would have to do a lot better than I had in the last forty years if I was ever to own an aircraft like this.

On arriving back in Simpson the first thing I did was to build a floating dock for the airplane, where it could be tied up to ride out a storm without the floats getting damaged. Our old boat harbour in the mouth of the Liard River a mile upstream from the town, which in the old days we referred to as Clay Point proved to be a safe harbour.

After arranging for fuel caches to be laid down at Dall Lake and Summit Lake with a Turbo Beaver and a Beach 18, and another thousand gallons to be brought to Fort Liard by barge, we were ready to go to work.

First I had to get a camp set up, cook tent and sleeping tents with propane stove, food and supplies. A couple of trips would do it, then I could take our two field assistants, Rolf and his cousin John (Stan's oldest son) out to the base camp. All would be ready when the helicopter got there on July second.

Summit Lake was at the head of the south fork of the Pelly

River, just inside the Yukon border and was nearly 300 miles north-west of Simpson. I found it took better than five hours for the round trip from Simpson to Summit Lake.

From the camp at Summit Lake the chopper had to take supplies into a fly camp at the 5000 foot level about ten miles north of the Northwest Territories border. Since Bill would have to be there to supervise the geological work, he came into Simpson on the mainliner and I flew him up to Summit Lake that night.

John Cranston a young geologist employed by Imperial Oil, was doing another project for the company on a separate budget. He would be working for a time in our area and we would both be utilizing the same helicopter. So that there were six of us for a time at the main camp until the chopper got Bill, Rolf and John moved up to the fly camp.

Summit Lake itself was a perfect lake to operate from with a float plane. It was at 3500 feet altitude in a valley where the hills rose to 6000 feet. The lake had good approaches at each end and there was room enough for seven planes to land and take off at the same time. For the three weeks we were there no strong winds blew. Twice only were there waves on the lake. I built a wee dock in the shallows near the camp for the airplane, where I could heel it in and tie it down so it would be safe.

So far things were going along too well and I knew there had to be some clouds in the sky somewhere, and they weren't long in appearing. The chopper got the men moved up to the fly camp while the weather was still flyable and then the clouds moved in and I don't think we got more than two consecutive days of clear skies for the rest of the summer. In fact there were not many days of even partially clear skies, or a ceiling high enough to allow an aircraft to go directly to a destination instead of following the valleys and sneaking in and out of high passes. Some mornings there would be sunshine breaking through the high clouds that were hiding the highest peaks; then by late afternoon the sky would lower and rain would set in.

During the month of July it never got dark at night, just two hours of dusk around midnight.

Up on the mountain at the fly camp John and Rolf managed

to get out most days in the fog and drizzle to get the geochem. and magnetometer work done, but the weather slowed them down considerably.

John Turner had done magnetometer work before so that he knew something of the necessary procedures. He and Bill gave me a rough idea of what it was all about.

The magnetometer itself is a recording instrument which measures the earth's magnetic field, and can be of various sizes and complexities. In this case the instrument was activated by battery power and was carried on the shoulders by means of straps. There are many different phenomena which can influence the world's magnetic pull in a perceptible manner, one of these is a body of mineral ore if it is fairly close to the surface. In this case there was some slight mineral showing on the surface, and if there was a significant body of ore below the magnetometer should indicate a higher than normal pull directly over the ore. The area to be checked was marked off accurately in a grid of stations, and a reading was taken at each of these. Then the readings were plotted on a graph, and with all the other available information taken into consideration, the geologists would decide if a drilling program was warranted. The ground we were working was an area the company had on lease and I am not at liberty to say any more.

The geochemical work consisted of laying out a grid on a particular ground area with stations at any chosen distance or merely at regular separated points along each creek. At each station, soil samples were taken from the creek bed and from the creek banks, with all information of location and type of soil etc. carefully recorded. These samples, often hundreds of them are then sent to a chemical laboratory which specializes in this kind of analysis. Modern methods are so precise and accurate that the analysis will be given in parts per million, for many different minerals. The theory is that water oozing from or running over a body of ore, will over thousands of years dissolve and pick up the mineral and deposit it in the soil down stream. Even if the indication is very slight, the chemical analysis can pick it up. This then is another one of the tools used to help trace down hidden bodies of ore.

There were many days when I arose in the morning to go on

a reconnaissance with Bill or John Cranston with the 185, to find the fog down in the hills on one side of the lake or the other. Often the chopper pilot Paul would be grounded too and we would listen to the rain pounding on the tent, drink coffee and smoke cigars. The rain would stop and one of us would step out and observe, "It seems to be lifting, it might be over for today." In a few minutes the rain would start again. Sometimes I would walk down over the squishy ground to the lake shore where the aircraft was tied. I would check to see that no rain was getting in, perhaps pump the floats, stomp around a bit and come back to the tent for more coffee.

Most every evening one or two moose could be seen eating lily pads in the swamp at the south end of the lake. They were so used to the sound of aircraft and the 'Flip-flip' of chopper blades that they would hardly raise their heads when a plane landed. Some mornings we would see moose tracks in the soft ground right near the tents; some tracks came from the lake shore along past the chopper to the cook tent. I told the boys not to start feeding them cinnamon buns or we would have them coming right inside.

Several nights I awoke to hear them calling to one another. The sound is about halfway between the soft moo of domestic cattle and the sharp deep grunt of a grizzly bear. It is a deep throated MMGHWHU-MMGHWHU, not at all unpleasant to the ears, once you know what it is. In the mating season of September the call of the bull is deep, short and sharp; the call of the cow is soft and quiet.

One rainy night when I was alone in camp I awoke to hear this soft grunting call right outside my tent. "She probably wants a cinnamon bun," I thought. "I will inform her that I am fresh out of cinnamon buns and that she had better go elsewhere," as I was afraid she might in desperation take a bite out of CF-RID. I got out of bed and slipping on my trousers peeked out from the tent. There, not over eight feet away stood a wee moose calf chewing on something. His mother was standing back in the shadows insisting that he come home. "You had better go back to your Mom," I told him, "or she won't let you come out to play again." And he scampered off into the bush. In the morning I found that the attraction for the little guy was a half eaten block of salt in a plastic bag that had fallen or had been pulled down from a cache of pack-horse equipment that had been left here years before.

Some mornings the clouds lifted enough for me to fire up RID and get out through the high pass to the Little Nahanni on past Cantung and down the Flat River to Fort Simpson for a load of supplies and to ship out soil and rock samples for the geological work. When a low ceiling forced me to skip around in and out of valleys it would sometimes take me three hours flying time into Simpson. Often with shopping to do and reports to make out I would not get back that night.

One day I got out as far as Landing Lake when the clouds came right down into the trees ahead of me. It seemed to be closing in behind too so I set down on the lake to wait it out, and taxied into an old campsite of mine at the end of the lake. I got the tent up when it started to pour so I went to bed and slept for fourteen hours. There was just no way I was going to travel in the rain. Out in the flat country, in the rainstorms the visibility would often get no worse than a mile or two and I could bumble along with visual reference. But I soon learned that at high altitudes cloud and fog would roll in and disappear then roll in again, which was not at all to my liking.

On this morning at Landing Lake, the rising sun was lifting steam from the damp bush and the mountain tops were glistening in the bright blue of the sky. Well rested and feeling fresh as a daisy, I soon had a crackling fire going and coffee on the boil. For it was a rare case indeed when I went flying without bedroll, tent, gun and grub box. After breakfast I stashed everything on board, checked over the aircraft, quick-drained the tanks for any sign of water in the gas and climbed aboard. With switches on and primed, I pressed the starter button, the engine turned slowly, coughed once and stopped. I primed it again and pressed the button. Urruh-Urruh—then silence. "Oh, boy, what now?" I thought. "The battery's down and I hadn't noticed the ammeter not showing a charge." I stepped out onto the float to see if I could swing the prop by hand. I couldn't even reach it, let alone swing it.

So, that was that. I guessed I would, like Piglet, have to wait until rescued. And by now the battery was too dead to activate the radio transmitter. After an hour's wait to see if the battery would build up enough charge to turn the engine, I tried again; the prop came over on compression then stopped.

I had read somewhere that a philosopher maintained that the human brain was a 'problem solving device'. "Now," I thought, "I have a problem here; I also have a container wherein a brain might be hidden, and Mr. Corliss Lamont says its function is to solve problems, so 'Get to work brain'."

And 'brain' replied, "how can I work when I need coffee and nicotine to activate my cells?"

"Yes of course Brain, I had forgotten."

A half hour later, well fortified with coffee and nicotine, Brain said "Build a platform you fool, whereby you can reach the propeller, grasp it with your right hand, swing with all your might and if you don't lose an arm or a head, the engine will start."

"Thank you," I replied, "I will follow your instructions."

With my sharp little axe I cut two substantial spruce logs and lashed them to the float struts. Standing on them I found I could indeed reach and grasp the propeller.

Brain spoke again, "Now before you try starting the engine you fool, you had better tie the aircraft firmly to a tree on the shore or you will find yourself with another problem if and when the engine starts."

"Give me time," I said impatiently, "I was going to do that anyway. What do you take me for, a fool?"

With the aircraft tied firmly, throttle 'cracked', a shot of prime and switches on I climbed up on the platform, eased the prop around on compression and gave a mighty heave. No fire. Once again, no fire. The third time and Barrrrrrrumh and she was away. Man, that was sweet music to my ears as the engine roared to life and the trees echoed with the soft rumbling purr. I climbed into the cockpit and advanced the throttle a trifle. After a good warm-up I removed the logs from the struts, undid one of the ropes and got aboard. I throttled back to idle, opened the door and leaning out, cut the remaining rope with my pocket knife. We were away. When I got to Summit Lake I unloaded and took off for Simpson to get the electrical problem rectified while I still had two arms.

While the props of many small planes are swung by hand I feel it is slightly hazardous when you are alone, to swing the prop of anything of 300 HP or more. Once in 1955 I saw Jim Murphy, an engineer with Associated Airways swing the prop of a Beaver when it had drifted away from shore on the Mackenzie. He gave it one swing and it started. The Beaver has a 450 HP radial engine and it would be too big a job for an ordinary man to swing the prop.

It was about a week before we moved camp to Big Dall that I went into Watson Lake with a load of rock samples from John Cranston's prospecting efforts. About four miles out from the airport which was right on the lake and close by the float base, I called the radio range. "Keep an eye out for the snowbirds," he said.

I replied, "Roger." Snowbirds at this time of year? I knew there was always danger from bird 'strikes' by aircraft, but the operators had never mentioned this before. Then I looked down at the runway and saw a large white V starting to move. Oh. Ho, he means THAT kind of snowbirds. THE SNOWBIRDS. And like one big airplane the formation of white jets lifted off and roared away south.

Next morning back at camp the sky looked somewhat unusual as I loaded up for the trip to Simpson. The clouds were high and there was little wind as I came by Cantung. I looked down at the Flat Lakes and thought perhaps I should stop and gas up as we still had some fuel left at the dock in 45 gallon drums. It would do no harm to have full tanks for the trip to Simpson and at the same time I would load a keg and drop it off at Landing Lake as I had used the gas cache there.

Soon after I lifted off Flat Lakes and headed down the Flat valley the airplane started to kick around a bit with peculiar little shuddering movements. On final approach at Landing Lake, it felt as if I was hitting small vacuum pockets and the wind on the surface of the lake seemed to be in vertical puffs instead of blowing in one direction like it should.

Unloading the gasoline I noticed that the high clouds were moving west at a good clip and felt relieved as I had never had trouble with an east wind; the hot westerly ones were those I dreaded. But I tucked in the load and roped everything down anyway.

Over MacMillan Lake I could see I was in for a ride. At 7000 feet I was just beneath the cloud layer and the turbulence was starting to get beyond moderate. By the time I was over the Caribou Hills the instruments were starting to come loose. (When the eyes due to short rapid movements of the aircraft cannot focus on a specific instrument, it appears that the instruments are coming loose.) The cloud layer was broken and appeared to be only a thousand feet thick, so I backed the trim and pointed the nose up. The plane leaped and shuddered and bucked as I tried not to fight the controls, but nothing seemed very effective. Now I felt I would just have to get on top as my kidneys would be jarred loose from their moorings if this kept up much longer. But what the hell was wrong? Eight and nine thousand feet had wound up on the altimeter and still I was in and out of cloud. At ten thousand the turbulence eased off a little. At eleven thousand I broke out on top and what a relief! Smooth air. I looked at my watch: I was an hour and a quarter out from Landing Lake. Holy Smoke! Ground speed was about 60 mph. That meant a head wind of 65 miles an hour. But not to worry man, I thought. I have 140 miles to go and three hours fuel left; should be no problem.

Looking down through the gaps in the clouds I could catch sight of the ground here and there. Below and just to the right I saw a tiny lake which I recognized as one ten miles west of Dead Mans Valley. Good. I was right on track with the Gyro holding nicely. Another fifty miles and I would be over the eastern edge of the mountain front and could let down to tree top level where the velocity of the wind should be much reduced. In a few minutes the clouds opened up again, and it couldn't be, but it was: there was the same lake in pretty much the same place it had been ten minutes before. At cruising power the airspeed was indicating 110 mph, ground speed would normally be 125 mph. In ten minutes I should normally have come twenty miles and as near as I could tell I had come two. Ground speed was working out to 12 mph! Good God, I must be in the Jet Stream. But it can't be, they go from west to east. No matter, I was burning up gas at twelve gallons per hour. I could sit here burning off gas until I ran out, or I could get back down into the turbulence where the velocity of the wind should be less. At no time did the thought of turning back enter my head as it would have had there been low cloud and fog in the valleys.

I was coming up on Dead Mans Valley and disliked the thought of submitting to the vicious winds that here were the most notorious in the country. None the less I took my seat belt up another inch, trimmed the nose down and watched the needle unwind. At 7000 feet I was below the clouds and was starting to move again. Over Dean Mans Valley, I could see the lowlands to the east but I could not take much more of the shaking up I was getting. Power had been reduced to 60% to lessen the impact when a wall of changing air currents was met and yet I felt there was imminent danger of the aircraft going over on its back. Although I had two sacks of rock samples on board, emergency equipment and six empty kegs, with gas being burned off, the overall load was light and therefore could withstand much more stress than if it had been fully loaded, so I felt there was no danger of the wings coming off.

Over the main Nahanni I swung to the right over the river, put the nose down again and reduced power still more. At long last over the 'Splits' I got down to tree top level and was able to advance the throttle to 'cruise'. What a relief it was. Although the trees were almost bent double, the wind speed here was much less than at high altitude and ground speed was good and the ninety miles to Simpson took less than an hour.

At Simpson the wind was coming directly across the rivers. I landed across the current and into wind on the Mackenzie, intending once I was down on the water to turn, and taxi back across the river and up into the mouth of the Liard. But when on the water I found I could not get the airplane turned around. Each time I got halfway around the leeward wing would dip almost to the water and I was fearful lest the plane would go right over. The gauges showed some fuel left in the tanks, so I poured on the coal, took off, and came around over the Liard where the banks were high, landing across the current. In the lee of the high east bank I got turned around and keeping the wind directly on my tail, taxied back across and under the high west bank where I was able to get down close to shore and into my little floating dock. It was now four hours since I had left Summit Lake. I had averaged about fifty miles an hour. I must have lost ten pounds of weight on that flight and didn't gain it back all summer.

I drove up to our trailer, had lunch and flopped into bed feeling exhausted but happy that I had sustained that ordeal without bending the wings.

21

The Quest II

On July 20th Bill had the work on the high plateau finished and we made plans to move to Little Dall Lake on the Redstone River. Paul brought Bill, John and Rolf down from the fly camp as well as their tents and equipment. Then the rain set in and the fog came down and for three days we slept and ate and drank coffee and slept some more. Rolf and John said that up on the hill they had not missed many days work as they dressed in rain clothes and went out for a few hours each day when it was drizzling. They acquired a pet marmot, or perhaps the marmot acquired them. It would come into their sleeping tent which it used as an outhouse. And when it went into Bill's tent its favorite perch was sitting on Bill's chest gazing into his face. Bill is such a gentle guy, maybe the marmot thought Bill was his mother.

Little Dall Lake was about 120 miled due east, over the divide between the Nahanni and the Redstone River. The mountains went to 9000 feet with the lowest pass at 5000 feet. There was no way I was going to attempt the flight unless I could see where I was going. Several times I took off, got about thirty miles and turned back. At last I made it through with John and a load of supplies. I circled Little Dall and didn't like the look of it at all for a camp spot. The elevation was 4300 feet, it was a mile across and circular. As Mark Fairbrother had said, there were no trees at all within two miles of the lake, with the ground all around the lake appearing wet and squishy. The map showed Big Dall Lake 20 miles to the east; it also was near the Redstone River, two miles in length and a thousand feet lower than Little Dall. It looked good to me and halfway down the lake we found a dry spot and there we set up the tents for the camp.

Back at Summit Lake the drizzle and fog moved in again and it was two more days until I could get Rolf and a load of supplies into Big Dall. Paul got over with the chopper all OK and Bill did a reconnaissance on the way.

The terrain from Broken Skull to the Redstone is all above timberline with sharp peaks and some glaciers. Minerals in the sedimentary rocks have produced a wide range of colors in the rock, soil and lichens. There are bands of purple, yellow and pink along the hills, mixed with the green, red and orange lichens. The few lakes on the route are emerald green with the ice and snow from the glaciers coming almost to the edges. On a nice bright day the beauty is breathtaking. But if the weather is down on the hills then the visual splendor seems gone. On the next flight over what I called the Eagle Route, I was returning from Summit Lake with the last load of odds and ends of supplies piled to the roof. I came into the pass at the head of Broken Skull with the tops of the hills obscured in fog. There was still plenty of room in the valleys to navigate but once I went into the pass on the Redstone I would be committed as I knew there would be no room to turn until I hit the main Redstone River thirty miles down. The divide of the Broken Skull River and the Redstone was the last place a 180 degree turn could be safely made and I had to make a choice right there and then. There seemed to be no wind; there was over 500 feet between the river and the cloud layer; there was only thirty miles to go and I didn't want to go back a hundred miles to Summit Lake where the camp had been taken down and it was drizzling.

I turned into the Redstone pass and very soon I wished I had not done so. While I was headed downstream into a lower altitude and a wider valley the cloud layer too got lower and lower. Now the beauty of the rock cliffs and the lichens was entirely lost to me, and the sides of the valley seemed to close in, building in me a feeling of dread and apprehension. As always in a sudden and tight situation I became what I term as 'psyched right up'. I was hoping against hope that it would not close in ahead, but if it did, while I had some altitude I would put on a notch of flap, wheel around on one wing and with the nose right down, hope to come around out of it. And if the ceiling became gradually lower and I was forced down close to the creek, I would continue on even if the floats were almost touching the water of the creek beneath.

The hands of my watch seemed to be stuck and a minute seemed a long time. Ten minutes were now gone and still the tunnel ahead opened at each bend of the creek. Two more bends and I would be out of it and able to relax. Then suddenly, what I had been dreading happened. Immediately ahead, the narrow valley was plugged with fog. In less time than it takes to tell it I thought of many pilots in these mountains who had been sucked into a similar situation and who had their lives suddenly snuffed out and their bones left among the rocks. Knowing the danger full well, I had, like the rest been tempted into a trap and the jaws were closing.

With the fog looming ahead I had about two seconds to make a decision. There seemed to be a space above the fog and another space below, but how far they extended could not be seen. I had either to go up and over or right down to the creek level. I dumped the stick ahead to take the low road, and when I was down I could see there was an opening below which extended into the valley ahead. I pulled up a little and could see ahead to where the valley widened. Little Dall Lake should be coming up soon on a plateau to the right. There I would land, regain my composure and wait out the weather.

Foiled again, Little Dall was completely obscured in fog, so I swung away from there and got down over the Redstone again, which at the junction here was now a river, very swift flowing but where a safe landing could be made if necessary. Now the clouds were breaking up with open spaces between low lying clouds. Twenty miles farther Big Dall was wide open and I thankfully settled into the safety of the water. At the camp I was told the weather had been unsettled all day with fog and drizzle coming in intermittently.

As I sat in the tent eating dinner with the boys I said, "I know now why Johnny Miller and Pete Cowie both together weigh not much more than 90 pounds. When I have as many hours as either of them there will be nothing left of me but a willing spirit with clothes hanging from it." (Johnny and Peter are two accomplished bush pilots who I try to emulate.)

From our camp at Big Dall, Fort Simpson was 200 miles south, one hundred less than from Simpson to Summit, and after breaking out of the mountains fifty miles to the east, it was flat country all the way to Simpson.

We kept thinking that perhaps August would bring a change for the better in the weather; but 'twas a forlorn hope. We'd get one clear day then two of rain and low cloud. When we had only about two thirds of the work done which we had intended for this area, on consultation with our employers it was decided to move to the Toobally Lakes in the southern Yukon.

Bill had gone with the chopper to Fort Simpson so that left only John, Rolf and me at camp. I thought we should all stay together for the first flight to Toobally which was 215 miles. With some camp gear and food and full tanks (62 gallons) we had an overload. But with two miles of lake I thought we could make it off the water. It was one of the few hot days we had all summer with not a breath of wind to stir the water. It was the first and only time CF-RID refused to fly. She would not get up on the step. Too much full throttle at slow speed can damage an aircooled motor so we called it off and went back to the dock. We unloaded 100 pounds of freight and in two hours the temperature had dropped to 60 degrees.

Now I was able to coax the aircraft up onto the step and we were away. There were some clouds in the high mountain peaks but when we crossed the Nahanni and headed south conditions improved and I was able to climb to 8000 feet. The Toobally Lake region was new to all of us; each of the lakes was about ten miles long and we flew low over them looking for a suitable place to establish a camp. We needed a sheltered spot for the float plane, an open glade for a heliport and a level place to erect the tents. We flew low the full length of the lakes and back again. The heavy timber around the lake went right to the edge. We landed anyway, found a place to beach the airplane and by the time the tent was up it was dark.

The worst feature of Toobally Lakes was a lack of harbor to shelter the airplane from a wind. The map showed Larson Lake was just the right size for a float plane and not too far away and in the morning we flew over to have a look at it. It was 'made to order' with a float dock already built and a fine abandoned camp site with a nice cleared heliport.

Paul had been doing some work with John Cranston in another area and was waiting in Simpson for a message from me. While the boys were setting up camp I flew into Fort Liard 80 miles east for a load of gasoline and to contact Paul to let him know where we had established the camp.

At Larson Lake the weather seemed settled at last and we had great hopes of getting an ambitious program of geological and geochemical work done. The next morning the chopper set Rolf and John down at the head of a creek to gather samples of that area while Bill and I planned a day's reconnaissance with RID. The geology of the country was very interesting and we mapped many areas that warranted exploration. That night at sundown I had supper ready when the chopper brought the boys back to camp, with their packs filled with rock and soil samples.

The third day at Larson Lake the weather reverted to its old tricks of rain and fog and more rain and low clouds. During this spell of weather we did get some work done close to camp, but it was a week before there was a nice enough day to get over to Dall Lake for the last load of supplies we had left there.

To the north and west of Larson Lake lay a land of timbered rolling hills that was the drainage system of the Beaver River where forty-two years before, Stan, Raymond, Pete and I had spent six weeks on an abortive beaver hunt that could easily have ended in disaster for Pete and I. From the air I recognized the spot where Pete and I had lost our first raft in the out-going ice, the canyon below, Happy Valley and the Chutes, where we had eaten the best part of the hind quarter of a grizzly bear. I had brought the present crew up to date on those long ago exploits, in the evenings in the cook tent.

We were four young trappers from the Liard River near the Nahanni Valley. Those were hard times; fur was scarce and the price for raw fur was low. For a number of years the Northwest Territory administration at Ottawa had prohibited the hunting and trapping of beaver for all white residents. In those years most of the species of land fur were at the bottom of their cycle and as we could take no beaver, the white trappers, especially new-comers like Stan and I, were having a very difficult time.

After all these years a wave of bitterness wells within me when I recall those early years. While not actually starving, I know that I suffered from malnutrition and a very inadequate diet, due in a great part to the restrictive and punitive game regulations instigated by the Northwest Territories administration in Ottawa. I sincerely feel to this day that the regulations were a deliberate attempt to drive the few white settlers out of the Northwest Territories and back to the Provinces.

In the Yukon Territory the game laws were not so restrictive so four of us young men embarked on a spring beaver hunt into the Beaver River area of the Yukon Territory. We were all inexperienced and had not been in this mountain area before. Reports were that beaver were plentiful here and we hoped to garner enough pelts to provide a small grubstake for the following winter. There was no industry in the north at that time and trapping was our only means of livelihood.

On April 6th, 1932 we set off from Fort Liard with a load of supplies, and a team of five dogs, westward into the mountains. We took just enough basic food, flour, beans and rice for about ten days, thinking we could live on wild game once we were into the mountains. We knew that the Indians when in this area killed plenty of moose and caribou. Through a series of errors and misfortunes we were able to kill no game whatsoever, and became very hungry indeed, trying to spin out our meager rations of flour and beans.

In a vain search for beaver lodges we split up into two parties; Stan and Raymond heading up one fork of the creek and Pete and I continuing on west. We ended up almost at the head of the Beaver River without finding any beaver lodges and without killing any game for food. It was May 4th, and we were on the point of exhaustion and starvation. With the snow melting and the creeks starting to break up we, in desperation, decided to build a raft and try to float back down the Beaver River. There would be at least one hundred miles of very fast rough water to navigate before we could hope to find a trapper's cabin or Indian camp where we might get food.

We built our raft from big dry spruce trees and waited three days for the ice to move out. In desperate haste we set off too soon and ran into an ice jam, where the ice from above came roaring down and tore our raft to pieces. We were fortunate in being able to escape to shore with the few items we had. We then hiked for over a day, to the foot of the next canyon where we built another raft and thirty miles downstream from there we found Stan and Raymond who had also come back to the main river. They had fared little better than Pete and I. Four days later we killed a grizzly bear, and by ten o'clock that night the four of us had eaten nearly a hind quarter. When the rain let up somewhat Bill marked out a program of soil sampling on some of the creeks that drained into the Beaver River, and Paul flew them off to the area early one morning. At about five in the evening he left to pick them up at the agreed rendezvous. The chopper failed to show up for supper and Bill and I ate alone. As the evening wore on Bill and I talked of everything and anything but the missing helicopter. Hour by hour I grew more nervous and apprehensive. What the hell could be wrong? It was only thirty miles to the pickup spot, which was an hour's return flight for the chopper. I started to imagine all sorts of calamities that could have befallen the chopper. Paul was a good pilot and the helicopter had not been giving any trouble all summer. But things do happen; the blades could have hit a tree on take-off, or one of the boys could have broken a leg, or maybe they had mistaken the pick-up place and Paul could not locate them. Hell. This was what I had been at great pains to avoid in our whole operation. All our careful planning and constant safety precautions had apparently come to naught. Before dark, in a few minutes now I would have to fire up RID and start the search. But wait—"Listen, Bill. HEY BILL, I think I hear the chopper," I said. The Flip-Flip-Flip of the blades in reduced pitch became louder and soon it appeared low over the trees, and circling into wind settled down on the pad.

"They're all there," Bill sounded relieved also.

As John and Rolf got out of the machine we saw they had no packsacks or axe with them. In fact they had nothing but the shirts on their backs and Rolf was minus a boot. "What happened?" I asked. And while their supper was warming, they related their adventure.

Paul had set them down on a sandbar on the Beaver River, and they were to walk down to a point ten miles below, sampling the creeks along the way. The river was too large to wade and seemed suitable for rafting; and in order to sample every tributary they decided to build a raft so that they could get stream samples from both sides, and at the same time avoid having to fight their way through the bush. In two hours they had constructed a sizeable raft out of driftwood and with a sturdy pole each in hand they set out. Everything went according to their expectations for the best part of the day and they were congratulating themselves on accomplishing a good day's work when they came around a bend and saw an island ahead. There seemed to be plenty of water in either channel and they guided their craft into the left hand one as it was narrower but deep. Then right ahead there appeared a fallen tree that reached from shore to island and which lay just barely above the water. The current was swift and the raft rammed the log and was flipped over by the force of the current. They were both thrown into the water and both swam to shore. The upturned raft disappeared down stream and their axe and packsacks with all their day's work of soil sampling were at the bottom and Rolf had lost one boot.

The only thing left to do now was to go on down stream until they found a suitable open space for the chopper to land, and hope that Paul would find them. Chopper pilots have eyes like eagles and have had much experience in locating men in the bush, so it was not too much trouble for Paul to find them when they failed to show up at the prearranged rendezvous.

"We were never in any danger really," Rolf said. "But we were pretty disgusted at losing all the samples which we had so laboriously and meticulously garnered during the day."

"We were so proud of that raft," John exclaimed. "And thought that we had devised an easy and efficient way of stream sampling. And then to go and lose the whole blessed caboodle on account of that one stupid log, rather set us back a bit."

They showed us on the map where they had upset and it was very near the place where Pete and I had swamped our raft forty-two years before.

The weather continued its non-cooperation and we had our work far from completed when the first frosts arrived and we brought our program to a conclusion for the summer.

CF-RID was delivered back to Prince George, and before Christmas I went to work for Hire North at Camp 3, near Fort Norman on the Mackenzie River. But after drinking that mountain water for all those years I was consumed with a desire to get back to the hills and continue the search for the riches that were yet hidden and waiting for a blow from my prospector's pick.

22

At Last

It turned out that Imperial Oil decided to withdraw to some extent from the expenditure of funds for mineral exploration in western Canada for the time being. So one set of our plans went out the window. Bill and I would have to look for other capital.

As is well known, hind sight is futile, but I can't help but speculate on the possibilities if Imperial Oil had backed Nahanni Placers with a budget for 1975. I would have been able to go to the men in the Calgary office who had recommended our program and say, "You stayed with us last summer when the weather was giving us a hard time. We did not complete the work we wanted to do, and now, here is your reward, we have found something that appears to be very promising."

But such was not to be. Bill had to go hunting for other capital. And he found it. One Simpson resident and a group of Calgary men came up with the funds for a summer's exploration work on a program I had been wanting to do for years. We would have a helicopter and a Cessna 185. This time it was not RID but its mate CF-VZP, a similar aircraft, except the colours were not so bright.

We had four prospects I wanted to go over with a fine-tooth comb, all not far from the Flat River, where I had been scratching around for fifteen years. One especially, Don and I had spent much time and money in trying to track down, without success. I called it Blue Moon Valley.

Once again Bill would plan the geology and I would organize the logistics. I would get the plane from Prince George and arrange to begin our program about July 1st. This year I would have to do the soil sampling for the Geochem. work myself as John had arranged to help his Dad, for the summer, and Rolf had gone to Australia to teach. And our budget did not warrant hiring extra help.

In order to get a good start on the summer's work, in case we had another terrible rainy year, I determined to get a chopper and go into Blue Moon Valley to do a week's program of soil sampling so that when the crew came in to start work, I would have the geochemical analysis back from the laboratory. Positive results from these tests might be a help in locating the body of ore which I was convinced had to be somewhere in the valley.

For eight clear and beautiful days I tramped that alpine valley. The creeks were small and slow and laden with silt. At every station I took three samples; one from the creek bed, one from each bank above flood level. I was careful to get samples from each creek in the valley, even those that were only a foot wide and three inches deep.

Legend had it that there was a rock cliff somewhere in the valley where the silver stuck out in gobs, but again, my searching failed to reveal it. But what the hell, a more pleasant place to spend a week or two could not be found. The mosquitos were few, the days were warm and I tramped around, up and down the creeks and over the hills, as happy as if I had been in my right mind.

At night I came back to camp tired and hungry and ate like a horse. Indians had camped in the valley forty years ago and I found their old camps where the logs and stumps had almost rotted away. Everything the old Indians had told me of the valley fitted into place except that I couldn't find that blessed rock cliff. But this just HAD to be the valley where one of them had found the outcrop of silver and lead.

Through the valley there were game trails here and there, with fresh tracks of moose and caribou and at least one grizzly had been there recently. I lugged the big rifle with me wherever I went, and at night had it beside me in the tent. About once a year in the north there would be a report of some grizzly bear taking a bite out of somebody or scaring the daylights out of him. A few years previously, not far from this valley, in fact just over the hill, a very old, lean hungry grizzly had sneaked up through the willows and attacked three friends of mine, and that also was in June. So, while not wasting much sleep over it I always kept the old 'equalizer' beside me.

One morning very early, soon after midnight, I awoke to a heavy snuffling and crackling of bushes outside the tent. Most small animals are so quiet that their thumping and scratching in the leaves are fairly easily identified as one of the many harmless creatures. But this sound that reached me was a big noise made by a heavy animal and the snuffling could only mean a grizzly bear. "Oh, boy," I thought, "After all these years at last I am about to have a run-in with some bold grizzly." I had left no garbage at all around the camp having meticulously burned and buried all tin cans and paper. The food boxes were piled inside the tent, and there was no opened bacon or meat that could be attracting him. There it was again, the tent was moving and I heard a snuffling and loud chewing.

Very quietly I got out of bed, picked up the rifle and the noise of the shell pumped into the chamber sounded like a hammer on an anvil. "I'll put one slug in his guts before he eats me, anyway," I thought, and with the rifle ready to fire I pushed the tent flap aside and immediately was eye-ball to eye-ball with a giant old harmless porcupine! He was chewing on the straps of my packsack I had left outside the door. On observing my startled, naked appearance, he backed off in amazement and waddled slowly away. "You old Buzzard," I shouted after him, "you should be ashamed of yourself, for scaring the daylights out of a poor old trapper." And as he disappeared I swear I heard him say, "This is my back yard you are camped in, and it's you that scared the hell out of me."

At last the samples were taken and it was time to expect the chopper. The appointed day was clear and bright and my ears, attuned to the snap of a twig or the chirp of a bird, heard the hum of the motor long before it arrived.

In two hours we were back in Simpson where my precious samples were soon on their way on the day-liner to the laboratory in Calgary. I had high hopes that the results would indicate something positive, but was not overly apprehensive during the two week waiting period as over the last fifteen years I had become reconciled to the negative results from dozens of rock samples sent in for analysis.

Now came word that CF-VZP was at Winnipeg and I would have to go there to pick it up. That was farther than I had been for many years, but what the hell, it was still in Canada and I could probably find my way back all right. So armed with an airline ticket to Winnipeg away I went. During the stopover at Edmonton I purchased about forty-five maps of eight miles to the inch, so that I could plot a course direct from Winnipeg to Simpson. My stops would be The Pas, Lac La Ronge, Fort Chipewyan and Simpson.

At the float base near Winnipeg on the Red River, I test flew VZP and was happy with the way it performed. It had the Edo instead of CAP floats, and they were not bent or beat up and did not appear to leak.

Late one afternoon I loaded up with tent, bedroll, axe, and emergency equipment and with an armful of maps on my knee headed northwest. The sky was clear, there was no wind and reading the map was easy and I landed at the float base at The Pas. It looked as if there was some weather sitting to the north so I spent the night there. I was late in getting away in the morning and got into Lac La Ronge about noon where I had a two hour wait to get some work done on the aircraft. At Fort Chipewyan I stopped for gas and had supper with Steve Yanik who had come north in 1927 and had trapped for years and now owned an air charter service at Chipewyan.

When I left the sun was in my eyes as I set out on a Bee Line for Fort Simpson. The air was still, without a cloud in the sky, and at 8000 feet we sped along doing about 140 mph ground speed. It was an hour before midnight and the sun had just gone down when I touched down on the Liard River and taxied into Airplane Bay at Clay Point. It was July 8th,

1975, exactly forty-five years to the day that Stan and I had crossed into the Territories with our canoe on a journey that was destined to bring us far more adventures than we had bargained for.

Perhaps it was coincidence, only blind chance, but I like to think it was Fate, making up for some dirty blows dealt out to me in the early days, that willed I get a letter from Loring Laboratories in Calgary, dated July 8th, 1975, giving the results of the geochemical tests of the soil samples sent in from Blue Moon Valley.

We had asked for analysis for silver, lead, copper and zinc. Results were given in parts per million and were only expected to give a slight increase in values if there happened to be an ore body close by to where the soil sample was taken. The columns under silver, lead and copper showed only very slight variations here and there, nothing significant. But in the zinc columns the values jumped from 50 ppm to as high as 2400 ppm. My eyes could not believe the figures. I phoned Bill in Calgary. No, the Lab did NOT make a mistake, the results had been verified. "It looks," said Bill, "that we might have found the big one."

Further samples taken from the same area and extending farther north and south showed zinc values up to 4400 ppm on some of the creeks, extending over an area six miles long and possibly two miles wide. As one geologist pointed out to us, the soil samples themselves in the high value zones amounted to one ton of zinc to 250 tons of soil, which almost constituted an economic ore body.

We are not getting too excited, the body of ore could possibly be very narrow and rich, but not sufficient to make a commercial mine. If so, we will simply go on over the next hill and find something better.

We had not found gold and we had not found silver; but I was not about to turn up my nose at zinc. Enough common garden variety of zinc could buy some gold, and with gold I will buy an airplane, a nice, shiny, sleek new airplane. And I will go flying away in the mountains, among the fleecy clouds, with the birds, in the blue, blue sky.

END

Glossary

Bannock— A mixture of flour, water and baking powder usually cooked over an open fire. A cup of flour, half tsp. of baking powder, pinch of salt. Mix thoroughly and add enough water for a stiff dough. Put in hot frypan with a tablespoon of melted lard. Brown on bottom over hot coals, then support the handle of the frypan with a stick and let the heat from the fire finish cooking the bannock from the top.

Batholith— Igneous rock that has melted and intruded surrounding strata at great depths.

Blowpot— An open flame heat generator (usually propane) used to warm an engine and its oil before starting.

Dead-Heads— Broken off stumps or tree trunks lodged in the bottom of a river or lake.

Dragging the Strip— to give a landing site visual inspection prior to landing to ensure there are no obstructions.

Empenage— The tail section of an aircraft.

Gauge Mineral— An easily identified mineral found in association with valuable ores that are not readily recognized.

Gossan— A stain on rocks indicating mineralization.

HF— High frequency, a radio frequency within the range between 3 and 30 megacycles per second.

Heel In— The heels of an aircraft are the hind tips of the floats. When the heels are drawn up onto a beach or river bank the aircraft has been heeled in.

Intrusive— Designating igneous rock forced into another strata while in a molten state.

Long Reach— A particular stretch of the Liard River that is wide with a slow current. It starts twenty-five miles below the Nahanni and runs for twenty miles.

LF— Low frequency. A radio frequency in the range from 30 to 300 kilocycles per second.

Open the Tap— To advance the throttle.

Overflow— This is a winter term used to describe water that has oozed out of the ground or has been forced from below ice, and that lies unfrozen for many days underneath the blanket of snow.

Riffle— A short stretch of rapids in a stream, often merely the back curling waves under a sharp drop.

Rudder— A vertically hinged section of the tail of an aircraft, used for effecting horizontal changes in course.

Snye— Any and all secondary channels of a stream. If there is no water in it at the time it is referred to as a dry snye.

Stall Speed— The air speed at which the lift to the aircraft becomes equal to the downward force of gravity when the aircraft refuses to fly.

Toggle— A loose wooden pole preferably of green spruce that the chain of a trap is attached to. This is to avoid the animal being brought up suddenly and perhaps break the chain or pull loose from the trap.

V.F.R.— Visual Flight Rules. The operation of an aircraft dependent entirely on visual reference with land topography.

V.H.F.— Very high frequency. A band of radio frequencies lying between 30 and 300 megacycles per second.

PRINTED IN CANADA